A Delicate Refusal

A Delicate Refusal

T. T. Thomas

2013

A Delicate Refusal

Published by Bon View Publishing, 2013

ISBN: 9780983918080

Original Cover Art and Design by Patty G. Henderson

Please visit: www.ttthomas.com

For Patty

ACKNOWLEDGEMENTS

I've always loved the story of Cyrano de Bergerac not only for Cyrano's spirited sense of life, but for the whole concept of letter writing as a means to express love. So when I happened upon a quote by the creator of the play, Cyrano de Bergerac, by Edmund Rostand, it struck me as the perfect way to capture the essence of people who maintain their heroism in the face of personal trials and tribulations. Rostand called it "panache" and it's one of those words that conjure up a personality type as well as an outlook.

But in the land of my birth, England, such an outlook might come off sounding a bit dour, as in "Right, well, get on with it, then, shall we?" There's a bit of fatalism in that last phrase, I think, but it's more a stereotype than a reality. In the real world of 1914 England, being an eccentric, or unusual in some outward way, was as much a display of panache as was Cyrano's expressions of passion despite his nose. I hope that A Delicate Refusal captures some of that sense of lifc for readers.

I have the usual cast of characters, and a few new ones, to thank for helping me get this book to you. Patty Henderson, to whom this book is dedicated, and Ann Herendeen, both authors in their own right, shape shifted between muse, editor, cheerleader, taskmaster and all around *bon vivants* who wanted nothing more than for this story to be told. I thank them both, and an additional thanks to Patty for the beautiful cover design.

To my spouse, Karyn, unending gratitude for providing me with the love, security, home and atmosphere conducive to my indulgence in thinking I must write. That is matched only by her unending appreciation and astonishment at my newspaper reporter ability to write in a noisy room with the screams, blood, laughter and tears that accompany such erstwhile media offerings as *True Blood* and *Game of Thrones*. And finally, I must mention my love for her strength and perseverance and belief in me during her many hours of alone time while I "just finish this one last paragraph."

I also want to thank Corinna Muller, Michele Drier and Terry Baker who provided valuable input and encouragement as the story unfolded.

My friend Dorothy Carter has been in my life for nearly forty years. I always try to name a character after her, or some permutation of her name, and this book is no exception. Only this time, I included her beloved partner, Caroline, because I thought it would be fun to make them a couple in my book. In the book, their last name in Tads. They will, eventually, forgive me.

After reading this book, a friend said, "This is *Downton Abbey* for lesbians!" Well...I think he was being kind, although it might be a start! The very first character we meet in A Delicate Refusal is Sir Ralph Whitmore, who lives in Highclere. As fate would have it, Highclere Castle, Hampshire, U.K., home to the 8th Earl and Countess of Carnarvon, is, in fact, where *Downtown Abbey* is filmed!

The village where I was born, Tadley, is not very far from Highclere. Tadley is also home to January Jameson, one of several main characters in my book.

Kingsclere, home of Rosemary Parker-Pryce, one of our more rambunctious and not altogether delicate protagonists in A Delicate Refusal is the home of the entirely fictionalized Parker House. In real life, Kingsclere is located approximately midway between Highclere and Tadley.

Finally, the acknowledgements in this particular book would not be complete without mentioning Barbara Whitaker, M.D., a psychiatrist by training and profession and a vital resource for this and the other books I have written. The mysteries of the mind are knowable; the trick is in knowing one's own mind first. Thank you, Dr. Whitaker.

T. T. Thomas
Thousand Oaks, California
July 2013

Main Characters

Rosemary Parker Pryce, landed gentry, heiress, lesbian

Margaret Mills, female majordomo at Parker House

Victoria Anne Cabot-Jones, Rosemary's neighbor

Winston David Cabot-Jones, former Estate Solicitor for Parker House, Victoria's husband

January (Jan) Jameson, reader and writer for Rosemary Parker Pryce

Mrs. Hope Jameson, Jan's mother

Miss Beatrice Graham, neighbor of Mrs. Hope Jameson

Michael Sullivan, M.D., physician to Rosemary Parker-Pryce

Additional Characters

Benjamin Carter, M.D., physician to Victoria-Cabot Jones

Camille Carter, Victoria's best friend, wife of Benjamin Carter, M.D.

Sir Ralph Whitmore, Knighted by the late Queen Victoria; Special Envoy to the War Council on behalf of her grandson, King George V.

Mr. Dann Tads, houseman, personal valet to Winston David Cabot-Jones

Mrs. Dorothy Tads, cook, lady's maid to Victoria Cabot-Jones

Bertie Betters, driver for Parker House

Locales

Hampshire, England, 1914, the village of Tadley, where January Jameson, Hope Jameson and Beatrice Graham live.

Kingscler (later, Kingsclere), where Rosemary Parker Pryce, Margaret Mills and others live in or near Parker House.

Highclere, estate of Sir Ralph David Winthrop.

Wulverton (later Wolverton, five miles north of Kingsclere) where Winston and Victoria Cabot-Jones have a country house.

Distance from Tadley, Hampshire to London, driving in 1914, about 75 miles.

Distance from Reading to Tadley, driving in 1914, about 14 miles.

Distance from Parker House in Kingsclere to Wolverton, 5 miles walking, riding, driving.

To joke in the face of danger is the supreme politeness,

a delicate refusal to cast oneself as a tragic hero.

Edmond Rostand, Author of Cyrano de Bergerac,
Address to the Académie Française (1903)

PROLOGUE

Sir Ralph David Whitmore sat in the back seat of his Mercedes and watched with admiration as his driver expertly maneuvered the vehicle through the rain-slicked streets of London. They approached Paddington Station where the traffic increased and came to a standstill. Whitmore could see that his driver had positioned them in the correct lane and would soon find an open spot to park.

Sir Ralph thought about the phone call and his mission here tonight. That was probably the last person on earth he expected to hear from. Still, the worry in her voice convinced him of the necessity of his trip to the train station. Her voice hadn't changed much in 36 years. Still soft, still sweet, still special to him. A whole lifetime had passed between them and yet they were lives lived separately from one another. The odd call every few years, updates really, the occasional note. He pressed his lips together in a sigh of resignation and acceptance. Some things were just not meant to be.

And some were.

"I'll get out here," he told his driver. "If the Bobby comes 'round to try to move you, show him our Diplomat placard."

***

Wolverton, Hampshire

Another man would have been on time—no, another man would have been early. Another man would have been able to hold onto his wife—no, surely it was never possible to hold onto Anne.

Winston Cabot-Jones trudged up the stairs to the second landing. It was a half hour later than his usual arrival. As he passed their bedroom, on the way to his own, he glanced through the open door and saw that her eyes were closed.

"Was there any mail?" she asked, barely above a whisper.

He paused. She was not going to last long. She looked thinner. Her skin looked greyer than it had this morning. Her eyes remained closed, even to him. Especially to him.

"Let me go look," he said.

She nodded, but barely. He walked downstairs to the table where the housekeeper would have put the day's mail. There were strict instructions that only he was to bring his wife whatever mail she received. As the mail came so late in the day, the dying woman had not questioned the routine. Or if she did, she kept it to herself. He saw that there was a letter. She'll rally when she sees this, he thought, feeling the substantial heft of the letter-sized envelope. He looked at the handwriting. It was a beautiful cursive, the letters elongated but curvy, like a woman's body in recline. To a woman's body in decline, he thought. From a woman's hand, the letters spread across the envelope like fingers across breasts. Gently, slowly, insinuating themselves into all the hidden areas below and alongside the curves.

Strange to think of his wife as a lucky woman, but he did. He had never read any of the letters. He didn't need to. He knew his wife's face, and she had never been good at hiding her emotions, her moods, her longings and her needs. He knew when those emotions were deep. He knew when her mood had improved. He knew when her longings had been answered, and he knew when her needs had been filled. All from the letters.

He turned the envelope over. The return address mocked him, but he felt no resentment. The contents of the letter were as a cuckold to him, but he felt no anger. When she was gone, he would wait until several more letters arrived, and he would bundle them up and send them back, but he felt no revenge.

He started up the steps but stopped as he put his hand to his head. He rubbed his eyes, and he looked up the staircase as a haunted man might look at redemption withheld. He had seen true love, though not for him. He had witnessed deep passion, though not for him. He teared up without meaning to, and wiped his eyes on his sleeve. He pulled his shoulders back and walked slowly but steadily up the stairs.

“You've got a nice heavy letter, dear,” he said.

She opened her eyes and looked at the letter before looking at him. “You are too kind,” she said. “I have loved you for that, at least.”

“Now Anne, you know you loved me for my money! And my elevated standing in society!” He smiled, and she smiled back. It was a standing chant between them. He was rich, and he was a pillar of polite society, but so was she before they met and married. He always called her Anne, now, well, for a couple of years really. They both knew why.

“Just so,” she said quietly. “Just so.”

“All right, dear, I'll be at the club with the boys tonight. Don't wear yourself out, promise?”

She smiled but said nothing. They both knew she'd spend from now until her last breath writing to the person who had been so many years writing to her.

"And send my regards!"

"I'll do no such thing, Winston, and you know it," she said, her laughter offered as a courtesy more than anything until it dissolved into a wracking cough. He paused by the bed and waited for the spell to pass. She reached over to her bed stand and picked up a small crystal goblet from which she slowly sipped.

She fell back on her pillows, the letter clutched to her breast as he quietly slipped out the door of the bedroom that once was theirs.

June 28, 1914, Sarajevo

"We'll start with the facts and work back: it may make it all the easier to understand how World War One actually happened. The events of July and early August 1914 are a classic case of 'one thing led to another' - otherwise known as the treaty alliance system. The explosive that was World War One had been long in the stockpiling; the spark was the assassination of the Archduke Franz Ferdinand, heir to the Austro-Hungarian throne, in Sarajevo on 28 June 1914. Ferdinand's death at the hands of the Black Hand, a Serbian nationalist secret society, set in train a mindlessly mechanical series of events that culminated in the world's first global war."

Michael Duffy, The First World War

ONE

Kingsclere, Hampshire, England June 25, 1914

"I cannot and will not interview another reader!"

When Rosemary Parker-Pryce waved her arms like an angry crow flapping harder and harder to catch up to and dive bomb an errant hawk, no one could cajole her into submission.

"One would think they ought to at least be able to read," Margaret offered.

Rosemary stopped waving her arms and looked at her housekeeper. "Right. Well, then, what are we doing wrong? We've advertised for a discreet young lady to come for six hours a day to read my mail, well, certain mail, and write my responses. We're paying good money for this small task."

Margaret nodded, her face absent of the emotion her voice conveyed. "We are indeed," she said.

The irony was not lost on either of them, so there was no need to mention it. Parker-Pryce paid for everything, but they both enjoyed the illusion of running the estate together. And in some ways, they did.

"I think I see the problem," continued Margaret.

"I'm all ears," Rosemary said gloomily.

"I don't think one can actually run an advert for 'discreet'."

"Speak English, Margaret, or British at least!"

"Think about it Pryce," she said, lighting one of Rosemary's expensive cigarettes. She always called her employer by her last name—it was Rosemary's first request when Margaret was hired. At the time, Margaret thought it the special kind of odd that her whole career at Parker House would probably entail. "What we need to do is find someone to whom discretion would be important, someone who, perhaps, was not so discreet in her youth, someone who—"

"You're right," Rosemary said, jumping up. "I understand. Not exactly a fallen woman, although that would be its own kind of wonderful, I suppose, for my purposes, but anyway, someone youngish, someone with a past, someone...who do you have in mind, Margaret?"

Margaret looked at her with a blank face.

"That won't work, Margaret, you forget I know you! You have someone in mind, and you know you do! You've heard things...in the village. You know things, Margaret. Why didn't I think of this?"

"Because had you the opportunity, which you would not remotely have availed yourself of, but if you had, you wouldn't have listened, and thus, you wouldn't have heard," Margaret answered snuffing out her cigarette. "I'll make an inquiry next I'm in for shopping."

"When will that be?" Rosemary demanded petulantly.

"I suppose it best be later today," Margaret said with the soft, beautiful and completely feigned sigh of the beleaguered.

Rosemary smiled. She couldn't see particularly well, but she could hear perfectly. Her sense of smell was flawless. Her senses of touch and taste, without equal. The blindness was not complete, at least not yet. Maybe it never would be. But things were in the shadows. Not the total darkness, more like a gauzy twilight. *Never mind. Margaret will find you a very good pair of eyes.*

***

Tadley, Hampshire, June 26, 1914, evening

January Jameson stopped before opening the gate to the small yard that fronted their bungalow. She could see the glow from the lights at the back of the house, in the kitchen where her mother would be having a cup of tea before dinner. Mrs. Jameson refused to sit in comfort in the small living room because that would require turning on lights. That meant a higher invoice from the electric people. She'd wait for her daughter in the kitchen, and after dinner, they'd both sit close to the fireplace for the duration of time it took one log to burn.

She put her key into the lock, turned the old brass handle and called out as she walked in.

"Hello! Mother, I'm home and dying for a good cup!"

"Just have a nice hot pot of it brewing, Jan," Mrs. Jameson said, standing in the doorway between the kitchen and living room with her blue cardigan sweater wrapped around her thin frame.

"Oh, Mother! You'll freeze to death in that thin thing. Let me get you a proper sweater."

"This is fine, Jan, just fine." Something in the slight steely edge of her voice stopped Jan in her tracks.

"All right, Mum, all right. Let me just go wash up a bit, and I'll join you."

The cold water was icy, but Jan slapped it on her face and felt the bracing tingle on her fair skin. She looked at herself in the mirror. One more week at that dirty old man's office and she was sure she would become ill. It was all she could do to keep from turning green each time he hovered over her from behind, trying, she knew, to catch a glimpse of her breasts. She could smell him and soaped up her entire face to get the odor out of her nostrils. More cold water rinsing. Towel patted her face. Towel rubbed her hands. She looked into the mirror again and practiced several faces. She settled on the 'Not a bad day at all,' face and opened the bathroom door.

The tea was hot, just the way she liked it. She spooned a tiny bit of sugar into the steamy liquid and added enough milk to make it change to the color of her favorite old camel hair winter coat. *Good heavens, that was twenty years ago. That thing is long gone.*

"You look a bit drawn, dear," Mrs. Jameson said.

"Really? Wasn't a bad day at all," she answered, stuffing a scone in her mouth so further talk of it would be impossible.

"Weather's turning a bit colder, I think."

"Maybe we should put on two logs tonight, Mum since it's Friday, and we should celebrate!"

"What are we celebrating?" her mother asked, pouring more tea.

"No work tomorrow! And today was payday!"

"Well..." her mother demurred. "I suppose it would be nice to warm this place up a bit. If you think we ought...?"

It was a question Jan had no intention of answering. "Right after tea, I'll get the fire going," she said. "What did you do today, Mum? Still reading that book?"

Jan listened while her mother chatted about the book. Then she launched into her usual tut-tut about Mrs. Graham, the elderly neighbor who was always borrowing 'a few' tea bags...all of it. But Jan wasn't really listening. It was the same ritual every evening, same cast of characters, the real ones and the ones in her mother's latest book. Her mother was exactly two years younger than the eighty-year old Mrs. Graham. That difference seemed to imbue her mother with renewed vigor, a certain superiority, and a calm resolve that she would never find herself in Mrs. Graham's impoverished state at eighty. Mrs. Graham should have had children, her mother always said, as if that alone could have stayed the inevitable outcome of diminishment that not having children apparently held for Mrs. Graham. And yet, Mrs. Graham had a sunny outlook on life, thought Jan, but then Mrs. Graham had a heart full of gratitude for life.

"And to think we almost lost you, January," her mother said, adding more jam to her scone.

"I know, Mum. But you didn't, so isn't that brilliant!" She poured herself another cup of tea and lingered over the additive ministrations. Would her mother ever stop saying that? Didn't she know how it made her feel?

"Oh, sorry Jan, that was thoughtless. I keep forgetting. It was all so...not real."

"It was real, Mum. I had a baby. I lost a baby. The end."

Her mother reached across the table and placed her hand on her daughter's arm. "Darling, it wasn't all you. I could have been more understanding than I was. I caused you great anxiety. And, then there was the father, of course."

"Of course. There usually is."

"Well, it wouldn't have been good for you, Jan. You

know that. We've talked about it before."

"And it seems we are forever fated to talk about it." Jan rose from the table and carried her plate and tea service to the sink. She glanced sideways at her mother and saw the look of disappointment on the older woman's face. It doesn't do to lose patience with her, she thought. It just makes it harder for both of us.

"Oh, come on, Mum, let's us have a nice evening. We could listen to some music on the phonograph. Are you up for a listen?"

"Yes, dear, that sounds good. Maybe some of that American jazz?"

"Not too...lively for the hour, Mum?"

Mrs. Jameson looked up. "Well, I'm not planning to clean house afterwards."

Jan nodded. "Right, might just give us a bit of a lift."

They settled themselves in the small living room, and Mrs. Jameson took up her knitting needles. Just as Jan turned toward her reading chair, Mrs. Jameson let out a small cry.

"Darling, I'm so sorry, I nearly forgot!"

"What, Mum? Is anything the matter?"

"No, not at all, but I have to wonder at my mind! That Miss Mills came by today. You remember Margaret Mills who used to be at the Langston's place?"

"Margaret Mills? Whatever for? Are you and she that friendly?"

"Well, no, not really, Jan, but she does stop by on occasion. There are still people alive who wonder what I'm up to, you know."

"Well, of course, Mum." Jan wasn't going to go in that direction again.

"Well, apparently, the lady she works for has an opening."

Jan flipped through the pages of her magazine, starting from the back. Why ever would she order tulip bulbs from Holland when she could buy the Dutch bulbs right down the street at Harbingers Nursery?

"January?"

Jan looked up. "Yes, Mum?"

"Aren't you interested?"

"Well, who is the woman and what is the opening? I've a decent enough job at present," Jan said. "For now."

"Apparently, the woman is Rosemary Parker-Pryce from the Parker House estate...she owns it, inherited it, I don't know, but she needs someone to read to her."

"Read to her? Is she illiterate? Or ill?"

"Gracious, no Jan, she's nearly blind!"

"Oh...sorry."

"It's for six hours a day and it pays double what you're making working eight hours a day."

January put her magazine down. "Really? Are you quite serious, Mum?"

"I am, although it's for six days a week. You have to be there to read her mail to her."

"Her mail?"

"Yes, and I guess it's all very hush-hush."

"What does that mean?"

"I don't know for certain, but I gather that...I'm not sure."

"You know something," Jan said, leaning forward in her chair toward her mother.

"Not really. Margaret said something about this Miss Parker-Pryce's confidential correspondence with someone, utmost discretion, trustworthiness—all the things you are, dear."

Something was tugging at Jan's brain, but she couldn't quite place it. She didn't believe in coincidences. Fate, yes. Destiny, yes. But a coincidence? It was just a word to describe a reality that someone who didn't understand fate and destiny would call it. How does it happen that she can barely face returning to that old geezer's office, and a friend–no, a casual acquaintance really–drops by to tell her mother of a possible job for the daughter?

"She said you should go 'round tomorrow after lunch if you were interested."

"Hmm, well, let's see how we feel about it when we wake up tomorrow. It does sound...intriguing."

"Very well, my dear, let's think on it overnight. I do think I'll toddle on off, Jan. Can't keep the hours I used to keep!"

Jan stood up and reached out to her mother. They gave one another a warm embrace and a sweet kiss. "Don't stay up too late, dear." Mrs. Jameson said.

"No, just a bit longer, Mum. I'll let this last log burn down a bit more."

As she heard her mother finally get into bed, Jan turned off the light and sat in the darkness staring at the fire. There wasn't much heat coming out of it. But she wrapped the Afghan blanket around her shoulders and contemplated her new opportunity. It paid the same. It was closer to home. It was working for a woman instead of a man. How difficult could it be to read someone's mail? In many ways, it sounded like a dream job. Maybe this could lead to something. Maybe she could get her life back to something resembling normal. All right, she cautioned herself, at least not so terribly *abnormal* as a randy old man hoping against hope to 'accidentally' brush against her ample bosom.

***

Tadley, June 27, 1914

This was not going to be a typical employment interview. As Jan applied a bit of rouge to her cheeks, and ever so slightly dabbed her lips with the same gloss, she wondered at the woman who had invited her to tea as a way of introduction to the letter-reading position. Well, it was hardly anything one could properly call *a position.* More like a daily task. One that apparently paid quite well. Who hires someone to read and write love letters? What else could they be? *She could be writing a tawdry novel, I suppose—one of those sensationalistic fictions so popular with the masses. My guess is love letters though. Has to be.*

Jan shook her head and turned in the mirror. *Did she look as good in profile as she hoped she looked straight on? Not really. Well, it's the truth!* Her mother was next door talking to the neighbor so this would be a good time to make her getaway. Jan looked at her watch. The driver from the Parker-Pryce estate would be arriving any moment. The thought had barely formed when she heard a sharp rap on the door.

As Jan walked through the living room to the entryway, she could see a long black car in front of the house. She knew her mother would be going on to old Mrs. Graham about her only daughter's rather "important" social engagement. Jan knew the two of them would be peering out the window of Mrs. Graham's cottage, hoping to see something, anything, they could talk about for the next week or so.

On the ride to the estate, Jan reviewed her qualifications for being a reader and writer of love letters. Well, one, she had been in love, once, so she knew that it was a state of near madness. Therefore, she concluded, the Parker-Pryce woman was probably quite daft. Yes, well, one couldn't exactly articulate *that* qualification in quite *those* words, now, could one? No, it would have to go something like, 'Yes ma'am, I am well-acquainted, intimately acquainted, actually, with the kinds of circumstances that require absolute and incorruptible discretion.'

Incorruptible? No. Better word, something that doesn't sound as though there's the slightest thing wrong with whatever her ladyship is writing and receiving. And *doing*—in between the letter writing, of course. Something that gets across the idea that Jan knows what sexual relations involve—does she ever—and finds it as natural and acceptable a condition—condition? No. As natural and acceptable as...as what? As so many worthwhile human endeavors. A bit formal, that, but better than *condition*. Right. What else?

'Well, two, Mrs. Parker-Pryce, I took top level in my Composition exams. I read a great deal, including current events, and I'm fond of poetry, although fiction is my first love. Oh, let's see, well, Willkie Collins, of course, Jane Austen, all the old standards and classics, I think one could say.

'Then, third, I am reliable. Meaning I show up each day. I stay until the work is done, and I don't impose myself upon one's personal life—except of course, by invitation, such as writing love letters.' *Perhaps I ought to refer to it in general terms. Such as 'handling your private correspondence, ma'am.'*

Was she to take dictation, she wondered, or was she to compose original lyrics to music scores of love? January smiled. She was approaching this new position—possible new position—with far too much *sans-souci-ism* than one ought when depending so completely on the income from it. Well, her mother had that small pension, barely enough for two weeks' groceries. They owned their cottage, of course, thanks to January's father who had the foresight to leave a small insurance policy on his life before he unceremoniously took it. I'm thirty-four years old, Jan thought, and literally half of my family is dead. My father and my son. My mother is staying alive through sheer will to find out what happens to Mrs. Graham, who has no family, few if any resources and a heart so generous she'd willingly give you her last scone.

Jan made a mental reminder to drop a five-pound note in the mail to Mrs. Graham come Monday. She'd been sending the anonymous bequests for three years. No one knew. She loved to see the look of glum forbearance on her mother's face when Mrs. Graham lived to die another day. Little did Hope Jameson know that under the little cloth serviette Mrs. Graham brought over once a month were the cookies she baked with the money Jan gave her. They were tasty, too. Oatmeal cookies.

As the car slowed to pass through the wide, open wrought iron gates, Jan looked up ahead to the large and sternly constructed manse. The stone was dark, but the wooden trim was a stately grey. Stately and a bit faded, even peeling a bit. A huge mahogany double door with a massive cast iron doorknocker was the only vaguely ornamental aspect of the facade. It could use a good polishing, she observed. Jan was no sooner out of the car than the massive door swung open, and a tall, thin, gaunt-looking woman wearing a long black skirt, a white blouse and a black shawl smiled at her. If she was self-conscious about a couple missing teeth, she didn't show it.

"You must be Miss January Jameson," she said. "I'm Margaret Mills. If I were a man, I'd be called a major-domo." She stopped and looked off somewhere over Jan's head. "But since I'm not, I'm called the head housekeeper. Welcome to Parker House. Pryce will be thoroughly enchanted!"

January hesitated at that last bit, but walked up the

front stone steps and extended her hand to the outstretched hand before her. Margaret Mills had quite a strong handshake. She was not a beauty, but there was something handsome about her. She seemed friendly, and her eyes held a bemused curiosity that Jan found unnerving. *What does she know about this meeting that I don't? Just about everything.*

Once inside the foyer, Jan slipped out of her raincoat and handed it to Mills. It almost seemed chillier inside the house than outside. Suddenly a loud and strong female voice emanated from behind the double doors of what must be the sitting room. "Well, bring her in, Mills, bring her in!"

"The Honorable Miss Rosemary Parker-Pryce," whispered Mills. She gave Jan a look as if to say, '*Here we go, then,*' and flung open the heavy doors to the large parlor.

So great are the psychological resistances to war in modern nations, that every war must appear to be a war of defence against a menacing, murderous aggressor. There must be no ambiguity about whom the public is to hate. Guilt and guilelessness must be assessed geographically and all the guilt must be on the other side of the frontier.

H.D. Lasswell, in Propaganda Techniques in World War I

TWO

Kingsclere, early afternoon, June 27, 1914

Jan expected to see a large woman, and she was not disappointed.

Rosemary Parker Pryce was not tall, and she wasn't heavy, but she was of compact and solid build and musculature, and she dressed like a woman who had spent the morning in the garden, with goats. Her long, heavy skirt nearly touched the tips of her well-worn work boots, and she had rolled her shirtsleeves up tight and high on her arms. She had grass stains on both the shirt and the skirt, and the boots were caked with dried mud. She walked briskly across the room, narrowly missing a table, and held out her hand to Jan.

"Sorry for the get-up, luv, just out milking the goats, mucking out the chicken coop and trying to kill that god-damn rabbit who keeps eating my petunias! Parker-Pryce," she added, "and you must be January!"

"Pleased to meet you Miss...Parker-Pryce," January said with a serious demeanor. She wondered how this sightless woman was able to do such chores.

"Oh, just Rosie or Pryce is fine," she said, waving away the formalities. "Do you go by January, then?"

"Or just Jan," Jan said, with a similar wave.

"Excellent. Come sit down and let's talk, then."

Jan followed Rosie–she had already decided she preferred that name–to the center of the room where a cozy seating arrangement was placed around an unlit fireplace.

"Still a bit warm for a fire, although I grant you the mornings and evening are unseasonably chilly, nippy even. Another few months, first week of October, I imagine we'll have the fire lit. So! Tell me about yourself."

"Well," Jan began, "I have been working as a secretary at Rennart Publishing and–"

"You worked for that dirty old groper? Good lord, Jan, you can't get out of there fast enough, I daresay!"

Jan opened her mouth to say something but she wouldn't have known what that was. Margaret Mills materialized with the tea service at that moment and offered the first of what Jan would come to rely on as perfectly- timed observations. January noticed Margaret had mud on her shoes, too.

"Well, Pryce, she's here now, so let's not dredge up old nightmares." Mills bent over to pour the tea. As she handed a cup to Jan, she offered another opinion. "He really is an old scoundrel, Jan. Pryce's father used to own that company and sold it years ago because Rennart was, well, he was disgusting. He once tried to grope Pryce, too."

"He did not, Margaret! He only told Daddy I was a sweet and pretty young thing."

Mills looked at Pryce and then back to Jan. "See? I rest my case. The man's a miscreant and a reprobate."

"The same thing, Margaret," Rosie said.

"Yes, Pryce, I know that. I'm being purposefully

redundant to emphasize the point."

"At any rate," offered Jan, "the old goat shan't be bothering me anymore. I resigned."

This announcement was met by silence. Jan sipped her tea demurely. Rosie coughed and Margaret busied herself with folding and unfolding her serviette.

"I don't mention that," Jan explained, "as any kind of pressure for you to hire me. I state it simply as fact, and in the event you would need a reference, I haven't one."

"Was Rennart your first position, then, luv?" asked Rosie

"No," Jan said. She took another sip of tea. "I was a mother for a brief period of time."

Mills stood up. "Perfect! Didn't I tell you, Pryce?"

Rosie looked in the direction of Jan, but her eyes seemed cloudy and unfocused. "So I suppose your husband works, luv?"

"No husband," Jan said. "Delicious tea, Margaret. May I have another cup?"

"Well, then, I believe you are my girl, Jan!" Rosie said effusively.

"I beg your pardon, Rosie?"

"Oh, she simply means you're hired!" Margaret cut in, fussing with the doilies on a nearby chair.

"Thank you," Jan said quietly. "And what is the remuneration?"

They looked at her blankly.

"The pay?" Jan said. "And the hours?"

"I'm prepared to double what that clumsy coot was paying you," Rosie said officiously. "And the hours are first post to last post."

It was Jan's turn to look blank.

"From ten in the morning until four in the afternoon," Margaret clarified. "Late letters go out in the next morning's post while new ones come in. Then answers to letters received in the morning go out in the three o'clock post. Then letters arriving in the afternoon get answered for the next morning's post, as I said."

"I see," said Jan. "So I would be writing about three letters a day, then, do I have that right?"

"Absolutely wrong," Rosie said with a big smile. "I write the letters, you take dictation and put it all in nice handwriting. Of course, if I make any mistakes, you are free to correct them. Never be reluctant to make me sound brilliant," she finished with a jerk of her head.

"Of course," Jan said.

"And don't forget the reading of the letters you receive," Margaret added. She turned toward Jan. "Sometimes they run for ten or more pages!"

"Rarely," Rosie clarified. "Don't frighten her, Margaret."

It all sounds perfectly acceptable," said Jan setting her teacup down on the nearby tray. "When do I report for work?"

"Oh, Margaret!" Pryce screamed. "Didn't you tell her? You know I have a letter that simply must go out today. Victoria is quite under the weather, and I can't have her sinking into ennui because I'm half blind and can't write my own letters! Margaret, you promised!"

"Victoria?" asked Jan.

"Oh, I made no such promise Pryce, and you know it. It was always understood that if January was unable to stay a while longer today, I'd write the damn letter myself."

"You'll do no such thing. Victoria knows your handwriting, remember?"

Jan watched this exchange, mesmerized by the easy, familiar banter between the two women. No one was seriously upset—Jan could see that.

"Well, if it can be done in time for me to be home by

supper, I'm more than happy to stay," Jan offered.

"Excellent!" Rosie said. "Margaret, let's set January up at the table, and, oh, let's move that table a bit closer so I'm not shouting."

"You're already shouting, Pryce," Margaret offered as she easily shoved a small library table closer to Rosie's chair.

"Because I'm happy, Margaret! I'm deliciously happy! I have a new scribe, and all is well with the world!"

***

Jan looked at her watch. She had to leave in twenty minutes or she'd miss the Kent's Coach back home. She hoped Rosie had arranged to get her to the station. It was only two miles from the Parker estate, but it would be getting dark in an hour. She watched Margaret bring another pot of tea in, and she rose from the table to partake. It was getting chilly in the big room.

"Excellent," said Rosie. "Let's have another cup, then read it back to me once more and we'll post it." She fingered the pieces on the chessboard placed on a table within arm's reach. Twenty-two pieces were lined up next to one another on one side of the board, while ten others were lined up on the opposite side. It didn't look like any chess game in progress that Jan had ever seen.

"Post will be here in fifteen minutes, Pryce," Margaret said.

Jan took her cup of tea to the table, picked up her notebook and began to read aloud.

Darling, I want you to be the first to know: I have a new scribe, a Miss January Jameson, an educated young lady with whom I feel I can entrust all of our confidences for the purpose of communicating with my beloved. I can't see her clearly, of course, but as I dictate this quick note, I sense that she is blushing! Oh dear! We shall yet turn her rose-white cheeks to crimson. Seriously, my love, do not restrain yourself—Jan, (she seems to prefer I call her that), is quite adult and dependable. She's from a small village in the area—Tadley, she informs me as she writes—and she is of great sustenance to her elderly mother who lives there yet.

Enough of the news of the day here! How is my darling? You mentioned being a bit under the weather—nothing serious I surely hope! You must let me know right away if I can send my physician to you. He would go for my sake...and he is the very meaning of discreet.

I've told January to read to me as she might a novel, a gothic novel, I think. She has a lovely voice (oh see, she's blushing wildly, even I can see it), and I've told her that it's actually not at all unlike your own. The timber, the accent, the inflection is so much like yours it's uncanny. Well, don't know if that's the right word, but you know what I mean. I miss your sweet smile and the feel of your skin against mine as you hold me closely. Perhaps I'd best save that for my evening letter!

Josephine is positively cantankerous today, and I heard her bawling out the poor postman for not delivering your letter to me first, Friday past. I didn't get it until midday Saturday and by then had missed the post. Forgive me my sweet—two letters from me today, I promise. Your new gown sounds divine. I've always loved you in black...very mysterious, exotic, tempting and wicked! Perhaps you'll wear it in September when next we sojourn to the Lake Country where I hope to personally...amend my equally wicked ways! Yes, I was too going to say that! I mean to make you smile when you read it.

Will write early tomorrow, darling. All my love, forever and ever, amen. R.

"Well, luv, what do you think of it?" Rosie asked.

"Hmm, well only that you said you'd write her back this evening..."

"Actually, I thought I said two letters from me today—and technically, I've written two letters because I wrote the part about Josephine earlier."

"You wrote it earlier?" Margaret asked.

"I wrote it in my mind, Margaret. Same thing." Rosie brushed an invisible speck off her sleeve. The look on her face indicated the speck might as well have been a bit of bird mess.

Jan stood up. She put the letter in an envelope, and addressed it to V.A. Cabot-Jones. She handed the envelope to Margaret, and walked to within a couple feet of Rosie. "Will that be all for today, then Rosie?"

Rosemary Parker Pryce looked up in the direction of the voice. She smiled. "Yes, well then, see you tomorrow at ten, unless you have any questions? I believe this will work out just capitally!"

"Tomorrow is Sunday, Pryce," Margaret said.

Rosemary didn't even look in Margaret's direction. Jan noticed this and wondered at the slight undercurrent of, what was it? Resentment? No, more like competition. "All right, then, see you Monday morning, Jan!" Rosemary said.

Jan nodded and then uncertain that Rosie could see the gesture, she spoke. "Excellent, see you Monday, then. Lovely to meet you, and thank you for the position." It was Rosemary's turn to nod, a small look of pleasant surprise shadowing her face.

Jan followed Margaret out the doors to the hallway and front door. Margaret helped her with her raincoat. “I do have one question, Margaret.”

“Only one? Do tell?”

“Who is Josephine?”

Margaret began to laugh softly. “You are a sharp one, are you not!”

“I try not to miss anything,” Jan answered, returning the smile.

“Well, then, I suppose it's best you know. I'm Josephine. It's my middle name. ‘V’ doesn't care for me, so we leave out the part about my living here. It's a long story. Maybe someday...ah, here's Rosie's driver.”

Jan blinked. “Very well, then,” she said, “I'll see you Monday.”

Jan was on time for her coach. Packages, boxes and one middle-aged servant with a small tote of produce surrounded her. Jan nodded to her and then sat with her eyes closed. She had a devil of a headache.

In any case, the bayonet isn't as important as it used to be. It's more usual now to go into the attack with hand-grenades and your entrenching tool. The sharpened spade is a lighter and more versatile weapon - not only can you get a man under the chin, but more to the point, you can strike a blow with a lot more force behind it. That's especially true if you can bring it down diagonally between the neck and the shoulder, because then you can split down as far as the chest. When you put a bayonet in, it can stick, and you have to give the other man a hefty kick in the guts to get it out.

Erich Maria Remarque, All Quiet on the Western Front

THREE

Tadley, early evening, June 27, 1914

As she approached the cottage, Jan was surprised to see every light in the house on. Even from the gate, she could smell the savory scent of a beef stew.

"Oh, hello, darling," Mrs. Jameson called out from the kitchen.

"Hello, Mother. Something smells so good!"

Mrs. Jameson poked her head around the corner. "Well, as you were gone all day, I imagined you must have been hired, and I thought we'd celebrate!"

"That's...wonderful, Mother. Let me just go freshen up a bit. Nice and warm in here."

Mrs. Jameson returned to her work in the kitchen.

"Take your time, dear, get comfortable."

Jan went to her room, closed the door and sat on the bed. She didn't really feel up to talking about her day, but she knew it was expected. The smell of the beef cooking almost made her nauseous. It smelled good from a distance, but, well, maybe it was that the house seemed so warm and close. Her head was pounding worse than ever. She rose from the bed and opened her door.

"Mother, do I have time for a quick bath? I feel the need to wash this day off me."

Her mother walked toward her. "Oh dear, was it awful?"

"No, no. Just that the coach was crowded and–"

"On a Saturday?" Mrs. Jameson asked.

Jan nodded. "Just a quick one, Mother. I got so chilled in that big house today."

"Of course, dear." Mrs. Jameson twisted the dishtowel in her hands. "But you did get the position, did you not?"

"Oh, yes, I did. I think it will work out just grand! I'll be out in ten minutes," she said, turning back toward the bathroom. While the tub filled with hot, steamy water, she splashed cold water on her face. The coolness helped her head.

Jan wasn't sure what she wanted to tell her mother about the day. It was, after all, privileged and private information. She was hired for her discretion. Jan reviewed the day and smiled as she recreated the Margaret and Pryce dialog. Those two have some kind of special relationship, she thought.

Jan leaned against the back of the tub and sank in the water up to her chin. She felt her muscles relax. For a few moments, she closed her eyes, but a sound from the kitchen made her start. She wouldn't get any rest until she went to bed later that evening. With that realization, she stood up and stepped out of the tub. She wrapped a thick cotton towel around her body and splashed the cold water on her face again. The headache was threatening in the background, but at least it had retreated from her frontal lobes.

"Oh my, don't you smell delicious," Mrs. Jameson said as Jan entered the kitchen in her turquoise lounging pants and top. "Will you be warm enough in that, January?"

"I'll be fine, Mother, it's actually nice and cozy in here." Jan peeked inside the oven. "Hmm. How soon?"

"It's ready when you are, dear."

"Mind if we have a libation, Mother? I mean if we're celebrating."

"Oh! Of course, although I don't think we have much liquor in the cabinet. Or mixer either."

"I can make us a lovely scotch and water. Would you like that, Mother?"

"Make mine very weak, Jan, or I'll be swinging from the chandeliers. Or would be if we had any!"

"Somehow, Mother, I don't see it. You swinging from the lights, I mean!"

As they shared a mutual laugh, Mrs. Jameson took the tumbler of scotch from Jan. "You might very well be surprised, young lady, at what your old mother has done in her youth!"

"Oh, tell me, Mother!" Jan said, smiling. They clinked glasses and took a sip of their drink. "Shall we sit in the living room a bit?"

Mrs. Jameson did not take her usual seat on the couch but instead sat across from Jan in one of the upholstered chairs. The fire was burning nicely and the glow from the table lamps gave the room a festive air.

Just as Jan was about to launch into some version of her day, her mother spoke.

"There was someone, in London—this is long before I met your father, of course. A dashing specimen, quite the posh background—not royalty but somehow connected to one of the cousins of the Queen. Eventually was given a knighthood."

"Is this someone who courted you?" Jan could barely hide her tone of astonishment.

"I suppose. In a way. It was doomed, of course, but I recall one evening when we went out dancing. Oh my! I can't honestly say we swung from the chandeliers, but it felt that way!"

"Why 'doomed,' Mother?"

Mrs. Jameson took a swig of her scotch. She coughed a bit at its medicinal kick. "I thought I said make it light!"

Jan laughed. "If I made it any lighter, it would just be water, and you know it!"

"Why doomed?" Mrs. Jameson repeated, gazing into the fire. "Oh the usual, I suppose. Different stations in life, different...interests, different everything, and yet, not different enough."

Jane was looking at her mother and waiting for more. She saw a small smile on her mother's face, and decided to let her bask in her own memories.

"Perhaps you should have married—" Jan began lightly.

"No!" Mrs. Jameson stood up. "I better get that dinner on, then, Jan."

Stunned at her mother's emphatic response, Jan sat frozen in the chair. "Oh Mother, I understand. You would never have had me! So I'm glad you married Father."

Mrs. Jameson looked at her daughter with amusement. "Are you going to help me, then?" her mother asked, pleasantly. "I can never get everything to stay hot at once unless you do."

Over dinner, Jan told her mother about the highlights of her day. She talked about writing the letter for Rosie but didn't mention the recipient's name. And Mrs.

Jameson didn't ask. “Now, how do you know Margaret Mills, Mother? I forget what you said.”

“Oh, I don’t really know her, January, not well anyway, but over the years, I’d see her around the village. You know how it is. I believe she knew Beatrice first.”

“Mrs. Graham? Our neighbor?”

“The very same,” Mrs. Jameson said.

Jan had rarely heard her refer to Mrs. Graham by her first name.

“I don’t think I’ve ever heard you call her by her first name!” Jan said.

“Oh, of course you have—you’ve just forgotten. Well, anyway, Beatrice knew Margaret from years ago. I understand she practically runs Parker House estate.”

“It does seem that way,” Jan answered. “Of course, it’s only my first day, but I rather liked Margaret. Seems a good sort.”

“And Miss Pryce? She is still unmarried?”

“Still? As far as I know,” Jan said.

“I just—I never heard that she had married. Just wondered.”

“Did you know her parents, Mother?” Jan asked.

“No, I did not. I may have met her father, once, at some town meeting, but I couldn’t swear to it. It was a long time ago. Now, your father, he knew Miss Pryce’s mother.”

“He did? How?”

“She was the very pretty Jahney Parker when she married Mr. Pryce. I think your father might have had a youthful crush on her. I believe they attended the same church, St. Catherine’s, over Wolverton way.”

“Mother! You know more about Rosie Pryce than I realized.”

“I know a few things, my dear girl.” Mrs. Jameson mashed up her potatoes with her fork and scooped some of the stew gravy on to them. She smiled at Jan. "So, how is it? To work there, I mean?"

Jan buttered her biscuit. Still holding the knife aloft, she looked off into some mythical distance. "They're quite different from us. Well, there's the wealth, of course, although I don't know how much of that is left. Place is a bit shabby, a little run down. Neglected, I'd say."

"Well, people are people Jan, whatever possessions they have or don't."

"Oh, I know, Mother," Jan said. She took another bite of her biscuit after dipping it in the gravy.

"Be sure to eat those carrots, Jan, they're fresh today."

"And delicious," Jan said with a smirk. She hated cooked carrots.

"Oh go on," her mother said, grinning. "Good for your eyesight."

"I mean, for instance, when they say, 'Hello, how are you?' they don't really expect you *to tell* them. Well, maybe Rosie's a bit different—I actually think she wants an answer, but some of the people she...her crowd. That's not right, either, as she hardly seems to have a crowd. Just Margaret. Oh, I don't know, but her kind is different. From us."

"Well is she pleasant to you, Jan?"

"Oh, yes, very. Asks my opinion, holds regular conversations, but..."

"What, dear?"

"I can't quite explain. It's as though her face is out in front of her. That is, she's a lot of performance, if you know what I mean. A bit dramatic. Good heart, though, I think. Lonely. Sometimes I wonder if the letters she gets and sends are her entertainment. And yet...I don't know, Mother, I can't quite figure her out just yet."

"Well, you may never have to, Jan. It's just a job, more or less, isn't it?"

"Yes, it is, and yet, it's something more, too. These people, well, Rosie and Margaret, pull you in somehow. I don't know their full story but I find myself wanting to. Is that strange, Mother? Am I the odd one?"

"We're all a bit odd, January, and it's frankly a miracle how the human race has managed to survive this long!"

Jan laughed. They both did. They finished the meal with the usual sounds of palates teased, then tantalized, then savored with the hot juices and flavors of the stew.

"Nice cut of meat, Mother, tender, falls apart."

"It is, isn't it? Of course, it did cook for six hours!"

"Oh no!" exclaimed Jan. "You had to sit in this house with that aroma all day. And poor Mrs. Graham must have been positively tortured."

"Yes...Jan, why don't you take a small plate over to her, the poor dear. It's still early, I know she's up, and I doubt she's eaten much today. Give her some extra potatoes, as she adores them, and plenty of gravy. A bowl of this will probably last her three days if she covers it and refrigerates it properly. Tell her that. I mean, remind her. Remind her to cover it when she puts it in the icebox."

Jan looked down at her plate, afraid to look up for fear of hearing her mother change her mind. "Lovely idea, Mum, and we've plenty for us for the next two days. I'll do it now, before it gets too late. Unless you want to take it over—"

"No, Jan, you go ahead. I visited with her today. One can only take just so much Mrs. Graham."

"...Kaiser Wilhelm II was finding himself largely frustrated in his desire to carve out a grand imperial role for Germany. Whilst he desired 'a place in the sun,' he found that all of the bright areas had been already snapped up by the other colonial powers, leaving him only with a place in the shade."

War of the Nations: The Caldwell Series by Dan Ryan

FOUR

London, July 1, 1914

Winston sat in one of the leather wingback chairs, a book about Leonardo da Vinci on his lap. He looked off across the room, seeing nothing distinctly, feeling everything precisely. He sipped his scotch. As he replaced his tumbler on the side table, a shadow crossed his face.

"Is that you, Cabot-Jones? By God, it is!"

Winston looked up but the face before him didn't register. The man put out his arm.

"Carter. Ben Carter!"

Winston started to rise, the vigorous handshake pulling him out of his chair.

"By damn, it is you, isn't it?" Winston said.

"Thought you were dead, too, old boy!"

"When did you get back from the States?"

"About an hour ago! Thought to come here to the club first as I've not let a place yet. Camille and the girls will be arriving in a couple of weeks."

Winston motioned Carter to take the chair across the table from him. Carter dropped a heavy-looking medical satchel on the floor and backed into the deep seat.

"Damn, I'm tired. Hell of a trip. Crowded. Didn't know if we'd sink or just die young from all the copious drinking at those American cocktail parties. Rough trip."

"Ah, sorry to hear that. Well, you're here now! What's the plan?"

"Not sure, yet," said Carter. "I've been offered head of the department at Middlesex Hospital. Doing some awfully impressive therapies over here. How is your lovely wife, by the way?"

"Not good, truth be known. Not good at all. Wasting away, basically."

"Who's seen her? Who's in charge of her treatment?"

"That's the problem, Carter, she won't be seen. But her general physician says there's nothing wrong with her. Nothing serious. A bit anemic. He says it's...it's emotional. Possibly depression."

"Sorry about that, Cabot-Jones," Carter said, closing his eyes. "If I take the position, I'll come see her. We have a new treatment for hysteria that—"

"I seriously doubt my wife is hysterical, Carter."

"No, no, of course not. The thing is, old chap, there's a therapy we use for...for this kind of thing. Especially women. Seems to work quite well on women."

"You don't say?" Winston said, his tone revealing his lack of interest. "Speaking of the Germans, you've heard the news? About the Archduke?"

"Yes, everyone in London is talking about it. People are wondering if Austria will declare war on Serbia."

"I doubt Germany is wondering," Winston said.

"We're going to be dragged into it, you know that, don't you? I don't see this ending well. Could change everything for Camille and me. I'm still young enough to be called up, I suppose."

"I doubt you'd be put in the actual theater," Winston said. "More likely you'd be assigned war hospital duties here."

"I didn't think we had that many war hospitals left after we got over the Boers shooting us up in Africa," Carter said.

"We don't Ben, but you know how fast that can change."

"True enough. Well, anyway, if you change your mind about me seeing Victoria, uh, Anne, let me know. I'll drop you a note next week. To let you know where I am," he added, rising from the chair. "Seriously, Winston, you should let me come by and see her."

"I suppose you could...she rarely leaves the bed these days anyway," Winston answered, his voice barely above a whisper.

"Yes, let me come 'round, take a look at her. Camille will want to see her too, I'm sure. They go way back, you know."

"Drop me a note," said Winston, rising to shake hands again. "Let me think on it. I've heard about some of the new therapies. It can't do any more harm, I imagine."

"Excellent," Carter said. "You'll be hearing from me."

Winston watched as Carter made his way across the room. A good man, he thought. Lucky, too. Loving wife, two pretty children, and his choice of medical positions at first-rate hospitals. He wondered what experimental hypnotic hocus pocus they would try on Anne. In addition, what if Anne's problem isn't mental or emotional? Does it matter? She's half paralyzed, she's slowly wasting away, she writes love letters to...to that woman, and she hasn't been the same since—how long has it been? Two years? A few months shy of two years, he remembered.

But Anne really took a turn for the worse earlier in the

month. It was when all the war talk escalated. The government was not so secretly declaring its preparing of contingency plans to help France if Germany invaded. That meant troops. How long before Britain would declare itself at war? They were all maniacs. Power-hungry lunatics. But Anne was no maniac. She had power she wouldn't, or couldn't, employ. She could have left him. He asked her not to, but he could not have stopped her. But no, she chose to waste away, blind to her own guilt. For God's sake, he absolved her. He told her so. But was it guilt? Or something else?

But why? Why did she suddenly become incapable of living? Incapable of wanting to live? And the other one! She actually *is* half blind. And all they do is write letters to one another. Something happened. Something happened to Anne. They don't call. They only write. What happened between them? Well, what happened is obvious—perhaps the question is why did it stop happening? *Did* it stop happening? It must have done. Anne hasn't been out of that bed much in the past three months, hasn't been able to walk of her own power for nearly six.

And when did she stop loving him, he wondered. He was always wondering that. Had she ever really loved him? Maybe not. Their intimacy had been—what? Strained? Yes. Infrequent? Yes. Passionless? Yes. Perfunctory? Yes. Predictable? Yes. His fault, he supposed. He couldn't move her...and then he didn't want to. Had he tried? Yes. Had he given up? Probably. But they got on so well in every other area. She was...she was a friend. More than anything, she was his friend. Or had been until the letters began.

The letters were everything now. He had no friendship with her now. Not like before. They used to laugh. To banter a bit. They had some friends. They had their home. They each had interests, differing and similar. They had...what? They had an agreement. Implicit yes, but no doubt an agreement. He would not approach her, intimately...sexually...and she would not reject him. But isn't lack of passion rejection? Isn't writing two and three letters a day to her beloved paramour rejection? Yes. Yes. And yes.

What drew Britain into the war was technically a pretext of honoring a long-forgotten 1839 Treaty of London agreement in which the British committed to defend Belgian neutrality. Using this old treaty and a newer 1912 one with France called the Anglo-French Naval Convention, Britain promised its protection of French coastline from its historical arch enemy, Germany. When Germany asked Belgium for passage across its sovereign lands to reach France, Belgium refused. Germany marched into Belgium anyway. German military strategists had long planned to take on both Russia and France, so they were ready for a war on two fronts. The Germans felt strongly that Britain would remain out of the fray to protect its commercial interests. They were half wrong.

FIVE

Tadley, Hampshire, July 3, 1914

Michael Sullivan did not enjoy being a physician. He would rather have been writing poetry, a book or a play. He pulled on his raincoat, picked up his medical bag and trudged out the side door of his flat for the quarter mile walk to the train. The skies were threatening and full of unshed moisture, but it was not yet raining.

Once inside the train car, Sullivan pulled out a novel he was reading. Everyone was coming into Reading on the approaching tracks, headed for London, no doubt, but his car was half empty and heading opposite for the countryside. He pulled out a pack of cigarettes and lit one. As he pulled the grey smoke into his lungs, he looked out at the misty morning, the soot-streaked mercantile warehouses and the odd itinerants cowering in the doorways for warmth before the workers arrived.

Rosemary Parker-Pryce. He hadn't thought about it before now, but it seemed all his patients were odd in some special way. He was affiliated with a hospital, of course, and had his small office, but most of his work was done in the mansions and country houses of the eccentric and wealthy patients who came recommended to Sullivan when no one else could help them. With war looming, his business would grow. But his healing arts would not attend to lost limbs or bullet holes. No, his domain was the mind. He supposed that was as close as he would come to being a philosopher, an artist of words, and a healer of broken minds. But Parker-Pryce baffled him like no other. He kept feeling that he was missing an integral second half of her condition.

Her condition. She wasn't blind, but she couldn't see, either. Not clearly anyway. There was no neurological cause. None he could find. All the tests for that had been given and the results were within normal range. There was no optic nerve damage. There was no brain swelling. Yet, 'twas her mind, that indecipherable, invisible part of her brain, that was traumatized.

By the time he reached Tadley, he was anxious. Why did he always wonder where his life was headed just as he was about to see his patients? No one challenged his sense of his own insignificance like Rosie Parker-Pryce did. She'd much rather discuss world events than her inner life. Sullivan needed other input about Rosie. He daren't approach Margaret Mills for further insight, as that would breach the trust he'd worked so hard to establish with his volatile patient. But he felt he was getting close to something.

When he walked into the cavernous, chilly room where Rosie was parked comfortably on the couch with several blankets around her, he noticed the brightness of her cheeks.

“Good morning, Rosie! You look quite flushed–have you a fever?”

“I don't believe so. Good morning, Michael! I've been up for hours, and I'm on my third cup of tea. Would you care for some?”

“If it's not too much trouble,” Sullivan said.

Rosie rang her little bell, and paused her hand in mid-air. “She'll know it's for tea, that's what two rings are.”

“What's one ring, Rosie, or three?”

“One ring is trouble! One ring is I can't bring up the strength to ring more! One ring is hard because you've got your one ring, then you have to wait a bit for a second one ringer, else she think it's two or three slow rings!”

“You have your own language of bells, then!” Michael said with a laugh.

“We do indeed. Ah, you see, and here is the tea! The language of bells works!”

Margaret Mills carried a large tray with a fresh pot of tea and service for two. “'Morning, Doctor! You must have let yourself in.”

“I did, indeed, Margaret. I knew that's why you left the door unlocked.”

“Here you are, Pryce,” Margaret said placing the tray on an ottoman between the patient and her physician. “I'll be back to the baking, then, before my breads burn.”

Rosemary watched Mills leave the room and sat with a quirky smile on her face looking at the closed door through which Margaret had departed.

“Don't know what I'd do without Margaret,” Rosie said.

"And yet..." Sullivan began. "And yet there are things you do not share with her I think. Am I right?"

"You are indeed. Some things, though not much."

"Name one," Sullivan challenged though his tone was soft and barely above a whisper. He placed the blood pressure cuff gently on her upper arm, an arm covered in a gorgeous grey silk pajama top. A man's pajama top.

Rosie turned to look out the French door windows that led to the patio. "She doesn't understand what happened to me."

"Do you? Do you understand, Rosie?" Sullivan asked gently.

"Yes and no. I understand that things became too difficult to see, so I stopped seeing them. I didn't even know I could do that, and I surely don't understand how to reverse it."

"But...but you'd like to?"

"I think so, yes. It's time. I'm tired of these cloudy eyes. Any ideas?"

"Well, just one, perhaps. What do you think would happen should you find yourself suddenly able to see as clearly as before the...before the shock?"

"No idea."

"Well, perhaps you could be thinking about that answer. You must sometimes wonder how it would all change if you could see again."

"I do wonder," Rosie said, "but I never get much beyond wondering. It doesn't cause me to make any new plans, or revisit old ones."

"Really?"

"Really. Oh, yes, of course, I'd probably try to make contact with Victoria...but..."

"Probably?"

"I don't want to hurt her again, or hurt her more."

"Perhaps with vision, the way to achieve that would be

more obvious to you. You know, your blood pressure is a bit high. Higher than last month. Has anything happened?"

"What do you mean 'happened'?"

"Any changes around here, any surprises, anything different in the past few weeks, Rosie?"

Rosemary shook her head. "Nothing I can think—well, yes, one small change but I find it most agreeable. I've got a new reader."

"Oh, excellent!" Sullivan said. "And you think this one will work out?"

"I do. She's very discreet...had some love gone wrong problems herself...even had a baby. Baby died, boyfriend took off, that kind of thing."

"And she's educated?"

"Quite. An excellent writer as well as my reader—someone has to write the letters I send Victoria, you know."

"And you're both still writing every day?"

"Of course!" Rosemary said. "Sometimes three times a day! Oh, yes, there is something that's changed. How could I not think of it first? I fear my Victoria is failing or fading or both. She's taken to lying to me about her activities."

"Lying? What do you mean?" Sullivan asked.

"Just that she wants me to think she's up and about and doing fine. I know her well, Michael, and when she's extra bright about things...well, I know it's quite the opposite for her. I have no way to know for sure, of course."

"Who is her physician?"

"I don't know, she never mentions him. I've asked of course, but she says he is the husband of an old friend. That's all. I do know he's somehow associated with Middlesex Hospital, though."

"Hmm."

"Is that your hospital, too, Michael?"

"It is, indeed. But there are so many physicians..."

"Are there a lot of psychiatrists, though?"

"No, not so many. If I had a bit more to go on, perhaps I could look into it for you."

"Oh could you, Michael, could you really?" Rosie sat up straight and clapped her hands together with undisguised joy.

"It's not quite proper, you understand...but, well anyway, I'm curious myself. What did you tell me is the matter with her?"

"She's evidently paralyzed, but only on her left side. And not fully. She has use of her legs and arms, but I suppose the left side is very weak. But you know, it's not really her legs I'm worried about. It's her state of mind."

"Oh?"

"She's so worried about war coming. Then there's her situation with her husband–I'm not sure what that situation is, but they don't carry on as man and wife in the, ah...in the conjugal sense. So, that has to be a strain.

"Is it?" Sullivan asked.

"Well, anyway," Rosie said batting away his question or, more likely, the thought that parented it.

He watched her movements and saw that she expressed her most intense emotions with her hands.

"Then I know she worries endlessly about me. We have plans to meet in the Lake District in a couple of months."

"Really? Is this a new development?"

"No, not really...more like a repeat performance, I fear. We made the same plans last year, and then she cancelled."

"I recall you mentioning it. Ever find out why?"

"Nothing specific, just 'circumstances,' she said. I let

her off easily because she was so worried about my reaction to the news. I think...I don't know what to think. She loves me, Michael, more than anyone ever has, more than she's loved anyone. At least I think so. I believe it. Oh it's all so upside-down, isn't it?"

"And what do you suppose keeps you from just showing up at her door? You're bold like that, Rosie, I know you are," Michael said. He smiled benignly, knowing she couldn't clearly see his face, and amazed, as always, that she trusted him with her most unusual story.

"I don't know," Rosemary answered. She fiddled with the fringe of her blanket. "I'm afraid, I suppose."

"Afraid of...?"

"Afraid that I won't be able to read her, to know, for certain, by looking at her, if things are good with us. They seem to be, but I must see her face, Michael, look into her eyes. I've always been that kind of person. This letter writing, well...letters are good, I love getting hers, but I'm not so prolific as Victoria. She can write volumes!"

"Well, what about this high blood pressure. What can we do today to get that down a bit? Are you getting enough sleep?"

"Probably not."

"Are you eating properly?"

"Probably not."

"Are you still smoking?"

"Probably."

"Rosie," he said. "I thought you told me you'd cut back. You've increased, have you not?"

"Well, you smoke, Michael!"

"I don't have high blood pressure, but at any rate, will you try harder to cut back?"

"Yes...I was only having a few in the evenings, but then, oh hell."

"Then?"

"Then this new reader started working for me and, well, it's not that easy, Michael to divulge one's entire private life to what amounts to a total stranger."

"But you knew that before you hired her," Michael said.

"I did, yes, but this one is different. I feel as though she reads my mind. Oh, I trust her, I don't mean that. I simply mean I find myself filtering things through her, asking her what she thinks of what I say in my letters, that kind of thing. I write, well, I dictate, as I always did, without restraint, but then, when she reads the letter back to me—oh gracious, I think I hear her in the hallway."

The door to the parlor opened and January walked in but stopped just inside the threshold when she saw Michael Sullivan.

"Oh, so sorry, I thought—" January waved her hand in an indeterminate direction.

Michael Sullivan stood up and turned toward January.

"Jan, meet my doctor, Michael Sullivan. Michael, January Jameson, my...associate."

Jan and Michael gave one another a smile and nod of the head. Jan stayed stuck in her position, unsure what to do next.

"Come in, come in, Michael was just leaving, weren't you Michael?"

"I believe I was," Sullivan said. He smiled at January again and raised his eyebrows as if to say, 'Do I have a choice?'

"Oh, Rosie, I was just here to say I'll be having a cup of tea with Margaret in the kitchen until...until Dr. Sullivan is actually gone." With that, she turned on her heels and left the room before anyone could object.

"Michael? Hello, Michael? Why are you staring at that door?" asked Rosie.

"Because I think I just saw an angel," he said, turning back to Rosie. "Is *that* your new reader?"

"Indeed, shall I mention that you asked after her," Rosie said with a lilt of humor in her voice.

"Well...no."

Rosie made a small noise of dissatisfaction. "Can't stop me, but don't steal my reader away from me, doctor!"

"You won't always need her, you know," Michael said, as he gathered up his medical bag.

"You believe that, don't you," asked Rosie.

"I do, Rosie, I surely do. See you in week or so. I'll show myself out."

Austria accused Serbia of masterminding the murder. Emboldened by the military support of Germany, Austria delivered an ultimatum to the Serbian government that, if accepted, would have made that country a virtual possession of the Austro-Hungarian Empire. Russia weighed in on the side of the Serbs. Surprisingly, Serbia bowed to all of Austria's demands -- except one. Austria would find Serbia's refusal the ideal justification to declare war, which she would do by the end of July.

SIX

Kingsclere, July 15, 1914

January entered the Parker house by the back door, which led through a large storeroom and into the kitchen. She had taken to doing so within a week of taking the position. Two weeks into the job, she was glad to come through the back as it gave her time to hang her cloak, have a cup of tea and go over the most recent letter of Rosie's to ready it for transcription. Jan and Margaret had taken to sharing a quarter hour or so before Jan had to go to work.

"Nasty little storm we've got going on out there," Margaret said. "Any trouble on the trains?"

"No, and I have to say it really helps to have Rosie's driver waiting for me at the station each day. I'd hate to have to walk that distance in good weather, never mind inclement," Jan said. Sitting down at the large farm table, she pulled her notebooks out of her satchel, while

Margaret brewed the tea.

"Made a full pot for this shivery day," Margaret said. She placed the teapot on the table and covered it with a cozy. "We'll just let that steep for a few," she said, waving back Jan's movement to pour.

Margaret brought a plate of something over from where they were being kept warm atop the stove. "Fancy a bit of Irish soda bread?" she asked.

"Oh, I do," said Jan. "With raisins, I hope."

"Is there any other way?"

"Well, plain."

"Well, we're not that poor just yet," Margaret said biting into a piece of bread spread generously with fresh butter.

Jan spread the butter on her piece and added a thin spread of marmalade.

"Ach, got a sweet tooth I see," said Margaret as she reached for Jan's cup to pour the hot brew.

Jan took the cup, added a bit of milk and a tint of sugar and washed down the bread with a careful sip of the tea. "Umm," she said, taking another sip. "I do think you brew the best tea, Margaret."

"The key is boiling water," Margaret said. "Most people think hot water's enough. It's not. Got to be boiling. My Irish grandmother taught me that."

Jan watched Margaret close her eyes as she drank the tea.

"So, are we on our way to the poorhouse, then, Margaret?" she asked.

Margaret's eyes remained closed. "I shouldn't think it will be any time soon," she said, "unless this blindness continues to keep The Honorable Her Nibs away from work."

"Work!" Jan exclaimed. "Rosie works?"

"Did once," said Margaret, "until the accident."

Jan wondered how Rosie's eyes had been damaged. “Horse riding?” asked Jan.

“No. Car accident.”

“Oh dear! Was she driving? Anyone else hurt?”

“No. 'V' was driving, and yes, she was hurt too.”

“When was this?”

Margaret looked at her a long minute, then poured some more tea in both their cups.

“If I tell you, you'll just have more questions. But since you're going to be working alone for a couple hours this morning, I'll tell you.”

“Where's Rosie?” Jan asked.

“A bit under the weather, but she'll be down from her quarters later this morning.”

Jan fiddled with her fountain pen. She rolled it around in her fingers for a moment, then set it down and reached for another piece of soda bread. “Delicious,” she said, pointing to the half-eaten loaf of the fresh bread.

They sat in companionable silence for a while, with only the sounds of the radiators hissing out a heavy heat generated from the boilers in the basement.

“What work did Rosie do?” Jan finally asked. She decided to wait on the accident subject.

“Well, basically she ran the estate and oversaw the other Parker house enterprises, too,” Margaret said. “Her father was in publishing, as you know, but he was also in coal mining, diamonds, land and some farming. Cattle, mainly.”

“And since the accident?” Jane asked.

“Oh, a series of bad solicitors, a decent managing director or two and me.”

“You?”

“I know, hard to envision, isn't it?” Margaret looked down at her housekeeper uniform. I was trained as a bookkeeper, almost a full accountant. But all I could do is see how much money was coming in and going out. I had no authority, really, until Winston Cabot-Jones became the Managing Director. He and his wife Victoria knew Pryce socially, so he was a natural to try to save the Parker House interests. He appointed me as his Deputy Director. Everyone was happy for a few years, the estate was profitable once again and...everyone was happy. A couple people were happier than most." Margaret shook her head and looked directly at Jan.

Jan took the measure of the look, but was uncertain which question to ask first. She held the other woman's stare.

"Pryce and Victoria had a torrid love affair, sort of."

"Sort of?" Jan asked.

"Well, I only knew this somewhat after the fact, but apparently they were close friends who became a lot closer one long week when Winston was unable to join them for a shopping and theater week in London."

"I thought they lived in London," Jan said.

"They stay there frequently, usually at Claridge's," Margaret said, "but they live full-time right down the road from here, in Wolverton. Charming house. He has business interests in London, of course, but he stays at his club and comes home weekends. Seems like yesterday, that accident. Was it really three years ago? No. Just a bit over two," she concluded.

"And the accident? Did it happen that week?"

"Yes. They were about thirty miles from here. It was thick fog everywhere. Evidently, they were pulling into a small hotel when a lorry plowed into them. Knocked them both unconscious. They were both hospitalized. I got the first telephone call. Winston got the next one."

"Why were they going to a hotel if—oh."

"Exactly," Margaret said. "They made up some story later. Unfortunately, they each made up a different story.

Winston figured it out. As soon as Victoria was let go from hospital, he moved her to London. Had a house let and all their things moved while she was in hospital. She was paralyzed."

"Oh God! Completely?" asked Jan, the shock vibrating in her throat.

"No, and not right away. She was fine, actually, a broken arm, some cuts, bruises, that sort of thing. Same with Pryce. She was fine too. Within a month, Pryce started losing her vision and Victoria's left side became paralyzed. Very odd."

"Odd indeed!" Jan said. "What did the doctors say?"

"Well, they had different physicians, of course, but, nothing. No one could figure it out. They both had every test and examination possible. There's nothing wrong with either of them."

"What do you mean? Rosie can't see and V can't walk!"

"I can only tell you what Winston told me. He evidently has some physician friends, and they say it's a form of hysteria or mental breakdown, something of that ilk. Winston resigned as Managing Director of the Parker House enterprises, and arranged for me to have a stipend to stay with Pryce. Most of the business have been sold or leased, and she lives off the interest. I should add it's been dwindling the last couple years with all this talk of war on the continent."

"Is that why the house seems in a bit of disrepair?" Jan asked. She saw the look of surprise on Margaret's face. "I couldn't help but notice the paint is peeling," she added, waving her hand generally in the direction of the front of the house.

"Right," Margaret said. "Right. Well, she can't see it, so I don't mention it. We've enough to keep the roof over our heads, for food and heat, and some necessities, but I had to let the full-time driver go. He drives you to and from the station and sometimes Rosie will take a short ride for fresh air. And we're down to a small gardener crew of three for the entire estate."

"How big is the property," Jan asked.

"Now? Now, it's down to about fifty acres. Was over a thousand acres. Pryce had to sell it off. Most of it is let go to seed, but I've kept the gardening crew for the immediate area around the house. There's even a small lake on the property. Sometimes in the summer, I'll go fishing there."

"Why do you stay, Margaret?"

Margaret peered into her teacup as if she'd find the answer there.

"I don't know," she finally answered. "Old habit, I suppose. I worked for the Pryce family years and years ago. In fact, I was Rosie's tutor." With that, she rose from the table and began to clear away their bread plates and the tea service.

Jan took the last swallow of her tea before handing the cup over to Margaret. She wasn't prepared to say with any certainty that Margaret was lying, but Jan knew there was more to the story. Margaret's uncharacteristic choice of referring to Rosemary as 'Rosie' instead of 'Pryce' told her that much.

"There's a letter from V in the morning post. Pryce likes to touch the envelope and open it herself, so why not take it into the library, and I'll go tell her you're here and so is a letter. That will probably rouse her."

"A bit of a cold, then?" ask Jan.

"No, I think it's called depression. The blues."

"Margaret?" Jan took a few steps toward Margaret. "Margaret, did they never see one another again? Rosie and V?"

"Well, they write. Every day. Sometimes several times

a day." Margaret forced a smile and turned back to the sink.

"But—but have they *seen* one another. Since the accident, I mean? Have they, Margaret? They are five miles away from one another!"

Jan saw her swallow hard, but Margaret did not speak. She shook her head in negation then left the kitchen.

***

When Jan entered the library, Rosie was in her usual place in her oversized chair, a blanket around her legs.

"Bit chilly in here, Jan," she said. "Do you have a cardigan?"

"I do." Jan reached into her satchel.

"Good color on you, Jan," Rosie said.

Jan looked up, startled. "You can see the color?"

"Well, it's shadowy, of course, but yes, I can see a blue blur more or less. Here," she said, holding out an envelope. It was unopened.

"Did you want to open it?" Jan asked.

"If I wanted to I would have done," Rosie answered.

"Of course," Jan murmured. "All right, then." She took the letter opener from the table and slit the casing open with more sound than she intended.

Good morning, dear heart! I've just a minute before we leave for the theater but wanted to send something for your breakfast. Of course, it's early evening as I write this but will drop in post on way to Mr. Shaw's Pygmalion, a divine new play. Well I've heard it's divine—rave reviews, not surprised are we!

That German Kaiser is making those awful noises again. I really think he means to cause the entire continent harm. How could our beloved late Queen Victoria have him for a grandson! It defies understanding. He'd best not cause any delay of our travel plans, isn't that right darling! Only two more months and I shall see your gorgeous face, hold it in my hands and kiss your lips with mine. Oh, don't let me start on that—we're leaving the house in five minutes!

Don't be too hard on poor Josephine, love! And that's wonderful news about January—was she born in January? I'll try not to be too inhibited when I write but you know how long it took me to get used to Josephine reading my letters to you. Still, after a while I do forget all about a second pair of eyes.

I moved a bit more today on my own I might add, and though we're rolling me out in the chair this evening, that's only because I tire easily. I can walk, however gimpy that left leg is. So! Better all around—and oh, did your doctor really say you might see again? Darling, that would be so very wonderful! I will redouble my prayers!

All right, my heart...until later, I kiss you good morning, and remain yours alone forever and ever, amen. V

"Lovely," said Rosie. She rested her head on her hand.

"Shall we write back in time for the afternoon post?" asked Jan.

"*Were* you born in January, January?"

"I was indeed!"

"Yes, well, we'll write something, after a while. I'm not feeling all that positive, today, January, so I don't want to write too much because she'll know."

"She'll know what?"

Rosie sighed. She looked the other way, out the large French door windows that led to a small terrace. "She'll know I'm feeling low."

"I see."

"Actually, you don't," Rosie said, turning in Jan's direction. "Sometimes I miss her so much, so very much. Did Margaret tell you the story? I supposed she would."

"A bit," Jan said. "Enough for me to know it must be very hard for you."

"It's very difficult for both of us," Rosie said. "We miss one another in all the same ways, even—even when we don't specifically say which ways. It's better sometimes to avoid specifics. Sometimes, though, and you'll eventually see this, the specifics are simply not capable of being avoided. Well, enough of this self-indulgent blather. Get your notebook, January, let's write the lady a letter.

Darling, I'm reluctant to send this missive as I'm in a bit of a foul mood. No, I don't think I can wait two more God-damned months until I see you! I want you now! A woman like me...a woman like me...oh darling, it's coarse of me to say but...needs, desires, wants. I cannot wait two months! I won't! Make it happen sooner, my love, or I shall surely dry up and blow away with the winds of war that thump, thump, thump against my constitution like that God-damned window shutter on the side of the house that I've been meaning to get fixed. Well, see, love, I told you I shouldn't write. But you'll be expecting some word from me, so, begging your forgiveness for my selfish, surly, sexually depraved tantrum, I kiss you good morning and I remain yours alone, forever and ever, amen. R.

January held her pen in position to keep writing and was surprised that the letter ended so suddenly.

"Is that all, Rosie?"

"Is that all what, Jan? Is that all the naughty I can be? Certainly not!"

"All right, then, shall I go transcribe, Rosie?"

"You think I'm being mean, don't you?"

"I said no such thing, Rosie."

"No, but I can hear it...in the other words."

"Well are you? Are you being mean? I'll admit it sounds rather abrupt, however endearing, all at the same time."

"Endearing? Hmm. Good. Abrupt is good, too. I've got to do it that way, Jan."

Jan waited for further explanation but as there was none forthcoming, she rose to go to her table and begin transcribing. It shouldn't take long.

"Jan?"

"Yes, Rosie?"

"She's failing."

"She is? How do you know?"

"I doubt seriously that she went out to the theater. Besides, she loves theater and would have seen it back in April when it opened, which she didn't. She's giving up. I must rouse her. This is one way I know to do it!"

Jan sat back down.

"It's complicated, January. Margaret couldn't have told you everything, because Margaret does not know everything about it. I frightened her. Victoria I mean. When it happened. When we...when we were in London."

"But I thought you were together for a whole week. Did you scare her on the last day, then?"

Rosie laughed with the hollowness of the haunted and bereft. "No, Jan, I did that in the first hour."

Jan said nothing. She knew she was going to hear something she already knew.

"Oh, don't doubt it, Jan, she fell in love. We fell in love. Deeply, grandly, furiously. We were a perfect match in more ways than we could have predicted, although, looking back, and we did look back in wonder, separately and together, the die was cast when I first read her first letter to me."

"When was that?" Jan asked.

"Oh, when they first moved into the neighborhood about five years earlier. She wrote to tell me she was new in the area and would I care to come for tea. I didn't answer. I had no idea who she was and frankly could not be bothered. Daddy was alive then, but ill. And ill tempered on top of it. I had my hands full and I didn't feel like having tea with some housewife."

"She was a housewife?"

"Well, no, but I didn't know that. I was being unfriendly. Until I saw her. Oh my. No, she was no housewife. She was, however, a wife."

"And how did that meeting come about?" Jan asked. She tucked her left leg under her for warmth and comfort.

"She brought the tea to me! I heard Margaret fussing at the door—no, wait, was Margaret back with us yet? Maybe. Anyway, in she walks as comfortable as you please with two servants trailing behind her bringing tea and tea service and the most delicious scones.

"'I've not been able to discern why you never answered my invitation,' says she in her beautiful accent with her beautiful eyes dancing a tango of seduction in my parlor, 'so, I've done the next best thing and brought the tea to you! Victoria Anne Cabot-Jones,' says she, 'at your beck and call.'"

"Were you speechless?"

"Stunning as that might seem, yes I was. Utterly. And that's how it began. Later, later she'd come to garden with me, we'd ride out to see about the cows together, and she charmed that nasty little old man I called Father."

"Was he really nasty or was it the illness."

"No, he was nasty," she said, "but never to me. Everything he did, he did for me. But he was nasty to others. He wanted what he wanted when he wanted it."

Jan thought that apple didn't fall far from the tree, but she kept her own counsel. Something about Rosemary, though, told her it was more bark than bite. She'd supposed that from the very beginning, and her experience thus far confirmed it. She liked Rosie, liked her spirit and her passion. She liked her ridiculous but infectious joy at life. Not a quality Jan possessed but she could remember a time and a place she did, and a person who evoked it in her.

"We did everything together, Victoria and me, and most of the time Winston was there, too, or somewhere in the near background. I liked him. Anyway, he seemed...he seemed devoted to her. Yes, devoted."

"And was she?"

"Was she what? Devoted to him? Apparently not, Jan. But no one knew that at the time, least of all Victoria. That's part of what ended up frightening her. She was not who she supposed herself to be. Indeed, she was literally shocked by who she discovered herself to be."

"And how did you frighten her, then," Jan asked.

"Ah...Victoria was a wonderful woman, a very giving, loving woman, by nature. But she hadn't realized she was a passionate woman, and I neglected to see that the discovery completely frightened her."

"So, it wasn't a good discovery, then? For Victoria, I mean?"

"It was at first, I think, but after we were released from the hospital, I came home expecting her to arrive right after me. A day or two later, anyway. Instead, Winston took her to London, for an extended stay, and she..." Rosemary stopped. The memory cut her short. Her mouth was open, but no words came out. She put her hand to her mouth as if it were two years earlier, and she had just discovered Victoria was not coming back.

"It must have been very, very devastating to you," Jan whispered. She saw that Rosie's face had become more pale than usual.

Rosemary twisted her mouth a bit, pulled her shoulders back, and reached for the little bell she kept by her chair. "Let's have Margaret join us for a quick cup of tea before you go, Jan. It's cold out there." She rang the bell twice.

"And how did you reconnect," Jan asked. She felt she had to know.

"I wrote her a letter," Rosie said.

"So, you still had your vision?"

"Yes...that came later. About six months after she left the area. But I wrote her and quite surprisingly, she wrote back. We didn't speak of it, at first, of what happened, even, or even of us, but we started up a correspondence. At first, it was every couple of weeks. Then, every week. Then, every day. Then, several times a day. It was our lives. Each of our lives. She had come to realize she didn't love Winston, possibly never had, the way he would have wanted, and yet she couldn't leave. She felt so guilty for how it came about, how *we* came about, in London. She felt unable to leave."

"But Winston couldn't possibly have been unaware of her feelings about you, could he have?"

"I don't know. I don't know what they worked out. Sometimes I'm very jealous of him. She knows that. Did you know Winston handled all my business affairs? I suppose Margaret told you."

"Yes, she mentioned it."

"She and Winston handled everything. Margaret knows more about me than I know about me!"

"And why does Victoria dislike her?"

“It's a mystery to me!” exclaimed Rosie. “I only found out when we resumed our friendship. She simply said, 'I do not care for Margaret, but as she is of some help to you, I would be happy if you simply not mention her name.'”

“Hmm,” Jan murmured. “Curious.”

“Indeed, and I do feel rather badly about the 'Josephine' ruse, but I can't get 'round at all without Margaret, and it's nigh on impossible not to mention her, so I merely changed her name. I suppose I'll have to come clean someday, but I'll do it in person, not by letter.”

“And do you really think the rendezvous in the Lake District will take place in September?” Jan asked.

“No. Well, I'm not sure. I doubt it will be in the Lake District, but I will see her in the near future because I'm going to insist. That may involve talking to Winston, and good Lord, that could be a disaster of another kind altogether!”

Jan had the feeling that Rosie may have taken this line of thinking in the past. She seemed willing to force a meeting with Victoria and yet unnerved by the prospect of actually having one.

“Well, everything happens in its time,” Jan said, aware of the leeway she was providing Rosie. She wondered if Rosie would take that offer.

“I suppose you're quite right, January,” Rosie said with a big sigh, “and you're far too wise for your age. Incidentally, what age are you?”

Jan laughed and Rosie joined her. “I'll be thirty-four in six months.”

“Strange that I'm ten years older than you, but I feel much older.”

“So do I,” said Jan, laughing lightly, “I feel fifty-four!”

They sat in companionable silence while January transcribed Rosie's letter onto her personalized stationery. The scratch of her pen was the only sound. When she finished, she blotted the ink and then silently reread the letter.

"Does it still sound mean on a third reading?" asked Rosie.

"Oh, Rosie, it doesn't sound mean and you know it. It sounds...it sounds like something she'll be compelled to answer right away."

"That's the point, isn't it? Need to get her blood flowing. Even raise her ire a bit."

"Oh, I don't think she'll be angry. Alarmed, perhaps, but not angry. Will she?"

"She'll think me too given to the temptations of the flesh. Or rather, without sufficient fortitude to keep it to myself."

"Is that so? Truly?" Jan asked.

"No," Rosie said, "not actually. I exaggerate. She's deeply passionate, but our circumstances...our circumstances inhibit—no, that's not right either. We're both too afraid to see one another, and, speaking strictly for myself, I'm afraid not to! Damned either way!"

"So, we've gone full circle then," Jan suggested. "It began in fear and—"

"It didn't *begin* in fear, Jan, it became crippled by it. The fear I mean."

"And blinded by it," Jan said.

Rosie looked up suddenly but said nothing.

"I'll be off in a few," Jan said, standing up to gather her notebook and pens into her satchel. "So, see you Monday, then, Rosie."

Rosemary said nothing, but Jan saw her nod and turn her face toward the window where the sun's light was filtered through the trees and fell lazily to the ground in a free-form dappling of browns and beiges and grays. Jan left the large room quietly, afraid to turn and look back, but she wondered what sentiment those cloudy eyes would reveal if they were clear.

Excerpt from telegram exchange between Baron Tschirschky, German ambassador to Austria, and German Kaiser Wilhelm II, July 14, 1914: "But as soon as the period allowed Serbia to reply has elapsed, or in case she does not accept all the conditions without reservations, mobilization will be ordered. The note has been drafted in such a way that it will be practically impossible for Serbia to accept it." (Twice William II underlined the last sentence.)

SEVEN

Tadley, July 19,1914

Jan stretched leisurely, arching her back, raising her arms and flopping over onto her side so she could see the clock. Early Sunday morning. Her mother would have gone to Sunday services, so Jan knew she had a couple hours to herself. She got out of bed, slipped into her robe and headed for the kitchen. Coffee. It would be coffee today, not tea. A nice bold roast, a little cream, a half-teaspoon of sugar...ahhh.

Jan looked out the kitchen window while waiting for the coffee. She saw Mrs. Graham across the way, tending to her small garden. The old girl seemed in good shape. She was tall, slender and had a shock of white hair, bluntly cut but chic somehow. Jan watched as the neighbor pulled weeds out of the ground and threw them over her shoulder in a ferocious gesture of strength that seemed unnecessary to the task. Jan saw her stand up, put her hands on her hips and look up at the sky. Was she upset? Angry? Something Jan had never seen in her neighbor:

emotion. Jan poured her coffee and walked out the side door of the cottage.

"Good morning, Mrs. Graham! Looks like you're going to murder all those weeds!"

"I've a mind to murder something," Mrs. Graham growled.

"Oh." Jan stood awkwardly, warming her hands on her cup. "Would you like a delicious cup of coffee, Mrs. Graham?"

Beatrice Graham looked at Jan as if seeing her for the first time.

"It's fresh brewed," Jan added.

"Well, maybe I will, then," Mrs. Graham said. She took off her gloves and followed Jan into the Jameson kitchen.

"I don't suppose I could interest you in some of the best Irish soda bread this side of County Kerry, could I Mrs. Graham?"

Mrs. Graham smiled. "A girl after my own heart, she is! Of course, you could interest me. You'd have a hard time keeping me away from it now I know you have it!"

Jan brought the round loaf to the table, along with two small plates and a crock of butter. "Orange marmalade?"

"Of course," Mrs. Graham said, smiling.

The two women buttered their bread and drank their coffee in silence.

"You weren't for making up tall tales, now were you, January? This is the best I've had since Kerry."

"How long have you lived in England, Mrs. Graham?" Jan realized she knew precious little about her neighbor, although they had lived next to one another since shortly after January was born. Odd how you can be right next door to someone and never really know much about them.

"Oh, I've been here over forty years, now. Came in

thirty-four. Eighteen thirty-four," she clarified, as if there were any doubt.

"You've no doubt seen a lot of changes, then," Jan said. As soon as she said it, she thought it sounded vaguely insensitive. Or just dull.

"That I have, that I have."

As Mrs. Graham didn't offer to elucidate the changes she'd seen, *and by the way, who would want to sum up forty years over coffee?* Jan took a different approach.

"You know, this bread came from my new employer's house, the Parker Pryce estate."

"I thought it might. Margaret Mills was always good at baking. I didn't know common Irish soda bread was her specialty, though."

"Oh, you know Margaret, then?"

"I hope so," Mrs. Graham said. "She's my sister."

***

Kingsclere

When Jan climbed the stairs to her train platform, every muscle ached with anger and confusion. She found a seat next to a distinguished looking elderly man dressed smartly in tweeds, his mackintosh draped neatly across his lap, his umbrella lodged between the window and his leg. He tipped his hat to her and went back to reading his newspaper. *An old country gentleman. Back home after an evening in the city. Maybe the theater, maybe dinner with an old friend. He looked a bit lonely, though. Well dressed, wonder where he's from?* Jan shook her head. The things she made up about people! She sat back and closed her eyes through the lurching departure, the familiar sounds of steam and the smell of early morning humanity soothing her fevered brain.

She had claimed a headache. She spent most of

Sunday in her room, the shades down, the lights off. Concerned, her mother suggested calling the physician. *No, no, it wasn't all that bad. It was just a headache. Probably the winds. She'd have a bit of soup later. Go ahead, Mother, have your dinner.*

Hope Jameson said she'd do that and probably turn in early herself. She took January at her word about the headache and didn't seem to think anything else was wrong. Good. Jan wanted to think this through. She thought all day Sunday, and now again on the train.

Nothing made any sense. Why had her mother not mentioned the familial connection between Margaret and Mrs. Graham? Surely her mother knew of it. And come to think of it, why didn't Mrs. Graham seem even the least bit surprised to discover Jan did not know of the connection? It was one of those disclosures that seemed almost incidental, and yet not quite accidental. Something about Mrs. Graham's fraught demeanor yesterday bothered Jan. She had never seen the woman in such an animated state of distress.

She had mentioned the difference in last names but Beatrice just shrugged. "Well, Margaret isn't a 'Mills,' and I'm not a 'Mrs.'," she had said, as if it were the most natural thing in the world. Somehow Jan felt she already knew about the 'Mrs.' part. There had never been a single mention of a 'Mr. Graham,' and Jan thought it was just something older women sometimes did—added a 'Mrs.' to their name if they didn't want to be thought of as an elderly spinster.

Jan also wondered why she hadn't merely come right out and asked her mother about Margaret and Mrs. Graham. *Mother, you'll never guess what I just today discovered! How did I not know Margaret Mills and Mrs. Graham were sisters? I was so amazed!* Something like that. Let her mother fill in the blanks. But she hadn't done that. She chose to sit with her new knowledge and brood because not having known seemed unnatural. It left Jan feeling ill at ease. It was probably nothing. Mere oversight on her mother's part, something that simply never came up.

But Jan knew that wasn't the case. She knew because, for the time being, at least, she wasn't planning to ask Margaret Mills about it either. She wondered why.

When she opened her eyes, the older gentleman was smiling at her.

"Have a good rest, then?" he asked. "I tried not to rattle my newspaper too much."

Jan smiled. "Thank you, but I'm not sure I was sleeping."

He extended his arm across the aisle. "Ralph Whitmore," he said, "I've seen you on this train before, thought I'd introduce myself."

Jan shook his hand, which was fleshy, firm and warm. "January Jameson," she said. "Heading to Kingsclere."

"Ah, going onto Highclere myself. Do you live in Kingsclere then?"

"No, I work there. I live in Tadley."

She saw the amused twinkle in his eye. "I work at Parker House," she clarified. She knew she didn't look like most of the manor house help that travelled by train. "I'm actually an assistant of sorts to Rosemary Parker Pryce."

"Ah, yes, I've met the lady," he said. "Well, I knew her father, Walter Pryce, quite well in the old days. They've got an astounding library there—have you seen it?"

"No," said Jan, "but I expect to. I've heard about it. Extensive collections I'm told."

"One of the absolute best collections of maps, too," Whitmore said. "Well, here's your stop, Miss Jameson," he said, standing up in polite deference to her departure. "Awfully nice to meet you. We'll speak again, no doubt!"

"Thank you, Mr. Whitmore. I'm sure we will." Jan gave him a warm smile, and as she stepped off the train, she marveled at how a chance meeting with a pleasant person can change one's entire outlook, at least for a few minutes. She looked around. No driver.

By the time she walked from the station to Parker House, she was drenched. In her preoccupied state, she'd forgotten her brolly, so though her Mac covered her body, her head was dripping from the deluge.

Where was the driver this morning? Had Rosie run out of money for that, too? As Jan stomped through the kitchen door at the back of the house, she was annoyed, wet and cold. Margaret Mills was nowhere to be seen, but a cup had been set out for Jan and the burner under the kettle had been turned low. At least she'd have a good, hot cup of tea for her troubles. Jan dried her hair off with one of the clean kitchen towels in the pantry while her tea brewed. Once she got it mostly dry, she went to the mail table near the front door and was surprised, and pleased, to see a big, thick, heavy envelope on the table.

Margaret came into the kitchen during Jan's second cup of tea. "Good morning! Or not," she added.

"Why not," Jan asked warily. "Is she unwell?"

"Not unless you consider a foul mood a condition of being unwell, which, frankly, I do. She's on some tear about having to hire a new driver. Sorry about that, by the way. He simply didn't show up. He wants to join up."

"The army?" Jan asked.

"No, His Majesty's Royal Navy. The man can hardly read or write, but he's handy with engines, so he told me he was joining up."

"Do you think we'll have war, then, Margaret?"

"Frankly, yes I do. Things on the Continent are in turmoil, Germany is arming itself to the teeth and Russia is being friendly to *us*—that alone is suspicious!"

"I should learn to drive, Margaret. I could probably be more useful around here if I did," Jan said.

"Now there's a capital idea, Jan!" Margaret enthused. "I know who could teach you, too. Bertie Betters, local handy man to just about everyone. He's the only one knows more than I do about everyone. Difference is, he doesn't gossip. I'll mention it to Her Royal Arse."

Jan giggled at Margaret's blasphemy. "I suppose I best get in there, then. This envelope portends much writing today!"

Jan opened the door to the parlor and was pleased to find a fire had been lit.

"Come in, good to see you. So very sorry about that driver business, Jan. Oh my, is that an envelope I see in your hand?"

Jan handed it to Rosie and arranged herself in the chair next to the writing table. "Oh, do come closer, January, at least for the reading of this deliciously heavy missive! It appears that Victoria has had some kind of epiphany!"

"Perhaps your letter did its magic," Jan said.

"Well let's see," Rosie said. She fondled the envelope, placed it in her palm as though she were weighing it and fingered each of the four points.

"She always had such lovely stationery," Rosie said. "Used to be that every note came written on something different—a different color, a different weight, a different texture." She held the envelope a moment more before handing it to Jan.

"Do you wish to open it?" Jan asked.

"No, you go ahead."

Jan slit the envelope with Rosie's pearl-handled opener. She pulled out a dozen or more pages of large-sized stationery. "Ready, Rosie?"

Rosie nodded, but she sat stiffly, as though

anticipating something unpleasant.

Jan began to read. She heard rather than saw Rosie lean back as the words poured out. The tension left the room and was replaced with expectation.

My Darling,

There is nothing lacking between us...nothing missing, no one left wanting, is there, my Blessing?

So many ways to make love, my darling...in my heart we've had, and have, them all...even parts you might sometimes think we don't---oh but darling, we do! Every night I hold you in my arms, and I kiss you to sweet distraction, to the farthest reaches of your imagination, to the outer bounds of worlds unknown. There, dear heart, we tangle and paw and pant as mated felines might in the deep, green grasses of our souls. Do you not know how the heat from our bodies creates a rain-fragrant, rain-gorged, rain-sweet bed that births so tenderly, so naturally and so fiercely, the love children of our deepest bonds: those words! Words of mine, words of yours, those words of ours, the children of our fertile imaginings, no less real than the paper upon which I write...And yes, as fragile, our words are sweet and young and trusting, like children.

Ah, but we are not young, my angel, and if I had but one chance to redo something in my life—please don't let this hurt you—it would be this...it would be that I would have loved you perhaps just a little less (impossible, my heart!) but only so as to lessen the pain of ever losing you.

Do you not treasure those moments, my sweet, where our grasping and clutching imprint upon our skin that singular, special stamp of fingerprints of our moment? Our moment forever memorialized in the words upon the vellum formed from the latent heat of our love? Do you not marvel, as I do, when the fire within us burns the old growth forest with lapping flames blending yellows and reds like the red, red, red sun? Beloved? I'm whispering to you of the kisses of our sacred seasons in the valleys where the bluebells and lavender pave a path of passion unheard of, as I find your secrets and give mine to you...oh, my love can you feel the yearning and the hunger in my naked limbs, my naked heart, my undressed soul? I feel your touch in every sweetened syllable of your words, your voice breaking in ecstasy, your body shuddering in surrender.

And in the dusking skies of our goodnight, pillowed and buried in the safe underbrush of our world, the nightingales sing a lullaby to our sweet dreams of one another. So many ways to make love, sweetheart, and I shall think of many more. You will not have enough life years left to take in all the love I have for you...but should I die first, let your heart be not unsoft toward another (Yes, as of this moment, it is hard for me to say such...I can share you with no one! May I repeat it: no one!) Still, the sheer volume of my love is meant to sustain you, nourish you and inspire you until the end of days--and I mean for you to...(Ah, necessary vision unhinging my heart!) ...to perhaps, share it. Quiet! Shhhhh. There, there, darling, no hard tears from my beloved...we're not going anywhere for now.

And God alone decides our final breath. But when it comes, and only one of us is left, that one must go into the world and share the love bequest, for surely there is plenty for two...as we know! But why talk about something so magically and majestically out of our hands? No, love, we shall not speak of death further: We shall not, my heart, we shall not.

Today I went to our place to have a coffee. It was a lovely day, and you were never out of my thoughts. I sat and watched a young couple in love—no, darling, they did not see me staring! You've taught me not to do that! Remember the Savoy? (Well, of course you do!) But I mean that day we had a late tea in the courtyard cafe? Need I say more about my tendency to stare at lovers and my own lover's utter astonishment (and disapproval? Yes, but gentle I think, and not really disapproving) at the temerity I revealed in my unabashed stare? 'Twas a love of the looking glass, darling, for that young couple was but a reflection of you and me: lovers.

And didn't I see you staring too? I smile to recall our laughter, each stifling the urge to look at another version of us. God how I love you! (God, be kind in how you test our faith! God, we are in your hands).

And I remember that kiss, my treasure—when we stepped inside the suite, and you closed the door and held me against that door (but not at all against my will!). You held my hands at my side, my palms flat against the smooth, rich, warm mahogany door, and you teased my lips, and you asked me what I wanted, and I was confused and said 'you,' and you gave me a mysterious smile.

"I asked you what you wanted," you said, "not who."

I was dizzy with a need for you, and I tried to put my arms around you, but you held them at my side, my damp palms against that hard, cold wood. And when I saw that you held your lips so close to mine and yet offered them not, oh my darling I nearly swooned for want of the feel of your mouth on mine.

"A kiss," I whimpered, "I want your kiss!"

Then in a blessed moment of compassion, you favored me with the most delicious kiss of my life! Of my life, my wonder, of my life! Oh, you were wicked to have withheld for even a moment. And when your lips met mine, and our bodies melded softly into one another, then leaned hard into one another, I swore if you teased me and pulled away again I would faint. As I recall...oh yes I do, 'twas you who nearly fainted, sweet tease, when you released my arms from my sides and that horrifyingly cruel door so that at last I could kiss you fully, as I wanted, with my arms around your neck, your hands upon my breasts.

And then—and then, my love. Oh dear...and then! Oh my God. Oh Blessed Mary and all the saints and all the angels singing and bless you my darling, good God, bless you!

Yours alone, remembering the Savoy, forever and ever, amen. V

Rosemary laughed loud and long. "Jesus Christ," she said fanning herself with her hand, "I do believe that dear woman has a sexual problem!"

January was warm by the time she finished. *This table is too close to the fireplace.* She didn't move a muscle, didn't fold the letter to return it to its envelope and very nearly forgot where she was. She saw that Rosemary's cloudy eyes were closed. January felt intrusive, trespassing. This was surely the most...effusive? No, something stronger, much stronger. Fiercest damn love letter! She glanced again at Rosemary, and her employer's eyes were open. Her head was turned towards Jan.

“Right, well, good job, Jan, good job. I believe I'll lie down a spell before lunch, though I can't imagine anything more savory and flavorful than that letter. Can you?”

Jan was not expecting the question. She began folding the letter and slowly replaced it into the envelope.

“The author is a very passionate...person. It was, well, I've never read anything quite like it, I must say.”

Rosemary ran her fingers lightly across the chess pieces at one end of the game board. She touched each piece. Jan thought she might not say anything else.

"Yes, well, V. is the great love of my life. There were nineteen darlings, sweethearts, and dear hearts and..." Rosie trailed off.

“You've counted them then?”

“I don't count the *my dears*.”

“Why not?”

“Too much like what one would say playing bridge. 'Oh, *my dear*, you're not going to do *that* are you? Well, are you *my dear*?' See what I mean, Jan?”

“Yes, I think I do,” Jan said laughing, “although I don't recall reading a *my dear*.”

“No, you wouldn't have done. V. only says *my dear* when she is a bit frustrated with me. So, I only count the good parts.”

"Yes, well, I do believe the good bits are the only ones that do count—the rest is just in need of a good strong cup of tea.”

“Excellent!” Rosie said. “I believe we'll have a cup before I rest for a bit.” She picked up her bell and rang twice.

Jan looked at the chessboard. She counted the chess pieces that had been moved to one end of the board. There were twenty. Either Rosie had lost count or there was a word she hadn't noted. She glanced at the first page of the letter again. Then she saw it. *Angel.* January would have missed it but for the number of chess pieces. *Angel.* Imagine someone loving you *that* much. *Angel.*

***

Wolverton, late evening

Winston picked up his overcoat from the cloakroom attendant, put his hat securely on his head and walked out into the foggy night. How would he even approach her about Carter's idea? She would resist. She would fight him. Winston sighed as the doorman hailed the approaching taxi.

Maybe that's all it would take. He slid onto the cold seat and met the driver's eyes in the rearview mirror as he directed him to the train station. Just frighten her a bit. Maybe she would improve. Maybe she would come to her senses. Maybe she would have a miraculous recovery. When the train pulled in, Winston exited quickly and hired another cabbie. He sat in stony silence until the cab pulled up in front of his address. He paid the cabbie and looked up at the white stone building he shared with his wife. But if she is cured, he thought, that Parker-Pryce woman would be on the doorstep to collect her. He stuck his key in the lock and pushed in on the heavy front door. As he removed his hat and coat, his houseman Mr. Dann Tads ran down the stairs.

"Sir, happy to see you, sir. You've arrived just in time!" Tads' face was flushed, and he was frowning.

"In time for what, Tads?"

"It's your wife, sir! We, that is Mrs. Tads and myself, we think she's dead. We think—"

"Jesus!" said Winston under his breath. He took the stairs two at a time and rushed to Anne's bedside. Her eyes were closed, her breathing was shallow, and her albicant skin was frightening.

"Has an ambulance been called?" he shouted at Mrs. Tads.

Before the startled woman could answer, he heard the sirens approaching his street.

Winston watched as the ambulance drivers gently

placed Victoria on a stretcher and carried her downstairs and out the front door to the waiting ambulance. He gave Mr. Tads some ten-pound notes.

"Take care of the household. I don't know when we'll...I'll, be back."

Winston strode out the door briskly, and hailed a cab.

"Middlesex Hospital, Reading" he told the driver. "And hurry, man! It's my wife."

"Sorry Guv, aye, I'll do me best."

By the time he found where the staff had taken Victoria, Winston managed to get a message to Ben Carter. He met the physician in the entrance to the hospital. Before he could say anything, Carter raised a hand.

"Let me find out what's going on, Winston. You know I'll get to the bottom of this. Was she conscious?"

"Apparently not. The Tads found her when Mrs. Tads went up to run her bath."

Carter nodded while he walked quickly down the hall to the physician's lounge and entrance. "Wait right around here, somewhere, Winston. There," he said pointing to a single club chair placed in comfortable counterpoint to the rest of the hospital's sterile environment. "Sit right there, and I'll be back as soon as I can. This could take a while, Winston. We'll have tests to run."

"Can you just let me know she's still alive, Ben?" Winston asked. The pleading in his voice was masked and muted, but there.

"Look, old chap, if I don't come right back out, she's alive. I'll be too busy trying to keep her that way. Trust me, Winston."

Winston nodded his agreement and slumped down into the chair to which he had been assigned.

It could have been ten minutes or ten hours when Winston felt a hand on his shoulder.

"You can see her now. She's sedated, so don't expect a welcoming party."

"What is it, Ben? What happened to her?"

Ben Carter looked down the long hallway, his eyes unfocused and red rimmed.

"At first we thought it was a stroke. It wasn't. Then we thought heart attack—some blockage or another. It wasn't that either."

"Good God, man, tell me what it was," Winston pleaded.

"It was nothing. Absolutely nothing. There is nothing wrong with your wife, Winston. She evidently fainted, and she's extremely weak. She hasn't been eating, old boy. Did you know that?"

"No, of course not. I ask Mrs. Tads every night, 'Did she eat?' and the answer is always that she did."

"She's been pulling the wool over everyone's eyes, then, because this woman is dangerously underweight."

"What about her paralysis?"

"Paralysis? Are you quite mad, my friend? What paralysis?"

Winston explained about Victoria's frequent inability to walk, her muscle weakness, her general malaise.

Carter shrugged and looked perplexed. "I saw no paralysis, Winston. We had her stand and walk a bit a few hours after we got her stabilized. All her vital signs are consistent with near starvation. We're getting liquid broth into her. It's a start, and I think it's best for now. She's not at all resistant, curiously enough."

"Of course. Thank you, Ben, I'll go see her now. Thank you, my friend, truly."

"I'll want to keep her in here for at least a couple of weeks."

"That long?"

"At least. We need to build her back up. What's been

going on with her, Winston?"

Winston looked down the same hallway with a faraway look. "I don't know, but I do know what to do now."

Carter looked at him curiously.

"All right, well, go see her, but only for a few minutes. I would prefer you be her only visitor. Of course, on second thought, I think it would be good for Camille to see her."

"Yes, Camille, good. Good night, Ben."

The men shook hands under the harsh hallway lights.

"I think you mean 'good morning' old chap. The sun's been up an hour."

The gates of mercy shall be all shut up, And the flesh'd soldier, rough and hard of heart, In liberty of bloody hand, shall range With conscience wide as hell; mowing like grass Your fresh-fair virgins and your flowering infants.

Henry V, Act III, William Shakespeare.

EIGHT

The sun glinted off the boot of the cab, but Winston stared straight into its blinding light without blinking or flinching. She hadn't even looked at him. She never opened her eyes. If she heard him, she hadn't let on. He thought she was asleep considering the drugs.

He sat stiffly until the cab turned left down his street. He knew what he was going to do, and he was angry that he hadn't done it sooner. He'd send them back. Whatever letters came over the next few days, he'd send them back. A small note. *So very sorry. Anne has passed. Thought you might like to have these.* No services. No announcement in the papers, just his note. Then he'd take her to Wales, as soon as she could travel. He'd nurse her back to health. There would be no more letters. It was cruel, he knew. A lie like this was almost crueler than death. He was sorry for that. He was sorry. But there would be no more letters, and without those, there would be no life to feed that sad, little...little what? Affair? Romance? Make-believe trysts? Fantasy rendezvous?

When Victoria—Anne—first told him she had resumed her correspondence with Pryce, he hadn't said anything at first. It was an announcement, really, not a request for permission. Finally, he said, “If that's what you want, Anne.”

“It is what I want, Winston,” she had answered.

That was the end of it. Everything else about it was a series of glances, nods, tones, undercurrents, and silence, lots of silence. It became a dance.

"Have I any mail?" *one, two.*

"Let me see," *three, four, and, turn. One, two, three, four and turn.* “Ah, here you are darling,” *one, two.*

"Winston, thank you," *one, two, three, turn.*

It was a dance of the dying. That's how he thought of it. A dying dance.

***

After he had his breakfast, Winston called Mr. and Mrs. Tads into his study. They both looked nervous and worried.

“She's going to be fine,” he began, “but it's going to take a long time...months maybe. For the next two weeks she'll be in hospital, and then home. As soon as she's well enough to travel we're moving the household to Wales. Indefinitely. I'll come into London once a month to take care of my business affairs, but I won't be gone more than two days. We'll have very specific duties and responsibilities while Anne recovers. For starters, beginning when she returns home, one of you is to sit with her while she eats.”

The Tads glanced quickly at one another.

“It's not your fault, either of you,” Winston continued, “but for whatever reason, Anne has not been eating the food you've been providing her. Perhaps she flushed it, perhaps she threw it out the window, I don't know, but she's not been eating it, and consequently it's made her quite ill."

"I should imagine it would," said Mrs. Tads. "She leaves about half of what I serve her on the plate, but I assumed she was eating the other half."

"Anne is clever," Winston said, looking off at some point above their heads. "Very. This is...this is a most unusual illness. It's more emotional than physical, but it can lead to exactly where she's got herself—half dead."

The Tads nodded solemnly.

"So, first, let's set up the house for her return from hospital. I want Anne's bed right here in my study. I want her to be able to walk outside, get a bit of sun if there is any, and sit in the garden. No more hiding in that bedroom upstairs. Bring her toiletries downstairs, Mrs. T., and put them in the little powder room."

"But there's no proper bathtub down here," Mr. Tads said.

"I'll bathe her," Winston said abruptly. "Also, Mr. T., please begin to pack our trunks, including your own, for an indefinite stay at Mumbles."

"Ack, Sir, the Misses didn't much care for Mumbles when we were there a couple years ago. Do you recall?"

"I do, Mr. T., but a cousin of mine owns the property, and it's perfect for us. My cousin Jane goes off around the world with her husband, who is a chemist. They'll be gone this time to China for five or more months. We'll have the house to ourselves. Besides, I want Anne to get as much fresh air and healthy food as possible while we are there. She loves the little galleries and shops."

"Sir, there are only four galleries and a dozen shops," objected Mrs. Tads. "That's some of why she went so batty last time, begging your pardon."

"I know, I know," Winston said solicitously, "but Mrs. T., we're just going to have to keep her busy with long walks, hikes, maybe some swimming—"

"Swimming in Mumbles, sir? The waters are still quite chilly." Mrs. Tads stifled a giggle. "I don't doubt Madam would be most expressively against *that* one!"

"Well we can't exactly sojourn in the south of France, now can we, Mrs. Tads? Anyway, we'll sort it all out when we get there," Winston added, a bit softer. "That will be all, and thank you for your dedication to me and Anne."

***

Jan was taken aback when she opened the door to the library and found Rosie sitting at her writing table.

"I just want to get the feel of actually writing," she explained without preamble.

Jan shrugged and took her seat at the table.

"Are we ready to start, then, Rosie?" she asked.

"No, not yet. Just thought maybe I'd see what you think."

"About what?"

Rosie shifted in her chair, fiddled with the cufflinks on her tailored pin-striped shirt and tapped a couple of fingers on the table. Jane proceeded to pull her writing notebook out of her satchel.

"Tell me the truth, Jan. Do you think she's batty?"

"Who?" Jan asked, pretending to be occupied with the contents of her satchel.

"God, will you put that damn bag down and just talk to me!" Rosie cried.

Jan placed the bag flat on the table, folded her hands on her notebook and sat calmly waiting.

"Do you think V has lost her mind?"

"I don't see how'd I'd be able to know that, Rosie. I don't know her, and I only have her letters to go on."

"Then, just going by her letters?"

Jan crossed her legs under the table. She'd been

thinking of Victoria's letters, especially the latest one, quite a bit. A great deal, actually.

"Well, Rosie, based purely on her letters, I'd have to say, no, she doesn't seem batty or crazy at all."

"You don't think it's all a bit much?" Rosie asked. "I mean love is swell, and all that, but, honestly Jan, I don't think I know how to answer that last letter. I mean—well, there are things you don't know."

"I'm sure there is a great deal I don't know," Jan said. "But we said based purely on the letters, and that's what my answer was based on."

"Of course, yes, thank you."

"As for not knowing how to answer that letter, Rosie, do you think it's perhaps harder because I'm here? After all, these are quite personal letters, are they not? Maybe you're just self-conscious. That would be perfectly understandable."

"Well, I can't exactly have you leave the room, now can I, Jan?" Rosie said, standing up.

Jan watched as Rosie made her way to the couch, picked up the afghan warmer and plopped herself down heavily.

"Well, Rosie, do you love her? I mean the way she loves you? I know you said she was the grand love of your life, but are you in love with her?" Jan waited for the answer she suspected she'd get.

"Well, of course I love her, January! What a thing to say! I love her with all my heart! Isn't that obvious? I—I believe we love one another the same way." Rosie fiddled with her blanket. "But you might be touching on something I've been wondering about. And I'm not through wondering about it, and until I finish wondering about it, I can't write a letter in kind, so will you do it?"

Jan opened her mouth, but nothing came out. *All right, I wasn't expecting that last bit, no, not at all.*

“You're so good at this kind of thing.” Rosie said.

“I am?” Jan answered. “What gives you that idea?”

“I don't know, I can just tell. It's instinct. Your still waters run deep, and all that. You could write a letter that is more like the one she sent me than I could. Of course, I'd approve it, so it's almost as if I wrote it, not exactly, surely, but close enough!”

“I don't know, Rosie. Those kinds of letters have to be felt—one doesn't write that way about just anyone.”

“Well, haven't you ever felt deeply about someone, Jan? Oh, look at you getting all fidgety. I'm not prying, Jan, but, look, I know a bit about your background, and—”

“Is that why you hired me? Because I have ‘a background’ as you put it?” Jan sat up stiffly in her chair. The hair on the back of her neck and on her arms was standing up, the electrical currents of humiliation pricking at her skin.

“No, of course not, Jan. Please don't get defensive. I hired you because of your discretion. Margaret told me about...about your child, what happened, and what became of the father, and well, I knew you'd know about discretion.”

“I do, yes, but apparently someone I know does not. How did Margaret know?” asked Jan.

”I don't know, exactly, but she hears things, in the village, and Jan, I would never mean to hurt you! I bring it up only so as you'll understand that I understand.”

Jan looked at Rosemary and saw the woman staring at her from clouded eyes. She doubted seriously if Rosie did, or even could, understand, but she kept that to herself.

“I could try to write such a letter, Rosie, if you wish, but I won't be able to write it here. I'd have to go someplace else.”

“Like where?” Rosie asked.

“Like the library or perhaps a coffee house or...I don't

know yet. I'll have to think about it."

"Well, could you think about it today and come back tomorrow with a letter? I'll have to get something off to her by tomorrow latest."

"Yes, fine, I can do that." Jan began to pack her bag back up.

"By the way, Jan, Margaret has mentioned something about you wanting to drive."

"I'd love to know how, Rosie, and I feel I could be more useful to you if I had another skill."

"I'm not against it. Indeed, I think it a capital idea. I'll have Margaret call the person she knows, and all next week will be set aside for driving lessons. Don't forget to mention that in your—my—letter to V so she'll know if the missives next week are brief it's because you're in driving school."

"Yes, of course, I will mention it! I don't have a vehicle; you know that, don't you?"

"Of course I know that! You're to learn on the Mercedes, and you'll drive it back and forth from home to here each day. No more trains, and no more drivers who don't show up. Naturally, you may have to make a stop or two on your way here as we may need supplies."

"Well, and I could take Margaret into town on market day," offered Jan. "She'll want all the fresh vegetables and meats. I can pick up the dry goods on my own."

"Excellent. Off with you, Jan! You've got a love letter to write!"

Jan hesitated. "Rosie, how much, that is, do you want as much passion as V wrote?"

"Oh heavens, no, Jan! I want gobs more!"

Rosie laughed her full-throated way, and Jan smiled weakly. *Oh, yes, very amusing, Rosie. We'll just see about gobs of goo.* "Great," Jan said aloud, "I'll do my utmost!"

***

Jan returned the next morning and found that Margaret had gone to town and Rosie was still in her pajamas, smoking, and drinking a very large mug of coffee.

"No tea, today!" Jan said, placing her bag on the table. "Good morning, Rosie!"

"You're in a very bright mood this day, aren't you just, now," Rosie said unsmilingly. "I trust you've got the letter. I've been up all damn night worrying about it."

"Worrying? Oh Rosie! That's what you pay me for. I did complete the letter, and I want to apologize in advance if it's not up to your personal passion standards." Jan pretended not to notice the slight double take Rosie had. "I am so new at this, Rosie, and you...well, you know the woman, and well frankly, you know women...in that way, I mean. So I hope my clumsy attempts won't further ruin your already anxious day.

"Jesus Christ, get on with it, will you, girl!" Rosie placed her feet on the ground and sat on the couch as though preparing for punishment from a superior.

"Shall I begin, then?" Jan smiled sweetly.

Rosie lit another cigarette. "Yes, Jan. Yes!"

Jan began.

My Angel...oh you delicious, God-sent morsel of Heaven! Surely, God would not send you to me if he weren't just showing me the eternal future that awaits us. Paradise!

Darling, I have to tell you, you have me in such a state I hardly know if I'll make any sense whatsoever. Yes, of course, everything you say, my love, everything is true. And yes, how I love it when we make love! And, sometimes several times a day, and don't pretend that at least two of those occasions weren't special requests from you! I believe you are a naughty woman, and perhaps some personal restraint would be in order. Oh, nothing awful, darling...just thinking, well, just thinking of that morning, was it the second morning at the Savoy? You remember, don't you, darling? Of course, you must! When I awakened, you were there, up on one arm, looking down at me, the sheet fallen from your breasts. Sir Walter Scott was watching you when he said, "Her full dark eye of hazel hue."

And you wanted to make love to me, and you began to touch my body, still warm from sleep, but awakening quickly to your touch. Yet I was not awake, my love, not really, and I murmured my good-natured dissent and rolled over (hard as it was to leave the view of your fulsome, perfect breasts). Ah, but you were not to be dissuaded, were you? You know what you did, don't you? You remember, I think, don't you? The way you slipped your hand under me and touched my belly, lingering there with the palm of your hand while a slip of the fingers moved lower. And then you touched me, and you heard me moan, didn't you, darling? You felt me move upon your hand and you sensed my motion encouraging you to push deeper, didn't you, love? Do you recall what you did then? Surely you must!

Do you recall the way you crawled gently but quickly upon my back, your body imprisoning me in the clutch of your hand, and then, and then darling, how you slipped your other hand beneath me? Did you plan to pull me apart as you did and grab at the fleshly, earthly, dangerously close love awaiting your touch, only yours, awaiting your possession...There was no stopping me, love—for I was possessed with the silky softness of your legs wrapped around mine. I was moved beyond thinking with the feel of your taut nipples brushing against my back.

And then, and then, I felt it didn't I? I felt you moving lower on my back, and I felt your movement stop as you pressed into me, and the feel of it, darling, ah the feel of you. I was lost, my love, lost in sharp delirium, lost in blinding need, lost in the possessive touch of you, lost, willing, lost, wanting, lost, needing to give you what you came to claim. Quickly, darling, quickly, quickly, please hurry to me and...now darling! Now! Now! Now! Now!

And in our moment of magic, you told me, didn't you? You told me you would always love me, never leave me and must forever have me. Didn't you tell me that—I'm sure you did. I heard you say it! I couldn't see your face, but darling, you whispered it to me, didn't you? Didn't you say it over and over and over?

And as I turned over to face you, I saw a small runlet of water between your gorgeous breasts, and I had to taste the sweat of you, the heat of you, and the passion of you. I had to lick it, I just had to. I had to kiss those bright red nipples, hard and erect and perfectly formed to my mouth, perfectly prepared for my teasing bite, perfectly pushing into my mouth for hard suckling and then...and then soft soothing, I just had to, darling, I just had to. I was delirious, I know, and my sincerest apologies for the fierce kisses on your abundantly responsive breasts, and oh, I could not choose one, so I had them both, and as a second wave of passion overcame me, I nearly missed your muffled cries and calls for my mouth upon your lips. As you were spent, or, as it turned out, half spent, I easily turned you over on your back and crawled atop you. Forgive my wanton hunger, my love; forgive my mindless and repetitive devouring of every inch of you.

Forgive me, darling, yes, my mouth; I bring you my mouth, darling, now.

And you remember, don't you, how in my delirious abandon I misunderstood? How I slipped down the length of your waiting body, instead of up to your lovely face? How I got it wrong I'll never know, but I knew no better as I buried my face in all your curves, kissed every soft channel of your body, and—as I thought you asked—gave you my mouth. It was an acceptable mistake, was it not? Was not the slow undulous readiness of your hips a sign of your acceptance? Was not your incoherent pleading an indication of your approval? And darling? When the love became the sweet slaking of my thirst for you, when love was on the melt and I wanted nothing more than to drown in the wave after wave of you...wasn't that what you meant when you said we tangle, pant, and paw like mated felines in the deep green grasses of our souls? Wasn't it everything you meant, in your letter? Please correct me if I've misunderstood, and, naturally, I beseech your forgiveness if I got it too wrong...darling.

Remembering the Savoy, I remain, yours forever and ever, amen. R

P.S. Darling, January will be in driving instruction all next week, so if my letters seems little more than notes, remember that I double my passion in short missives!

"Absolutely not!" Rosie shouted.

"No?"

"No! Jan, I wouldn't say those things! I couldn't! It just, well, it, she would know, she would—look, Jan, I know what I said, but this might be more than she can take."

Jan leveled her gaze at Rosie. "More than *she* can take? Do you really think so, Rosie?"

Rosie was sputtering as she took a large gulp of cold coffee. "Bog water!" she fumed. "Where is Margaret when one needs her?"

"I can make us a fresh pot of tea, Rosie. I'd rather like one myself."

"Oh. Right. Yes, of course. I can't send that letter though. Jan?"

"Yes, Rosie?"

"I think she might like it too much."

"This would present a problem, then?"

"Well, God damn it, Jan, I didn't write the bloody thing! I could never write a letter like that."

"Oh, I'd be happy to write them all for you, Rosie. Truly."

"That's lovely, thank you for the offer, but then she'd fall in love with you!"

Jan smiled but said nothing.

"Awful lot of *darlings* in there, don't you think?

"I believe she likes it," Jan said without elaborating.

"Well, let's have that tea. I need to think about this a bit," Rosie mumbled.

Jan nodded and left the room. *Then she'd fall in love with me? Oh really, Rosie, you are overly dramatic. It's just a little letter.* She brewed the tea and a thought occurred to her. She couldn't recall ever seeing a picture of Victoria. She wondered if she might like to see one. She thought she might.

(World War I) was the most colossal, murderous, mismanaged butchery that has ever taken place on earth! Any writer who said otherwise lied. So the writers either wrote propaganda, shut up, or fought." Ernest Hemingway

NINE

Wolverton, July 21, 1914

Winston gathered up seven pieces of mail from the table near the front door. He saw three from Pryce. One from his tailor. One from Camille Carter to Anne–probably sent at the urging of Ben, one from his brother in Philadelphia, one from his Mother in Cornwall. It was the last one, though that caught his attention. He starred at the return address. It was from Field Marshall, The Right Honorable Earl Kitchener, the War Department seal below the name. He opened that first. As he stood in the entry hall reading, Mr. Tads hovered nearby to take his coat.

"Bloody hell," Winston said. "The General wants me back."

"We, that is, Mrs. Tads, actually, thought as much when we saw that envelope," Tads said. "What does he want of you, sir, if I may ask?"

"He's reinstating my commission and wants me to be ready to leave for Belgium within the month. 'Personal request, my good soldier, my dear friend,' etcetera,

etcetera. My bloody arse, I'll wager. That place is a hellhole."

"Belgium, sir, or the War Department?"

"Both, I suppose. I have no idea of the condition of my uniforms."

"Mrs. Tads has ordered them up from storage, sir, should be here by tomorrow noon."

"If they even fit," Winston said. He began a slow circular pace. He stopped, coughed and waved the letter at Tads. "This will certainly affect our travel plans."

"Yes, sir, it will indeed." Tads seemed placid but Winston knew that underneath he was jumping for joy. No one liked Mumbles, it seemed.

"Right, well, let's make a different plan, then, Tads. I want her out of this house. Perhaps someplace in the country...in the opposite direction of Hampshire of course."

"Of course, sir," Tads answered evenly. "Which direction opposite Hampshire, if you would, sir?"

"Oh hell, I don't know. I'll be in London, so maybe London?"

"Could be dangerous, sir."

"Everywhere is going to be dangerous, Tads. We're not even officially in yet, but mark my words, Tads, Germany is about to find out how dangerous we British can be!"

"Indeed, sir!"

"Maybe we should book a suite of rooms at Claridge's. I'll be with the men, of course, but I can make it there on weekends, or whenever I get leave.. I can't imagine I'll be leaving for Belgium immediately."

"Shall I book it, then, sir?"

Winston nodded his approval and took the mail to his study. He smiled at the letter from his mother, always asking when she might expect a visit. His brother was doing well, as was his tailor, judging from the size of the invoice. He picked up one of the letters from Pryce. He had not the slightest desire to read it. Indeed, he stacked it and the two others on a small pile on his desk. Nine. There were nine letters from her, three a day for God's sake. When the next one came in the morning, he'd be ready. He'd put them all in a large box, with all the others, and send it down to Tadley with a driver. A bit of an extravagance, to be sure, but that's the only way he could ensure there would be no more. He didn't want to have to send any more back. He didn't want anything more to do with that woman.

He looked at the small stack. What if he were killed in the war? Shouldn't Anne have her beloved Pryce in that case? *Ask me again when I'm dead. For now, no. Enough of this moonstruck puppy love.* He wanted his wife back. He wanted the mature woman he married. *And by God, I'm going to get her back.*

Winston poured himself a drink and walked to his desk. He began to write immediately. It wasn't anything he wanted to linger over long for long.

Dear Rosemary,

I regret to inform you that Anne has passed. It was sudden and unexpected. There will be no services, no memorial, no notice published. That's how Anne would have wanted it. She'll have been buried by the time you receive this package, which contains, among other letters, your recent 10 letters to her. The last letter she read was the one that arrived four or five days ago, although I see nothing with that postal date, so I cannot say what became of that letter. I've also enclosed all the letters she received from you in the past year. I believe the total is close to a thousand. Apparently, she kept them all as I found these in her papers.

Your private communications with her remain

intact, and, though I don't suppose my feelings make much difference, I am sorry to have to be the bearer of this news.

Yours, respectfully,
Winston David Cabot-Jones, OBE

Winston took a big gulp of his drink. He supposed he'd eventually hear from Margaret about this. Well, it couldn't be helped. Besides, when he spoke to Margaret about the...situation between Anne and Pryce, the old crusty was no help at all. She, of all people, should have helped him. Yes, she was good with the books; good with figures and always on top of the details he didn't care for. But she would be nowhere were it not for him suggesting she manage the daily existence of the estate. What had she been—a nurse? Or was she the librarian and her sister the nurse? Whole place was odd.

Should never have allowed my wife to even visit that house. Winston finished his drink and went upstairs to dress for dinner. He decided to stay home in case the hospital called. Besides, something about the club seemed, what would he call it—almost too festive? Well, there are many people who would say a bunch of half-drunk, dithering old men and the randy young bucks that made fun of them were a far cry from festive! Still...he'd be going to war soon. Best to stay home. When Tads woke him a couple hours later from his resting place in his comfortable, overstuffed chair, he hobbled up to bed and left all his clothing on the floor as he stripped and fell face first into a deep and troubled, alcohol-fueled, dream-laden sleep.

The next morning, Tads brought a strong cup of coffee to his room. After bathing, he threw more cold water on his face and braced himself for the day's activities. His head hurt, but he warned it off.

During breakfast, he had Tads call for the car. As it was brought 'round, he told the houseman he would be taking a drive.

"You know the Parker-Pryce estate, don't you, Tads?"

"Of course, sir; you used to be there all the time."

"Right. Well, I want you to take this package around to the house. Try to give it to Margaret Mills—she usually answers the door. She may or may not recognize you, but say nothing, you understand?"

"I doubt she'd remember me, sir. She spent more time with Mrs. Tads when...when Mrs. Cabot-Jones would visit."

"Well, just in case, say nothing. Just act like a delivery driver. 'Package for Parker-Pryce,' like that," Winston said.

Tads took the large package.

"And if she or anyone asks you what it is, you don't know."

'True enough," said Tads, "I don't know. Good day, sir."

"I'll be here when you return, Tads. Should take..." Winston looked at his pocket watch. "Three hours total coming and going. Stop on the way back for a tea if you need. I'll see you here about noon, then."

***

They both heard the doorknocker at the same time. It wasn't as loud as it could have been, and Jan's first thought was that it was someone who knew how very loud that knocker could be and wanted it not to be.

"Who in heaven's name would be knocking at the door in this downpour," Margaret said. She wiped her mouth with her napkin, and rose to go answer the door.

"Do you want me to come with you?" Jan asked. The

look on Margaret's face said the request was not only out of character, it was an unnecessary gesture.

"Drink your tea. I'll be back in a jiffy. Probably a delivery for Pryce."

Margaret opened the door, and a man in a black mac thrust a sizeable box into her hands. "For Pryce," he mumbled.

He turned away to return to his car, but stopped when Margaret called out.

"Is everyone all right, Tads?"

He stopped, frozen in his tracks, but he turned and gave a single affirmative nod of his head.

Margaret closed the door and carried the box to the kitchen. "Very odd," she said, drying it off with a dishtowel. "Winston's driver just brought this box to Pryce."

"His driver?"

"Yes, Mr. Tads. He's been with the Cabot-Joneses for a hundred years. He and his wife have. I know her better, but it was him all right."

"Well, didn't he say hello?" Jan asked.

"That's what was odd. No, he didn't. But when he called Rosemary 'Pryce,' I knew immediately who it was."

"Well, shall I take it to her, then?" asked Jan, rising from the table.

"Let it dry a bit. I'll bring it in when I bring the tea. Probably some old business correspondence Winston found. I'm sure it's absolutely nothing important. I hear he's been spending a lot of time in London...probably moving back there, cleaning out things here."

Jan nodded and left the kitchen to go see Rosie. As she passed the mail table, she saw there was nothing. Again. This was going to be a difficult day. In the end, Rosie had allowed her to mail what Jan had come to call 'the sex letter,' although she didn't call it that aloud.

Rosie insisted she change a couple of small things but nothing important. Jan thought the changes added nothing to the letter, but neither did they take away from what was left in. Ten more letters had gone out since that one was mailed, and still nothing from Victoria. Jan was glad her driving lesson was this morning, although she didn't relish the notion of driving in the rain. Still, that's what she would usually be driving in, so why fight the inevitable. Besides, she loved the feel of driving. The old black sedan was a thoroughbred. Smooth, powerful and sleek. The tyres were large and the spokes on the wheels shone like rotating silver daggers.

"Good morning, Jan, I've figured it out!"

Well, good morning, Rosie. You figured what out?

"You don't even have to tell me. There's no letter again today. But mark my words, there will be one by tomorrow! That's so typical of Victoria. Ha! Doesn't fool me, though."

As Jan was not going to be writing a letter today, she sat in the chair nearest Rosie's couch.

"Is it? Typical I mean? I thought she wrote you nearly every day."

"Oh, she does! But that was a silencer, that letter. She's thinking about it. She's going to come up with a response that will amaze and astonish even me! Mark my words," she said with a grin.

"Really? You think so? Well, good, that will be...that will be interesting to read."

Jan stood up.

"Driving today, right?" Rosie asked.

"Yes, through the mud and the muck. This will be the farthest drive yet. We're going into the village. Can I get you anything, Rosie?"

"I'm going to be needing some new stationery soon. But I usually send to London for that. Well, check Branson's, see if they've brought anything posh in."

"Will do!" Jan said as she headed for the door. She was about to mention the large box, but something stopped her. "All right, then, I'll see you tomorrow."

"Have Betters drive you into Tadley, Jan. I don't want you taking the train home in this mess. You can come by train tomorrow. Besides, in another week or so, you'll be driving the car to and from here every day."

"Why, thank you, Rosie! That's very sweet of you to offer to have me driven home."

Rosie waved her away and fell back on her pillows, eyes closed. Jan closed the door quietly behind her. A letter had better come by the morning. Jan went out through the kitchen and saw the large box still sitting on the kitchen table. Margaret was nowhere to be seen. On impulse, Jan took the box with her. Before she put it in the back seat of the car, she shook it. Sounded like a box of loose envelopes. She'd have to go through it for Rosie, anyway, so, may as well take it home and get a head start on whatever it was.

"Ready, Betters," she said to her driving teacher.

"Happy to get out of the rain, Miss, very happy indeed."

"It's raining my soul, it's raining, but it's raining dead eyes."

Guillaume Apollinaire (1880–1918), Italian-born French poet, critic.

TEN

Wolverton, July 22, 1914

Mrs. Dorothea Tads answered the phone—a task usually given to her husband, but he was on an errand. She listened to the stream of words coming out of the other end. She raised her hand to her cheek and nodded. She looked toward the stairs, put the phone down on the table and ran up to Victoria's bedroom. She went to the closet, looked around and saw it on an upper shelf. It was tan, expensive, large. She grabbed the large purse, went to Victoria's night stand, and under the sheath of scented paper that lined the top drawer, she found the envelope. She opened the purse, lifted up the false bottom and slipped the letter under it. She went to the bathroom, gathered up some bottles of makeup, cream and a couple of unopened bars of fragrant soap. Then she went back to Victoria's nightstand and placed a brush, comb and mirror in the bag, along with a couple of books. She ran back down the stairs, picked up the phone and spoke breathlessly into the receiver.

"It's done, ma'am. Yes, I'm sure. No. Of course. You

have my word—you know that, I believe. Yes. No. Probably in the next quarter hour if he just left you. Shall I say you called? All right. Do you think he'll agree? Yes, I put the books in, and the soaps. Will we see you soon? I hope so too. Goodbye now."

Mrs. Tads placed the leather bag on the floor next to the mail table. She paced around the foyer for a minute, deep in thought. She'd have to be casual but convincing. She'd have to focus on the caring. She drew herself up to her full height, her mouth set in determined rigidity.

When Winston came through the door, he glanced at the mail table and was pleased to see only a few bills. He turned at the sound of Mr. Tads approaching.

"Mission accomplished, Tads?"

"Absolutely, sir."

"Did she say anything? Did she recognize you?"

"I don't think so, sir."

"Which?"

"Sir?"

"Did she say anything?"

"No, sir."

"And she didn't recognize you?"

"No, sir. Or if she did, she didn't let on. Raining hard, sir, had me cap pulled way down."

"Good," Winston said, looking through he mail. "Tell Mrs. Tads I won't be having dinner. I'm going back to the hospital after I freshen up, then I'll stop at the club."

"Very good, sir."

Winston stripped to the waist and shaved. He expertly drew the straight razor up across the planes of his face. She was better today. Much better. Looked at him. Talked to him like a human being. Even laughed with him. He was pleased with her progress. He hadn't told her about the War Department letter, but she'd know within a few days. When they released her, she'd know they were going to be staying in London. Should he have let a house? No, better at Claridge's. More control. The Tads would be in a small suite next door with adjoining door. Able to look in on her, take care of her, take her out for walks. The hotel would provide the best food one could get Some items were getting scarce--butter, orange juice, sugar. However, the hotel would find some.

Winston finished his ministrations, put on a clean shirt and finished dressing. He was walking down the stairs when Mrs. Tads met him at the bottom.

"What have you there, Mrs. T.?" he asked amiably.

"Well, sir, knowing what the missus likes, thought I'd pack a few of her personal things and—"

"Like what?" Winston's eyes narrowed. He took the large bag and opened it. "Oh."

"What, sir?"

"Nothing, I...why would she want soap?"

"It's the fragrances she loves, sir. Helps her mood it does. Especially the gardenia bar. Then, too, her books, you know how she loves her romances, and then her hairbrush, her comb...just little things to show we care about her, sir."

"Ah. Hm. All right, I suppose it wouldn't hurt. As long as there's no writing tablets or stationery in there. I don't see any."

"No, sir, nothing like that. Just her little personal items that she fancies around her."

Winston took one of the books out and thumbed through it as though looking for something.

"That's her bookmark, sir. She loves her leather bookmark that you got her in Florence that time. Remember that, sir? She just loves—"

"Right. Right. All right then, Mrs. Tads. What about her own robe?"

"I could add that, sir, if you think she might like it."

"Yes, she mentioned something today. The cashmere one. I believe it's blue."

"Yes, yes it is, sir. I'll go get it right now."

While Mrs. Tads ran upstairs, Winston took the second book out of the bag. This one looked brand new. But another romance. Winston shook his head as Mrs. Tads came down the stairs carrying a nicely folded blue cashmere robe which she was pushing into a fabric envelope cover, also in blue.

"Here 'tis, and I found the lovely sheath it came in. She'll be very happy to see this!" Tads placed the robe in the open satchel, and Winston placed the book atop it, and closed the bag.

"Quite large for a purse, isn't it?"

"It's the fashion now, sir, in Paris."

"I rather think the fashion in Paris about now is to hide anything of value with the Germans in the neighborhood!"

"Ah, yes, well, that too. Please give the missus our warmest regards, sir. We can't wait to have her back again!"

"Yes, of course," Winston said as he shrugged into his overcoat. "Lock up, Mrs. Tads—I'll probably stay at the club this evening. In the morning after my meetings, I'll go over to Claridge's and settle for the suites. You and Mr. Tads best plan to be all moved into the hotel a week from today. Send two good suits and my tuxedo ahead with Anne's things, and of course my uniforms when the tailor is done with them. I'll need my medals, of course, and that awful greatcoat."

"But it'll keep you warm in Belgium, sir! I rather fancy them on a man. Reminds me of Napoleon...or something."

Winston allowed himself a small laugh and a smile. "Yes, well, we know where it got *him*! All right, I'm off—see you tomorrow evening."

After the front door closed, Mrs. Tads sank against the nearest wall. Her heart was beating loudly in her ears and her scalp was hot. She sat on the lower step of the staircase and calmed herself. A few minutes later, the phone rang.

"Yes, ma'am, he's bringing it. Yes, I found it under the mattress where you put it, and I put it under the false bottom."

Mrs. Tads listened while Victoria spoke.

"A bit, yes, although not suspicious so much as curious, I think," Mrs. Tads said. "No. No pen. Oh! I didn't see that, but I didn't check that inner pocket, and I don't suppose he did either. Well, good then. The hotel will have stationery, of course. He says we're to move to Claridge's a week from today."

Again Mrs. Tads paused to listen.

"All right, ma'am," Mrs. Tads said. "Please take care until we're back together again. Mr. Tads sends his best, too."

Mrs. Tads smiled at what she heard.

"Yes. Yes, of course. Thank you, ma'am. We appreciate that."

***

Jan paced around the small backyard. The rain had stopped but the air was still heavy with unshed moisture. She was smoking, something she hadn't done in years. The cigarette was stale, by at least a few years. She had found the half pack in the far recesses of the gardening tools drawer on the porch. She smoked two in a row, and then realized she was freezing. As she walked through the back door, she knew what she had to do. There was no possible way she could tell Rosie. Not now. Not any time soon. It would kill her. Truly, it would.

Sitting at the table staring vacantly at the box full of all the letters Rosie had written to Victoria, she realized theirs was far more of a relationship than Jan had realized. The way Rosie spoke of it, it almost seemed...what would Jan call it? Something optional in Rosie's life? But Jan could see that this was not an optional relationship. This was a love beyond Jan's imagining. She felt silly, even wrong, for having played with Rosie's feelings when writing that wild letter to Victoria. What had she been thinking? It must have been even more upsetting to Rosie because it was the kind of letter she would write if she could, but it wasn't at all her style. It was the kind she liked to receive from Victoria, certainly, no doubt about that, but not the kind she would write herself. Rosie was far too shy and too modest for all her riotous and loud explosions.

Jan wondered what Victoria would think when she read that letter. In the end, and very reluctantly, Rosie had allowed Jan to mail it. She added some ordinary news at the end of it, and that part sounded like Rosie, which is probably why she had wanted to add it.

Jan read a couple dozen letters from the box in front of her. They were from last year, and though she felt a pang of guilt at eavesdropping on a private conversation, Jan was compelled to read them. They were apparently written before Rosie's vision loss, as various references to color, sunshine, clouds and people were described in Rosie's unmistakably brisk but surprisingly poetic tones.

I see a cloud and she has your nose, Rosie wrote, *and she is sniffing the air for the scent of me...oh, I do believe she has found me!*

Another letter described Rosie's last conversation with her father.

I said to him, Daddy, you really are quite a grump, today. What is the matter?

And do you know what the son of a bitch said back to me? He growled first, as usual, then looked over at a photo of him and mum on their honeymoon—he always kept that frame on his desk or nearby—and then, after what he considered a suitably terrifying growl, which frightened me only for its weakness, he said, "Rosie, the only good thing that's come of your life is that woman. Don't muck it up."

Although I secretly agreed with him, I objected just to keep the conversation going because I could see his eyes were closing, and I never knew if they'd open again. I said, "Really Daddy, don't you think I've done rather well with the gardens?"

Well, his eyes flew open, he mouth pulled back in something resembling a grimace, and he said, "Yes, dear, all except for those goddamn pink tulips. Do everyone a favor, my girl. Get rid of them before they come popping up out of the ground this spring like pastel teacups on laudanum."

Jan smiled as she read the letters. One written three weeks later was more somber.

Darling do you recall the day we walked around the botanical gardens at Kew? How we laughed when we saw that array of pink tulips? Well, the pink tulip aversionist is gone. Daddy died, Vicky, and I want you here and you can't come and what should I do? How can I do the hard things without you?

That was so Rosie. The resident expert on everything save herself. As Jan looked at the postmarks on the bundled envelopes, she began to see how the two women complemented one another in virtually every way. Was there perhaps a way in which they did not complement one another? She couldn't find anything, but something must be holding them back. They kept delaying their rendezvous. What happened during their first encounter during that week? What could have happened? Some demon surfaced, for one or both of them...some fear or some pain. It's as if they have some unspoken bond of agreement that theirs is a love in another realm. Or is it? Jan rose from the table and went to her mother's writing desk. She removed five sheaves of paper and an envelope. She wrote quickly and barely paused as she filled up four pages. She folded the letter, put it into the envelope and sealed it. She stamped it and placed it into her satchel, next to the letter from Winston to Rosie.

Once in bed, Jan tossed and turned in a state of half sleep tormented with images of Rosie finding out about Victoria. She imagined Rosie's face, her screams, her tears, her sobs and her weeping defeat at the hands of God. The hands of God. Jan sat upright in bed. Why hadn't Victoria's husband mentioned how she died, what she died from? Jan had a queasy turmoil in her stomach and as dawn was finally peeking in through the sides of the draperies, she rose, went to the kitchen and heated the kettle. Something was gnawing at her brain, but she couldn't quite capture what it was. She put it aside and made a pot of tea. She could hear her mother stirring in the other room, just like she did every day. However, today felt different. Today was a new day in a way all the others hadn't been. She closed up the box of letters and resealed it with tape. She took it to the porch and shoved it under a bench with the galoshes.

***

Margaret Mills waited outside for Betters. She had told Rosie she was going into the village to pick up some sultanas for bread pudding. Rosie liked the golden better than the brown raisins. Mills hadn't mentioned to Rosie that she was going to pay an old friend a visit. Betters dropped her off at the green grocers, and Margaret told him to pick her up in two hours. As soon as he drove away, she headed toward Pamber Lane. It was a short walk, no more than ten minutes, so she calculated how much time she'd have to spend visiting. She slowed as she approached the cottages. She was sitting on the mental fence between fear and flight. She walked up the short path to the front door of the cottage and gently knocked. Maybe no one was home. She raised her hand to knock one more time when the door opened quickly.

"Margaret."

"Hello, Beatrice. May I come in?"

Beatrice Graham didn't vocalize her answer but pulled the door open wider.

"I didn't realize these cottages were attached," Margaret said, looking around.

"Just by one small wall, but I'm sure you're not here to discuss uninspiring architecture, Margaret."

They stood awkwardly, appraising one another. "I was just having a pot of tea. Care to join?"

"I'd love a cup, Bea."

They sat in Beatrice's kitchen, which provided a view of the small back yard. "Do you tend to her garden, too?"

"Usually, yes. Sometimes January will get out there and pull a few weeds, but she's not got the green thumb of her father, and Hope never had much luck with growing things, so, yes, I usually keep it in order."

"Of course you know January is working for Pryce."

"Of course."

"Well, that's what I need to discuss with you."

"With me? Why ever would you need to discuss Jan's employment with me?"

"Please, Bea. Can we just let the past go for a bit? Just until I explain a few things."

Beatrice Graham shrugged, but her eyes were clear

and alert and Margaret could see a spark of interest in those eyes.

"I've been talking to Pryce about teaching Jan to drive, and she's had a few lessons. Betters says she takes to it immensely."

"Probably the freedom it gives her," Beatrice said. "I wish I had learned."

"Well, me too—I mean, I wish I had learned too, that we both had, but..."

"I suppose it's never too late," Beatrice noted.

"Well, you know, you might be on to something. I think I could get Betters to teach us both. After Jan learns. Would you like that?"

"I have no vehicle, Margaret, so although I like the idea, I'm not sure the reality makes much sense."

"Well, that's what I wanted to talk to you about. It's clear to everyone, I think, that war is coming. England will be fully in before long. Pryce is thinking about turning Parker House into a rehabilitation hospital, and I thought..."

"You thought what? That I could be a nurse again? No."

"But Beatrice, you were an excellent nurse. You—"

"No! I said no," Beatrice said. She got up from the table and stood at the kitchen sink with her back to Margaret.

"She still doesn't know, does she? She has no idea."

"None. And that's the way we—I want to keep it. Was there anything else, Margaret?"

Margaret sighed but began to gather up her hat and gloves. "I only thought I could appeal to your love of country."

"My country is Ireland, Margaret, same as yours."

"Oh for Christ's sake, Bea! I say, you are still as stubborn as Da. Well, that's where you get it!" she added seeing the frown on Beatrice's face.

"And you're as diplomatic as Mother."

"Bea, I never wanted us to be so apart like we've been. I never wanted that."

"You never wanted someone of my kind in your life, either," Bea said, the old anger cutting the air between like a scythe. "And I'm not the one who changed my name."

"My mother's maiden name was Mills."

"But our father's name was Graham. Why do it at all?"

"I...I don't even know. I wanted to be my own person."

"Separate from me, you mean. That is what you mean, isn't it?"

Margaret sighed. "Yes. Yes, and now I regret that. My false pride."

"No reason to punish me, Margaret. No reason at all."

"And I'm sorry," Margaret said. "I'm truly sorry, Bea. I...I didn't understand, Bea. I didn't know what it all meant to you. I am so sorry, Beatrice, and I should have come to say it sooner. I am so sorry."

Beatrice stood frozen in place, eyes on the floor between them. "I know," she said softly. "And I've missed not having you in my life. You were the big sister I always looked up to."

"I'm two years older than you, silly."

"At my age, that's a triumphant note in an otherwise dreary performance," Beatrice said, a small smile playing across her soft, delicately lined skin.

"Well, I'll be off then. I'm...I'm so happy to see you Bea."

Beatrice looked up at her sister. "You can hug me if you like, Margaret."

The two of them hugged gently as if anything too tight, too close or too earnest would break every bone in their bodies. Margaret could smell the garden in her sister's hair, the bouquet of a floral mixed with the fresh, clean notes of fresh cut grass.

"I wonder," Margaret said, "if—I'm not saying this is for certain, but if, just if, I were to make sure that you had fresh soda bread every week for the rest of your life, would you at least agree to *think about* helping us out at Parker House if Pryce goes ahead with this idea? She won't be able to keep the house, Bea, unless she opens it for wartime usage. I've already looked into it."

"That's very close to extortion, isn't it Margaret?"

"Oh, yes, I believe it is something quite close to it, anyway!" Margaret was smiling. She turned to leave the kitchen when Beatrice spoke again.

"The first loaf would have to be here within a week from today."

Margaret looked at her sister. She nodded, afraid to say anything that might break the mood. But her nod was quick and definite. Yes, indeed. She'd have a loaf of the stuff on her sister's counter inside of two days.

***

Jan continued reading the letter, trying to sound like it was the first time she'd seen the words.

And so my darling, I only tell you this because I know how you worry, but we shall be back within a week, two at the most. You know I will try to get a note off to you whenever I can, but you also know it's a bit harder to do so discreetly with Winston underfoot. I hope that he'll have business to attend to, at least some of the time. Once again darling, I shall exist in divine exaltation as I re-read your letter, repeatedly, as I cover my cold, silly sorrows with the warmth of your words, the heat of your breath, the feel of your arms around me. I love you, my Bliss, I adore you my Beloved. I miss you every moment, and the only good thing about that is it eventually adds up to tomorrow when I might once again awaken and re-read your words. With all my love, forever and ever. Amen. V

Rosie coughed.

"Are you catching a cold, Rosie?" Jan asked, folding the letter up.

"No. No. Something's not right."

Jan shifted in her chair. "Meaning?"

"She's avoiding me. All right, they're going to London. Fine. She doesn't say where she's staying. She always tells me. It's always Claridge's, but she always tells me. I send letters to her there. And she's going to reread that last letter of mine over and over? Your letter." Rosie almost spat the last two words.

"She doesn't know that, Rosie. And why wouldn't she reread it—I reread hers to you all the time."

"But that's a sex letter. I have you reread regular ones."

"And the sex letters, too, Rosie. Come on, you know it's true. You're getting upset about nothing."

"I never, ever get upset about nothing, January! There's always something, even if it turns out to have been nothing much—it was still something! To me."

January took a deep breath. *At least she hasn't said Victoria didn't write it.*

"I think I do understand, Rosie. I think I really do."

"What do you understand, Jan? What do you think you understand?"

"I think this is the greatest love either of you have ever experienced. And yet—"

"What? And yet what?"

"And yet," Jan continued, "you have somehow scared yourself to death nearly. And, maybe...maybe Victoria has too."

"I'm not at all scared, Jan, and don't know why you'd say that."

Jan shrugged. "Don't know, really, it's just something I feel. Probably wrong though, as you say."

"Well that's just voodoo. Poppycock. The thing is, I know something's not right with her. I mean more than usual."

"Do we have any way to confirm that?" Jan asked.

"Maybe. Michael Sullivan said he'd look into things."

"Michael Sullivan?"

"My doctor! You met him, Jan. The nice-looking man?" Rosie said that as though there had been other men Jan had met at her employer's house, maybe ones that weren't so nice looking. But, no, there had only been one.

"Oh, yes, I do recall now," Jan answered lightly.

"I should hope so—it was barely two weeks ago."

"How will he check?" Jan asked, now curious about the man and his investigation.

"He's on staff at Middlesex, where V's doctor is. I don't know exactly how he'll do it, but he'll find out something."

"Do you think V is in the hospital, Rosie?"

Rosemary sighed. Jan could tell she was mildly agitated. Restless. Dangerous in this mood.

"How's your driving education going, Jan? Is Betters a decent teacher?"

"Oh, I think it's going splendidly, Rosie! And I love driving! I really do."

"Well, here's the thing Jan. I'm thinking...I've been approached to turn Parker House into a kind of rehabilitation center for this area of the country. Everyone seems to know we'll be in the war soon. The War Department is trying to arrange for the seriously wounded to be located in the general vicinity of their hometowns and villages so their families can visit them."

"Oh, Rosie! I think that would be a wonderful idea. Will they pay you to open the house?"

"Well... just a small stipend for supplies. Everyone has to be a volunteer. Duty to country and all that. But they will waive land taxes for participants. That's a substantial amount right there. And of course there's the honor of being chosen...or..."

"Where do I come in?" ask Jan.

"Well, we'll need someone to transport the soldiers from the air base and the train station to Parker House. They'll land them at Beaulieu or bring them by train as far as Reading. These will be mainly trauma and head injury cases, some blindness, some...some emotional upset."

"Won't we need a lorry of some kind?" Jan asked.

"We're going to use the Mercedes to start. Ought to be able to get three soldiers in that way, as long as they are mobile."

"And if they're not?"

'I don't know, Jan," Rosie snapped. "I don't have all the answers just yet. Yes, I suppose we'll have to contract someone with a lorry that can be modified for a gurney or two. I must know someone who could help."

"I think we should ask Betters, Rosie. His sons have some kind of a lorry business. I don't know where, but if it's around here..."

"If it's around here I should think I'd have heard of it," Rosie said flatly. "But maybe not. I've lost track of things. Check on that, Jan? Please."

"The next time I see him, yes."

"Well, Jan, I think there's no point of writing Victoria. Theoretically we don't know where she is."

As Rosie looked to her left and out the large French doors to the garden area, Jan stole a glance at her. She was going to have to tell Rosie the truth. Just not today.

ELEVEN

Tadley, July 23, 1914

Jan walked slowly up to her front door. She was deep in thought and jumped back startled when her mother whipped opened the door.

"It's Beatrice, Jan. She's ill. I fear it could be serious."

"Where is she, Mother?" Jan walked through the door. "Ill in what way?"

"She's in her house," Hope said, "I just got back from checking on her. She's got a fever, dear. Should we call a doctor?"

"A doctor? Doesn't she have her own physician?" Jan asked as she shook off her raincoat.

"Beatrice is never sick," Hope said. "But no, I think not. For that matter, neither do we!"

"Well, we have old Stanbury, in a pinch."

"Jan, he retired five years ago."

"Oh. Well, I know of someone. Pryce's doctor lives in Reading."

"And how do you propose he get here? Does he have a vehicle?"

"I don't know, Mother, but he must. Or maybe he hires one in Reading. Yes, come to think of it, he must do that. I know he takes the train into London from Reading."

"Is he associated with a hospital, Jan? I think she might have to be taken in." Hope's brow creased in its vertical parallel frown lines.

"Well, let me ring him up. We can't know until we call." Jan walked to the wall closest the couch, and picked up the telephone receiver. She made a writing gesture with her other hand, and her mother handed her a pen and paper.

After a short exchange with the operator, Jan turned from the mouthpiece and whispered to her mother, "I think they've found him. She's ringing through now." Hope made gestures indicating she was going to go look in on Mrs. Graham.

Jan was surprised that Dr. Sullivan remembered her. She looked at the wall clock and saw that it was nearly six in the evening. "I can't thank you enough, Dr. Sullivan. I beg your pardon? Oh, all right, thank you then, Michael. Yes, Number six Pamber Lane. Yes, actually *in* Tadley." She replaced the receiver and stood staring at the phone. She had forgotten to ask him how he'd get to her house.

She heard her mother come through the front door.

"She's sleeping. She still feels quite warm to the touch, hot even, but she *is* sleeping," Hope said.

"Dr. Sullivan is on his way. He said it would take about forty minutes."

Hope Jameson looked at her daughter with relief and gratitude. "I can't thank you enough, darling, and Beatrice will be the first to know who came to her rescue. I wasn't sure what to do next."

"How did you know she was taken ill?" Jan asked. She knew Mrs. Graham did not have a telephone.

"Oh, I went over about 4:30 to see if she wanted company for a cup of tea. You know of course that we have each other's house keys, for emergencies. Just like this one, I suppose. Well, she didn't answer the door. I became worried so I let myself in. I found her in her bedroom coughing, moaning and cursing all at the same time. Evidently she'd been sick since yesterday."

Jan listened while she put her own kettle on for tea. "You know, I think I'll have a glass of wine while that water boils," she announced. "You, Mother?"

Hope hesitated. "Come on, Mother, you need to calm down. I don't think I've seen you this agitated since...for a long time."

Hope looked at her daughter, and they both paused in an unspoken moment of acknowledgement. *'Since father died,'* Jan was about to say, but didn't. They both knew neither of them would prolong that moment. "I think you're right, January. Pour me a glass please."

***

When Dr. Michael Sullivan knocked on the cottage door, Jan opened it and stepped outside.

"Hello, Dr...hello, Michael, I thought we'd go directly to Mrs. Graham...first."

"Yes, I'm right behind you," he said, following her closely.

Jan introduced Michael to her mother, and the women waited while Michael went into the bedroom to see about Beatrice. They both stayed standing in Beatrice's tiny living room. Five minutes later, Michael joined them.

"It's pneumonia," he said somberly. "At her age, I think she should be in hospital. Is there a telephone? I'll call for an ambulance."

"Oh dear!" Hope said. "Jan, take your good doctor to our house, and I'll stay with Bea while we wait for the ambulance. Maybe pack her an overnight bag. Will she be all right, Dr...Sullivan?"

"A bit too soon to tell," he said somberly. "The infection's gone quite deeply into her lungs, but she looks to be a rather strong girl, so I think we have a fighting chance if we get her treatment right away."

After Michael called for an ambulance, he walked into the kitchen where Jan was brewing some tea. "I thought you might like a cup while we wait," she said.

"It will take them about forty minutes to get here from Reading," he said, "but I do think that would be best for her. She's a very close friend to your mother, I take it?"

Jan looked up suddenly. "Well, yes, she is a good friend, to both of us, actually, and she's a lovely neighbor. She does our gardens."

"You don't garden?" Michael asked, smiling.

Jan laughed. "I do, a bit, and I do enjoy it, but Mrs. Graham has no patience with my hesitancy when it comes to dirt and the things that need it to grow."

"Is it the worms and the bugs?" he asked, grinning.

Jan looked and him and saw the twinkle in his eyes. She watched as he sat down at their kitchen table in a way that revealed his innate comfort with himself. He stretched his long legs and folded his arms across his chest as he looked at her.

"How did you know," she asked, trying to feign a certain level of indignation that wouldn't be taken too seriously.

"I don't know," he said. "You just have that I-don't-like-worms attitude."

Jan laughed aloud. She brought the teapot to the table on a small tray with two bone china cups and saucers, two spoons, a small crock of sugar and a small pitcher of milk.

"Ah, you make a delicious cup," he said after taking a sip. "And we take our tea the same way, I see."

Jan looked first at his cup and then at him. He had

put milk in his tea.

"I add a tint of sugar," she said.

"Agreed, just a tint."

She smiled at him and drank her tea. "I ought to offer you a biscuit or something."

"You ought," he said, his tone teasing.

They both heard the siren at the same time. He thanked Jan for her hospitality, and headed for the front door.

"I'll see her into the ambulance. I'm having her taken to Royal Berks."

"I know the hospital," Jan said, lowering her eyes. "Why did I think you were affiliated with Middlesex Hospital?"

"Oh, I am," he said, "but just for psychiatric. Royal Berkshire for general practice patients, of which I have very few. Say, perhaps Rosemary will lend you the car and driver so that your mother can visit Mrs. Graham," he said, as he leaned against the doorjamb.

"I won't need a driver," Jan said. "I drive myself now! But, yes, I would have to borrow the car."

"Do you now?" Michael said.

"Is that so surprising," Jan asked. "That a woman knows how to drive?"

"Not at all, Jan," Michael said gently. "In fact, it's exactly what I would expect of you."

She gave him a look. "Are you mocking me, Dr. Sullivan? You don't even know me!"

He stepped outside the door, placed his hat on his head and gave her a generous smile. "No, but I know Parker Pryce and anyone who can work with her, well..." He tilted his head.

"Right, well, it can be a challenge, you're right. But I enjoy it. Good night, doctor, and thank you so much for seeing to Mrs. Graham."

"Goodnight, Jan, perhaps...goodnight."

Perhaps what? Perhaps not, Michael Sullivan. But...perhaps. She closed the door and looked out the window. A few minutes later, her mother came through it.

"Lovely man that Dr. Sullivan, dear. I feel that Beatrice will have the best care now. She'll come through it. She has to."

"Oh yes, Mum, I do believe she will. He'll see to it. He is a good physician, I'm told. Anyway, Parker Pryce thinks the world of him."

"Well, that seals it then," Hope said, a note of irony slipping out almost invisibly. Jan caught it, though, and raised her eyebrow.

"Fix me a drink, January, will you please? A real drink. Have we any whiskey?"

***

Hope walked quietly into the room, dark except for a side-table lamp. She stood there and looked at her neighbor. When did Beatrice get old? The fine lines on her handsome face seemed deeper, her skin thinner, her hair gone from a stately grey to a near white. Hope looked at Bea's hands resting on either side of her body, the veins standing out through the fine skin.

"I don't want you staring at me, Hope, even if it is with love," Beatrice said.

Hope smiled. "I wasn't staring, darling, I was evaluating."

"Well, am I worth the trouble? And by the by, what the hell is wrong with me?" As if in answer to her own question, her body became wracked with coughing, her face turned red and her breath hard to come by.

"Shh, now, my sweet," Hope said. "You're to rest, not engage in philosophical discourse. You've got pneumonia, and you were about ready to leave this earth if I hadn't gone in to check. We've got to get you a phone!"

"Why? I live five feet from you."

Hope walked around the bed, and peeked out the blinds. They were on the ground floor. "Oh darling, look, you have a little garden! That Dr. Sullivan is a prince. I'm sure he arranged this."

"Who?"

"Dr. Sullivan, a friend...a friend of Jan's, dear. Someone she knows. We called him in from outside Reading where he lives, and he came straight away to see to you. It's him who got you admitted here."

"How long am I to be cooped up in this facility?" Beatrice whispered. Talking was an exertion.

"I'm going to stop talking and staring at you until you stop talking, Beatrice Graham. Now, shush, and rest. The more rest you get, the sooner you come home."

They looked at one another. "Home," Beatrice repeated, and then closed her eyes.

Hope stayed the entire day and helped Beatrice to eat a bit of soup. By late afternoon, she realized she was starving herself. Jan was due to arrive any time, and perhaps they could find a pub to get some dinner before driving home to Tadley.

"I'm going, now, darling, but I shall return in the morning. I'm to meet Jan outside, and she'll want to come in, but I'll hold her off until tomorrow. You need rest. She leaned over to touch Beatrice's cheek. "Get well, sweetheart, for me."

With the arm that wasn't attached to a machine, Beatrice opened her eyes, nodded and reached up to pull Hope to her. She kissed her, once, on the mouth, and they looked into one another's eyes. "You'll have to tell her sooner or later," Beatrice said.

"I know. I will. Soon. Rest, my love, and I'll see you

tomorrow."

Hope walked out to the front of the hospital and looked up and down the drive to see if Jan was coming. Amazingly, Jan pulled around the corner and stopped right in front of her mother in the long black Mercedes.

"I always feel like I'm going to my own funeral in this big thing," she said by way of greeting.

"Mother, it's not a hearse. It's the most expensive model Mercedes offers."

"Maybe it's the color. White would have been better."

"They only come in black," Jan said. "Well, how's the patient?—I was prepared to park and come up and say hello myself!"

"I thought you might," Hope offered, "but she is so very weak, dear. I thought maybe tomorrow you'd drop in for a visit. I'll want to return in the morning, so perhaps when you pick me up in the afternoon."

"You want to spend all day tomorrow here, too?" Jan asked, surprised.

"Well, she has no one else...not really. And I—"

"She has her sister, mum. Margaret Mills."

Jan hadn't intended to blurt it out but there it was. She feigned intense interest in the oncoming traffic, and held her breath.

"I had a good reason for not mentioning it prior," Hope began. "They weren't close, really, and Beatrice preferred not to discuss it."

"Well, I wouldn't have told the other neighbors, or anyone else," Jan protested, a bit put out at her mother's attempt to rationalize leaving her out of the confidence.

"I know, darling, I know." Hope patted Jan's arm. "What would you think of stopping at The Tumble Down Dick?"

"Bit of a detour, mother. The pub is in Farnborough."

"I know where it is, dear. I used to go there all the

time."

Jan felt her head begin to throb. She had questions, but she would not ask them. She would not besiege her mother the way her mother had once beleaguered her. *Whose baby? Where is the father? What do you know about children? How will we support a child? A million questions. No answers. And in the end, no need.*

***

They ordered fish and chips and a couple of bottles of malt beer. While her mother went to the ladies room, Jan absently ran her fingers through her hair and then smoothed it back down with her hand. Looking around the old pub, she saw a happy group at the bar, with families seated in the room next to the bar. Two waitresses scurried back and forth between the family dining room and the few tables in the bar area. Jan saw her mother approaching the table.

"The old place hasn't changed much in thirty-five years," Hope said.

"You came here thirty-five years ago?" Jan asked, the look of surprise shadowing her uneasiness. "Was that with Father?"

Hope poured her beer into a tall glass, waited until the foam reached the rim, and set the bottle back on the table. She raised her glass, and Jan hastily reached for her own. They clinked, wordlessly.

"No, not your father, dear. With Beatrice. Beatrice Graham."

"Beatrice!" Jan exclaimed. "I...I never would have guessed you were friends before I was born. I thought...I thought you were just neighbors. I mean, I thought that's how you met." Jane took a large gulp of her beer. She signaled the waitress for two more.

"Actually, I was friends with Beatrice before I met your father."

"I didn't know that, either," Jan said. The waitress placed two more bottles on their table and said the food would be up within minutes. "And how did you happen to know Beatrice, Mother?"

"I actually met Margaret, her sister, first. I hadn't known Margaret long when we came here, right here to the Tumble Down Dick and ran into her sister, Beatrice. Beatrice was with a couple of friends, and we all joined tables and made a party of it."

"But...? Hmmm, yet you didn't remain close with Margaret?"

"No, that would have been impossible."

"Why?"

"Her sister, Beatrice, and I, we became...we were lovers. I cannot say with any certainty that Margaret had such designs on me—I always suspected as much—but when she found out about me and Beatrice, she went crazy."

Jan looked into her glass of beer. Finally she looked up and met her mother's steady gaze.

"Were? You and Mrs. Graham were...?"

"It was love at first sight, one of those things. There's more to the story, Jan, as I'm sure you can imagine. But not tonight. We've had a rough day."

The waitress brought the food. Stopped by the steaming plate of fried fish and fried potatoes, the conversation ended. They both sprinkled malt vinegar over their plates and forked their first bite.

"Is it just me or is this the best fish and chips in all of England?" Hope asked.

Jan had a mouthful of the crunchy, savory filet, but she nodded, swallowed and raised her glass of beer. "It is tonight, Mother, it is tonight.

If you insist upon fighting to protect me, or 'our' country, let it be understood soberly and rationally between us that you are fighting to gratify a sex instinct, which I cannot share; to procure benefits where I have not shared and probably will not share. Virginia Woolf

TWELVE

Tadley, July 24,1914

The next morning, Jan rang the Parker Pryce house and spoke to Margaret. As she dialed the house, she realized she should have made this call yesterday. She explained to Margaret that she wouldn't be able to make it in to work, and when she told her why, Margaret became alarmed.

"Well, how bad is it? Should I go to her?"

"Well, it appears she will recover, according to Dr. Sullivan."

"Dr. Sullivan? However did he get involved?"

"I called him. I hope that was all right. We didn't know who else to call."

"No, no, that's quite right," Margaret agreed. "And he put her in hospital then?"

"Yes, he said she needed monitoring."

"I should go to her," Margaret said absently.

"Well, of course, Mother will be with her all day today..."

"Of course, yes, yes," Margaret said. "Well then, perhaps I could go tomorrow. After you come back with the car and see to Rosie for a couple hours, maybe you could drive me to the hospital?"

"Yes, that sounds like a good plan," Jan agreed. "All right, Margaret. Shall I ring you this evening with an update?"

"Would you mind?"

"Not at all. Explain to Rosie where I am, will you please?"

"Of course. Good day, Jan, and...and tell my sister I send my best wishes."

"I'll do that, Margaret, and then tomorrow you can tell her yourself."

Jan walked out into the back yard with her cup of tea. Her mother was still dressing, so she had a few minutes to kill. She saw the weeds beginning to poke up through Beatrice's planters and she made a mental note to do some weeding. She walked slowly between the two yards, and she began to see the plants and flowers in a new light. Everything in one yard was the mirror image of the other yard. Without the fence between the yards, the gardens combined would have been quite a study in symmetry—of color, texture and layout. As Jan looked around, the only difference she could see was that her mother's roses were white, while Beatrice's were a joyful yellow. *White roses. My favorite.* But even those climbers joined with one another over the fence to create a cascade of compatibility on each side.

Jan finally sat on a bench at the back of the yard. *Her mother and Mrs. Graham.* Not only was this news astounding to her, it raised more questions than answers. *Had her father known? Why did they live next to one another all that time if Hope was married to Jan's father?* Jan thought about her mother's tendency to always try to put some kind of distance between her and her neighbor. *That must have been for my sake, to keep me from guessing. They needn't have bothered. It was surely the absolute last thing on earth I would think of! That anyone would think of!*

Jan rose from the bench. She felt slightly agitated and walked slowly around the small yard. The things her mother had put her through when she told Hope she was pregnant. And then losing the baby. And then suffering alone with the baby's father not even coming by to see her afterwards, something she hadn't ever dealt with properly. He was a bastard—what else was there to know about him? And now, she supposed, he'd soon be fighting and probably killed in the trenches of a war he was too ignorant to understand. Why did she always go for the good-looking ones? If he'd had half the brains as he had good looks, she'd at least be a divorced woman, instead of simply a fallen one.

Everyone had secrets. She had to tell Rosie about Victoria. She couldn't very well justify upset at her mother for her sins of omission when she was doing the very same thing to Rosie. She would tell her tomorrow. She'd have to. The sky darkened, and Jan could smell the impending rain. The clouds were churning above her, and as she crossed the yard, the first fat drops began to fall.

***

Middlesex Hospital

No one wanted to pull an all-nighter on the psychiatric ward, but as Michael Sullivan was junior to all the other physicians, he took the assignment in stride. It was one weekend a month, and it paid for his hospital privileges. He was tired after his late night call to see about Mrs. Graham. Nice old lady.

His hospital office had a long couch where he could rest, and there were books and magazine for reading.

Sitting in the staff office reserved for the physician on duty, Sullivan opened the draperies covering the interior window that looked out onto the ward. He watched as the 11 p.m. shift staff came on duty. Most of the patients were asleep, drugged to it if not naturally given to it. Still, there were always a few who couldn't, or wouldn't, sleep, no matter what narcotic was given them. Sullivan suspected those few had fine-tuned the art of appearing to swallow the tablets only to spit them out when the charge nurse wasn't looking.

Sullivan looked through the patient folders. There were nine patients on the ward this weekend. Six women and three men. He looked at the names, but nothing popped out at him until he came to the records on a Mrs. Ann Smith. The NRN designation was in small printed letter next to her name. *NRN. Not Real Name.* So who is she really, he wondered. He thumbed through the file. Diagnosis: Potassium Deficiency, Fainting Spell, Underweight.

Nothing about paralysis. Must not be her. He was about to put the file down when he noticed the physician in charge of Mrs. Smith was Dr. Benjamin Carter. Hmm. He ruffled through the other papers until he came to the admitting chart. He looked it over and saw that Mrs. Smith was brought in by ambulance. Her next of kin was...wait! Ah, there it was. *Winston Cabot-Jones.* Nothing noted under Relationship. So! The ever-lovely Victoria of Rosie's disquietude. He put the folder back on the pile and closed his eyes. Of course he'd look in on her, on all of them, when he did the midnight rounds, but he didn't think he'd learn much that way. His eyes popped open at the sound of a woman yelling profanities. He jumped up from his desk and went out into the ward.

“It's Mrs. Smith, Doctor,” the head nurse said.

“What seems to be her problem, Crutchfield, other

than an impressive longshoreman's vocabulary?"

"Right, well, language usage is no problem for her! She wants out of here. Should I call Dr. Carter? Instructions say if it's anything serious—"

"No, let me see her first," Sullivan said.

The two of them strode down the long hallway, empty save for the man who mopped the floor. "Nasty stuff in Belgium, eh, Doctor," she said as they walked into Mrs. Smith's private room just in time to see a bedpan flung against the far wall.

"I do hope that was empty," Sullivan said, grimacing.

Crutchfield stifled a giggle but said nothing.

"What the *hell* do you two want, now?" Mrs. Smith shouted. "I want to be discharged, and when my husband discovers you held me here against my will, he'll have you sent to the front, where you can help people who *really* need help!"

"Mrs. Smith, I'm Dr. Sullivan, and this is the head nurse, Miss Crutchfield."

"What is this, a cocktail party? Why the *hell* do you think I even care who you are? Please leave my bedroom. Immediately!"

"What exactly are you shouting profanities at, Mrs. Smith?" Sullivan asked, leaning casually against the far wall, his arms folded across his chest in a relaxed stance.

"Not *what*, Doctor, *who*."

"All right, I'll bite. Who, then?"

"At my goddamn lover, that's who."

"Would that be your husband, Mrs. Smith?" he asked, a slow smile showing his perfect teeth.

"Oh for Christ's sake. Just leave, will you both?"

Sullivan turned to Miss Crutchfield. "I'll be fine, here. Miss C., you go on ahead, and I'll meet you back at the charge desk." He gave her a small wink. After she left, Sullivan pulled a chair up next to Mrs. Smith's bed.

"Mrs. Smith, if you're not angry at your husband, then...?"

"You wouldn't understand."

"Try me," he said.

"No, thank you."

"Is it a woman?" he asked, stretching his long legs.

"What?" she cried. "What on *earth* are you talking about? Why do you ask that?"

"Because the only one who ever drove me to such fury was a woman...so I thought, well, why not? Mrs. Smith is quite beautiful, she's obviously intelligent and there's someone in the world she wants to kill. Has to be a woman! Common sense. Logical. Almost predictable."

"Almost?" She was looking at him intently, her gestures of furious frustration calmed, her voice noticeably tempered, her skin glowing more with the rosy glow of embarrassment than the bright, blotchy red of anger.

"Well, almost, because of course, I could be mistaken. It's just—"

They held one another's look for a moment longer than necessary. She had already referred to the person as "my lover," or, more precisely, "my goddamn lover," so the next move was clearly hers. His face remained placid.

"You're not," she said. "Go on."

"Well, the thing about women, and believe you me, I'm far from an expert on the subject—in fact, I'm actually ridiculously inexperienced, for my age—but the thing I've noticed about women is how rarely they credit themselves with having a profound impact on other women. That they have such influence on men nearly goes without saying...but most don't realize they have any effect whatsoever on their own gender."

"Well, this is different."

"It always is," agreed Sullivan good-naturedly. "Well,

I'll leave you to your favorite epithets," he added, walking toward the door, "but really, Mrs. Smith, try to keep it down a bit, will you? It's after midnight." He gave her an amiable smile and left.

Sullivan passed the charge nurse station just as Crutchfield looked up from her charts. "I rather think the wildly profane Mrs. Smith will calm it down a bit. Just my guess, but I could be wrong."

Crutchfield didn't speak, but she nodded and Sullivan thought she might even be imparting a look of admiration. Well, he'd give Mrs. Smith time to think it all over. Perhaps, tomorrow evening, she would reveal more. Going back into his office, Sullivan looked at her chart more carefully. Her weight was grossly low for a woman of her height. She was 46. Dark hair, hazel eyes, medium build. Her lips were full, her nose perfect. Sullivan noticed noses. Now, that letter writer, that reader, the Miss Jameson—there was a perfect nose. Even more so than Mrs. Smith's. He supposed he'd keep calling her Mrs. Smith until given good reason not to. He thought about Miss Jameson again. He liked her eyes. Big, clear, blue like his. Nice height, healthy weight, lovely face. Small hands. He'd noticed that right away.

Sullivan stretched out on the couch and closed his eyes. He didn't think he'd hear any more from Mrs. Smith this evening, but he fell asleep thinking about what an unusual woman she was.

I think a curse should rest on me — because I love this war. I know it's smashing and shattering the lives of thousands every moment — and yet — I can't help it — I enjoy every second of it. Sir Winston Churchill, in a letter to a friend (1916)

THIRTEEN

Kingsclere. July 25, 1914

Michael Sullivan stood outside in the driving rain, the water running down his arm from constantly raising it to bang on the brass doorknocker. No one was answering, but he could see lights on the second floor. Desperation caused him to try the handle, and no one was more surprised than he when the heavy door slowly opened. He stepped inside quickly, stamping his wet goulashes, shaking his wet hair and generally dripping all over the small entrance rug. He jumped back when a tall woman in a nightcap came out of the library.

"Jesus Christ, Dr. Sullivan! You scared the *bejasus* out of me!" Margaret Mills glared at him in full fury.

"Ah, sorry, Margaret, I got here as quickly as I could, but no one answered the knocker, so I let myself in."

A crash from the library made them both start, and they hurried back in from whence Margaret had come.

Rosemary was laid out prone on the oversized couch, a damp washcloth across her eyes.

"What happened?" Sullivan asked as he knelt down to take her pulse.

"I don't know," Margaret said as she bent down to pick up the teacup that Rosie's errant arm had sent flying. "I came down to walk her up to bed and found her on the floor, unconscious."

"Rosemary," Sullivan said gently as he leaned in close. "Can you hear me, Rosie?"

"If you got any closer we'd be sleeping together," Rosemary said, pulling the cloth off her eyes. "What the hell is going on?"

"What do you mean?" Sullivan said.

"What do I mean?" she said, moving to a sitting position. "What I mean is that I can see! One minute the room is spinning and I faint dead away, the next minute you and I are practically kissing and I can see well enough to observe that you are dripping water all over my good Aubusson carpet!"

"Well, your carpet will survive, Rosemary," Sullivan said, opening his medical bag. "As for the kissing, you're a bit old for me aren't you, Pryce?"

Rosie laughed and swatted the air between them. "Seriously, Quack, what am I to make of this?"

Sullivan took his scope and listened to her heart. He looked into her eyes, waved his hand across her field of vision a few times and held up two fingers. "How many fingers am I holding up, Rosie?"

"Seven. Oh, Doctor, really! Two of course."

He placed a thermometer in her mouth. "Now don't talk, Pryce," he admonished.

"Oh, that's enough to make her lose her sight again," Margaret said. She grinned at Rosemary, who glared at her.

"Assuming she ever really lost it," Sullivan remarked.

Rosemary startled to gurgle as she tried to talk and keep the gauge in her mouth.

"Pryce!" Dr. Sullivan waved a finger in front of her.

When he took the thermometer out, he looked at it long and hard. “Perfectly normal,” he said.

“I could have told you that, my good physician,” Rosemary said. “I need a cup of tea.”

“It's nearly ten o'clock!” Margaret said.

“How did I get here?” Rosie asked, waving her arm around the room. Margaret sighed and busied herself straightening up the pillows.

“I came down at nine to take you upstairs and found you out cold. So I called Michael. Now, we have one ruined carpet, fully restored vision and a soaked-to-the-skin doctor who's already been up for twenty-four hours on his shift at Middlesex.”

“Perfect scenario for a nice hot cup, Margaret, and I certainly don't wish to send my good friend out in this rain without some warm sustenance.”

Feigning a low grumbling growl, Margaret stalked out of the room and headed in the direction of the kitchen. While she was gone, Sullivan sat in a nearby chair.

“I told you it was temporary, Rosemary. Didn't I?”

“You did, but forgive me if two years seems longer than temporary! And why now?”

“Have you had a shock?”

“I was shocked to find you here, certainly. Pour us a brandy, will you Michael?” She saw his look, and added, “It's wonderful with a tea chaser.”

Sullivan went to the small bar that sat off to the side of the room. He poured cognac into large snifters.

“What happened right before you fell?”

“I don't know, I don't recall falling.” Rosemary was rubbing her leg and her shoulder. “But I certainly did bruise myself; I can feel it now.”

“I'm not surprised. Did you hit anything on the way down?”

“I don't think so. I was—I remember! I heard that

bloody telephone ringing and I made my way out to the foyer. I answered it, and the whole thing came down on my head. That's the last thing I remember. Next thing I was aware of was Margaret clumping down the stairs yelling my name."

Margaret entered the room with a tea tray. "It was just the box part. I put it back together and promptly called you," she said, addressing Sullivan. "She knocked the earpiece off the hook, then apparently got caught in the cord and then yanked the box off the wall and onto her noggin. It's looking like it was a blessing in disguise, now isn't it! I'll be the kitchen in case you be needing anything else before midnight." She gave Rosie a look and left for the kitchen.

"She gets awfully Irish on me sometimes," Rosie said.

"Can you still see?" Sullivan asked.

"Good God, yes. You're wearing a window-paned wool suit with blues and burgundies. Bit 'club' for you, isn't it, Michael?"

"Yes, I actually went to a club earlier this evening. *Sodalitas Convivium!"* he said, raising his glass.

"Ah, the Savile Club," Rosemary said. "And you were a guest of...?"

"Well, you're right, of course, I'm not a member. And I don't want to be. Client took me. I saved his baby girl a couple months ago."

"I thought you were a psychiatrist."

"I am, but you know, Rosie, I have gathered a few regular patients over the years, non-psychiatric, and sometimes I'm called on to help out. Or, save a life now and then."

"Why are you not married, Michael?"

"Because I haven't found the perfect woman, Rosie, although you surely come close."

They both laughed at the ludicrous notion against the

backdrop of such a stunning evening. Laughter gave them both the release from tension caused by a most unusual turn of events.

"By the way, who called at that hour? Who telephoned you?" asked Sullivan.

"I can't tell you because I don't know. I heard a voice, and I jumped back and got caught in a cord and the whole apparatus came down on top of me."

"All right, Rosie, how's about some sleep for you," he said soothingly. "Why don't I help Margaret get you upstairs."

"Oh, that old drone can lift you and me both up, Michael. I'll be fine–but do have another warm cuppa with Margaret in the kitchen before you go out into the night again. You've got a driver, I hope."

"You're looking at him," Sullivan said. "I decided the fastest way here was also the best way out of here, so I took a car for the night."

Rosie nodded. "By the way, have you been able to find out anything about Victoria, through your hospital connections?"

"No, not yet," he said, "but I'm on the case, Rosie, and I'll find out something."

"I'm tired as old geraniums, Michael. Do I dare go to sleep?"

"Of course, why not?"

She looked at him and gave a wry smile.

"Ah, you're afraid when you awaken you'll be blind again, is that it, Rosemary?"

"Well, is there any reason I shouldn't worry, Quack?"

"Yes there is, Madam. I am the finest quack in Hampshire, and Berkshire, I may add, and if anyone's going to worry about this, it ought to be me."

"And why is that?" Rosie asked, stifling a giggle.

"Because I am an excellent physician, Rosie, and you

are not now nor were you ever clinically blind."

"Could have fooled me!" she shouted, laughing.

"And that's exactly what you did, my dear, you fooled yourself. It's a form of hysteria, but I don't think it will come back."

"And why is that?" Rosie asked, her voice shaky, her tone uncertain.

"There's no skin in it for you anymore. It's a pain in the arse, frankly, and now we're going to find out what it is you didn't want to see."

"Oh, God! Most of humanity, truth be told!"

"Well, I can't argue with you there, dear girl. Off you go to bed. You'll be fine, Rosie. I'll stay with Margaret for the tea, and you don't need any. Trust me."

Rosie moved toward him and gave him a warm hug. "I do, Michael, I do trust you. And I thank you."

***

Jan dropped her mother off at the hospital, and then she turned right around and headed back to Parker House. She'd sit with Rosie for a couple hours, even write a letter to V, if Rosie wanted, and then drive Margaret back to Reading. She supposed she'd have to find something to occupy herself with for a couple hours while Margaret visited with her sister, but then she'd take Margaret back to Parker House and her mother home. *Awful lot of driving*. The more she thought about her self-imposed assignment, the more nervous she became. If she broke the news to Rosie this morning, then it wasn't quite right to leave her alone all day. Jan knew the woman was quite capable of making her way around most of the living quarters without help, but it would surely be after dark by the time Jan got Margaret home.

It was nearly 10:30 a.m. by the time she pulled the

Mercedes into the circular drive of Parker House. Before she even got out of the car, Margaret was at her driver's side door.

"Prepare yourself," she said in a low voice.

Jan smiled as she climbed out of the car and shut the door with a solid thud. "Is it the blind leading the uninformed again, Margaret?"

Margaret didn't smile back. "No, Jan, this is immanently worse than ever before. She's got her sight back!"

"My God! Margaret, that's wonderful!" Jan exclaimed. They stood next to the car, both looking perplexed at the other.

"And she knows the last letter didn't come from Victoria."

"Oh."

"Yes, I think she'll demand some kind of explanation, Jan." Margaret looked uncomfortable, and Jan could see that she could not imagine the circumstances under which Jan would write to Rosie as Victoria.

"Well, I have one, Margaret, but I do wish you'd stand in while I give it."

"Of course, unless she throws me out. Let's go."

As she walked through the front door, Jan saw two female workers from the Voluntary Aid Detachment and a girl from First Aid Nursing Yeomanry going back and forth from the kitchen to a large sunroom situated off the back of the house. The sunroom, paired with its own hallway bathroom and supply closet, would eventually be the room that would house four to six beds when Parker House was put into War Service status. The first floor of the home was designated as the recovery quarters. Just outside the door to the sunroom, a small antechamber would serve as the physicians' space. The VADs had the unenviable task of cleaning everything from floors to bathrooms to sheets in preparation for what could be in the offing. Jan sniffed at the unmistakable odor of disinfectant.

"Come in, January!" Rosie boomed from the other side of the door.

Jan and Margaret exchanged looks and Jan pushed the door open.

"Margaret," began Rosie, her warning tone reverberating through the room.

"Is staying," said Jan. "I've asked her to...uh stay, Rosie. I have to tell you something."

"Just tell me why you sent me a letter that you purposefully misled me to think came from my Victoria! Tell me that, Jan!"

Jan approached the couch where Rosie sat upright, stiff as a board and ready for war. She pulled a nearby chair closer. Rosie shifted uncomfortably.

"Rosie, this is not the way I wanted to tell you what I must say—"

"Well get on with it Jan, and let me decide."

"Two weeks ago a driver brought a large box around. Margaret will verify it."

"It was Winston's driver, Mr. Tads," Margaret interjected.

"What?" Rosie said, "Tads was here? Why did no one mention this?"

"Frankly, Pryce, I forgot all about it what with all the comings and goings the past week...I supposed Jan had given you the box."

"And I was planning to give it to you, but I thought it was old estate documents. I took the box home, thinking I'd get a head start on sorting through it," Jan explained.

"What the bloody hell was in the box, Jan?" Rosemary was losing her last bit of patience.

"All of your old letters to Victoria."

"What! She sent them back?" Rosie moved to the edge of the couch and looked as though she might bolt off it.

"No, no, Rosemary, Winston did. And he sent a letter with it."

"Let me see the letter, January."

Jan reached into her satchel. "Rosie, I need to tell you something. He said that...he said Victoria had passed."

"Passed? Passed where? You can't mean...died? My God! You *do* mean that. My God!" she cried again. She was standing now, her face blotchy, her hands trembling as she took the letter from Jan. She turned away from the two women as she scanned Winston's note. Jan glanced at Margaret and saw her eyes were watery. She was shaking her head, which hung down heavy on her chest.

Jan suddenly realized that in her desire to soften the blow for Rosie, she had made everything doubly worse. Not that anything trumped death, but she could tell by the set of Rosie's shoulders that she was angry. Almost as if reading her mind, Rosie turned to her.

"It isn't—wasn't—right! I would have wanted to know I was reading her for the last time! I would have wanted to know that, God damn you! I will never—"

She stopped. She was gasping with fury, with pain, with betrayal. "But what could someone like you know of love. Even your own mother doesn't claim you!"

"Rosie!" It was Margaret. Jan turned to her and saw that she had turned white as a ghost.

"What does that mean?" Jan asked. "What do you mean, Rosie? Margaret! What is she talking about?"

"Jesus, Rosie." Margaret spat the words out and began walking around the room.

"I didn't mean anything, Jan, nothing," Rosie said unconvincingly. "I'm just...I'm just so bloody angry right now I don't know what I'm saying."

"No, but you meant something. 'Even your own mother doesn't claim you.' I want to know what you meant."

"And I want both of you to leave me alone," Rosie said. Then she marched out of the room.

"Margaret?" Jan heard the note of pleading in her own voice. "Margaret, was she saying someone other than the woman I know as my mother is my mother?"

Margaret kept pacing and shaking her head. "This is not my place to discuss, it's not my place to tell you," she said. "It's not my place!"

"Margaret, you're frightening me! What is going on? Who is my mother?"

Margaret stopped. She turned slowly, made the sign of the cross and opened her mouth to speak. Her mouth formed a letter, but her voice was stilled.

Jan stared at her, and in Margaret's tortured face she saw an answer.

"You?" she asked incredulously. "You?"

Margaret shook her head violently. "No! No! Not me."

"Then who?"

"Beatrice," she said. "My sister, Beatrice."

***

Jan glanced around the room as though looking for an exit. *Leave. Now.*

She walked briskly across the room and out the door. In the parlor, she grabbed her brolly from the holder and her raincoat from the coat stand. The moment she felt the cool rush of damp air she took off running. She heard the keys to the Mercedes jangling in her pocket, so she stopped, turned around, walked back toward the house and tossed them up on the top step. Then she turned around and began running again.

She ran, sometimes fast, mostly slowly, all the way to the coach station. Twice the rain fell but she didn't bother to put up her umbrella. She discovered the next bus was not due to depart for Tadley for nearly an hour, an hour spent pacing up and down, her nerves on edge, her anxiety palpable. She wanted it to come before anyone thought to stop her. Not that anyone would. Finally she was on the coach. She slumped back into a seat, one of only three people in the car.

The realizations, and their implications, hit her like blows to the head. *Your mum is not your mum. Your neighbor is your mum. But even she can't like you, or she would have told you. Victoria is dead and you pretended to be her to save Rosie's feelings. Now Rosie hates you too. Too? Yes. And Margaret? She knew since the beginning, most likely. That's how this so-called job came up in the first place! So, how much could she have really cared about you? Wait! How long has Rosie known? All along. She knew all along. Pity—that's what they all gave me. And Mother? Well, the one she called Mother?*

That question stopped Jan. It was a blur of betrayal and bad feelings all around. *So, who was her father?* She shook her head to clear out the tangle of relationships jumping up and down to get her attention. Mother and Mrs. Graham. Or Hope Jameson and Mother. *What a ridiculous—what were they thinking? Way back when all this was decided? And why? What other lies were they hiding? And what did her poor father know, or was he her father?* She didn't look like him. She didn't look like her mother, either. *Well, maybe a bit, the eyes, the nose. But how could that be? She couldn't look like either of them in this case, not really!*

But she didn't look one bit like Beatrice Graham. *Or her sister Margaret, heaven forbid. Not nice. No, but there you have it.*

Jan's thoughts were all over the place. *What did everyone want from her?* A flash of insight stunned her: *They wanted her to be what they themselves could not be.*

These people have silenced me into compliance. I shall comply with their innermost wishes and disappear—they thought they wanted me in their lives, but they don't. Not really. I remind them. Of what? Of their errors? Of their bad judgments? Of who they want to be?

I will finally give them all what they want. I will be no further trouble to them. They will not need to tiptoe around life because of their secrets. They can't give one another what each of them wants, but they want me to—write the love letter, don't write the love letter, we almost lost you, Beatrice should have had children, you lost a baby you shouldn't have had, take this to Beatrice, a little of Beatrice goes a long way, and on and on. Yes, I will give them all what I think they really want. I will disappear.

***

Jan thought about how her mother—or Hope—would get back from the hospital. An idea occurred to her, and the minute she walked into her house she headed for the phone. She put in a call to Betters and arranged for him to pick her mother up from the hospital at around 3 p.m. She supposed she should leave a note lest everyone think she was dead. Her dramatic moment notwithstanding, Jan knew her mother well enough to know an abrupt disappearance without *some* communication could cause the woman to become ill. The shock of it. The sadness of it. *Oh, really, who are you kidding?* Still, she found a plain piece of paper in the desk near the phone, and scribbled a hasty note.

Have gone to London for a while. There are things I don't understand, and I need a bit of time to think on it. Please don't look for me. I will send you money when I get some. I hope Beatrice recovers quickly. Jan

She left the note in the kitchen near the tea container. She looked at the clock. It was nearly noon. She went into her mother's room and reached up high in her closet for a medium-sized travel satchel. She wouldn't take too much. She packed quickly. The quietness was eerie. It was odd how someone's presence gave a charge to a room, an energy charge. She wondered if that was the kind of thing one only noticed when the person was absent. She wondered if Hope would miss *her* energy. As she passed through the living room, she looked around as one would when saying goodbye.

She walked over to a framed photograph of her with Hope and Bea taken in the garden fifteen years earlier. She tried to recall who had taken that photo but couldn't. She had never questioned why her mother had placed that particular picture in the main sitting room, but as she peered at each person in the picture she realized how ever-present Bea had been in her life. It always seemed natural. In the past few years, Hope had tried to put some distance between herself and Bea, and Jan realized it had made her uneasy—because she liked Bea. She considered Bea part of her family. She had no idea that her presence was what probably kept the two women apart for so long. *They should be living together. Well, now they can.* With that thought, Jan turned and quickly left the house. When she reached Reading, she discovered there was a two-hour wait for the next train to London. Already the trains were being rerouted and slowed or hastened for military purposes. She noted with rising alarm the increasing numbers of young men in uniform. *We could go to war at any minute. I wonder if I've made a terrible mistake.*

***

As the train neared Paddington, Jan decided she had better check her money. It didn't take long to realize she only had about fourteen pounds on her. She'd have to find lodging and she'd have to find a job. She waited until the three other passengers stood to leave the car. An elderly gentleman smiled at her and made a gesture with his arm that she should precede down the narrow aisle. She realized she had seen him somewhere. Once outside, she followed the wave of people heading for the station exits. Outside, the blur of lights, sounds, sirens and rain startled her. It was pouring rain, and there was little sign of a letup.

Everyone was trying to hail a cab, although a few fortunate people had their drivers waiting for them. Jan stood next to two soldiers who were trying to keep their heavy duffle bags from tripping people up.

"Bit of a mess tonight, eh, luv?" one said.

"Indeed," Jan answered. She looked around and saw that the familiar gentleman was walking toward the three of them.

"I say, Miss, gentlemen," he nodded, "I've got my driver here. Be happy to give you a lift somewhere. I'm going to Kensington."

"Sir, thank you, sir," one soldier said. "I think we're not going too far. Meeting our mates at the Lion's Roar pub—you don't happen to know where that is, do you?"

"Indeed I do," the man said. "It's on my way. We'll drop you. Miss?"

"Oh no, I'm not going to the pub, but thank you, sir. I'll probably just walk," she added, waving vaguely in the direction of...everywhere.

"To?"

January stalled. She was trying to think up an answer. She supposed she could go as far as Claridge's just to get out of this melee and the sogginess of wet humanity. She noted his distinguished manner; his face seemed even more familiar up close, but she was sure she didn't know him. She no sooner thought that than she remembered. *She had seen this old gentleman on the coach several times as she travelled from Tadley to Kingsclere.*

"Well, I've already paid for the driver; he's my personal valet," the man said, "so it's absolutely no trouble whatsoever to give you a lift."

She liked the way he smoothed over her unspoken concern about the cost and the utter lack of destination. "Well, then," she said with a smile, "I thank you and accept."

One of the soldiers got into the front with the driver, and Jan sat between their host and the second soldier. The traffic was moving very slowly. After about ten minutes the car pulled over to a curb. Jan could see the lights from the Lion's Roar shimmering in the rain. To her surprise, all four gentlemen got out of the car, and before the driver helped the soldiers to the door of the pub, the older gentlemen shook hands with the soldiers and said something to one of them as he patted him on the back.

He got back into the back seat of the brand new Mercedes Benz, oblivious to the water he brought with him. By now, Jan had moved over closer to the window. "Ralph Whitmore," he said, extending his hand.

"January Jameson," she replied, shaking his hand.

"Do you live in London, Miss Jameson?"

"No, I live in Tadley...in Hants," she added.

"I know it well," he said. "Been through there a few times. I have a suite of rooms at Claridge's, kept mainly for visitors and business purposes, and then a flat in Kensington, where I actually live," he said. "Most people think those two arrangements are grand, fine, but I'd rather the house in Hampshire."

"You actually have a home there?" January sounded surprised.

"I do," he said, nodding. "A place in Highclere."

"But you don't stay there, or live there, Mr. Whitmore?"

"He laughed lightly. "Can't, my dear. I have business here. I'm a widower, you see, and..." As he said nothing about children, Jan didn't inquire.

"What business are you in, if I may ask," she asked.

"I'm an advisor to...to other businesses, more or less," he replied. "And you?"

"Well, of late I've been a reader and writer of correspondence for a woman who lost her sight."

"Fascinating," he said. "It sounds like it could be an interesting position if one were to have an interesting employer!"

"Oh, yes, she was...quite interesting."

"Was?"

"Well...yes, was."

"Did she let you go then," he asked softly.

"No," she answered, "I walked out. It was...it was not interesting after all," she finished.

"Well, those things have a way of looking different with time. Will you be taking a similar position here in the city, then?"

She looked at him, her eyebrows rising ever so slightly.

"I'm sorry, January, it's just...no I don't mean to pry or seem at all forward...not my intent at all, not at all. You remind me so much of my daughter...she would have been about your age, I think."

"I'm thirty-four," Jan said. "I'm sorry about your daughter."

"Yes, well, thank you. She's been gone a long time. But I was just thinking I might be able to help you find a position."

"I'd rather not read or write for anyone," she said.

"No, no. I think I might be able to get you fixed up with something at the hotel. Sometimes they provide room and board."

"At Claridge's, then?" she asked, her eyes shining with surprise.

"Well, yes. Yes. Would you like me to find out if they have anything? I know the owners rather well. Of course I live there, sometimes, so naturally I'd know them."

When he was looking out the window, Jan stole a glance at him. He appeared to be in his late sixties or early seventies. He was of medium height, and dressed in Savile Row's finest. His overcoat had felt like cashmere as her fingers brushed against it when she was wedged in between Whitmore and the soldier. Why would a perfect stranger offer her so much in such a short period? This just wasn't done.

"January?"

"Yes, Mr. Whitmore?"

"Ralph, call me Ralph, please. I'm not actually staying in my suite this evening—I have a small flat in Kensington. I'd like to see my cat this evening. Would you like to stay in my suite and then meet me for lunch, tomorrow, perhaps, in the hotel cafe? I think I could determine by then if the hotel has any work you might do."

"Oh, Mr. Whitmore...Ralph, I couldn't put you out of your own suite! Why, you don't even...we don't even know one another. Although..." she paused to look at him, to see if she saw recognition in his face, "although I think we might have been on the same train once."

"More than once!" he confirmed. "I don't get to Highclere that frequently, but I believe I have seen you several times. Haven't we even talked a bit?"

"I think so," Jan said. "Yes, yes we have, actually now that I think on it. Well, hello, then! It's a small world after all, isn't it?"

"It is," he said with a sigh. "And this world is changing fast, my dear, and we have to change our old ideas of how things are done, how things ought to be. I can offer you this, with the purest intentions, and in so doing, it makes me feel as though I've helped out a fellow soldier, so to speak."

"Yes, well, we might all be soldiers soon enough," Jan said.

"You've heard the news, then. We are going to be mobilizing the entire country, January. Those two young men we met? They just finished their basic training. They'll be lucky to be alive within six months. If we don't go to the war, the war will come to us. It may come to us all the same. But nothing else will be the same. Expect rationing, women doing men's work, wounds and debilitations no one in your generation has seen before, families torn apart, and much more."

"Yes, I drive a car," she offered.

"Do you now? There you see, it's already happening."

"I believe I would have learned to drive without the war, sir."

"Yes, January, but I doubt our England would have been as willing to teach you or to allow it. Necessity really is the mother of invention."

"Exactly," she said with a smile. "And when Bertha Benz wanted to convince her perfectionist husband Karl that he really needed to test out his car, she took her two sons and Karl's vehicle, without his permission or knowledge, and drove sixty miles to her mother's home."

"I had no idea," Whitmore said.

"Yes, well by doing that, you see, she convinced her

husband that he had a vehicle that would run long distances. I doubt he expected her to recommend brake pads and a low gear to get up hills, though." Both January and Whitmore laughed

"Your knowledge of automobiles and female accomplishment throughout history is remarkable," Whitmore said with a genuine smile.

"Yes, and Mrs. Benz unclogged a fuel line with her hatpin and when an ignition wire got a short circuit, she improvised a piece of her garter to act as insulation."

"You know, you just gave me a brilliant idea!" he exclaimed.

"I'd loan you my hatpin, but I haven't a hat!" She said grinning. She liked this old man, and felt at ease with him. "What's her name?"

"Who?"

"Your kitty."

"Oh, Veronica. Yes, well, I often call her Ronny, if she's being playful or Vero if she's being especially naughty, but yes, Veronica."

"It's a lovely name," Jan said. "And I'm sure she loves you!"

"Not as far as I can tell, but she's reasonably fond of me at dinner," he said. He laughed lightly at the thought of his cat, and Jan saw the twinkle in his eye that told her he was a nice man.

Whitmore's driver pulled into the small circular drive beneath a *porte cochere* alongside the main entrance to the hotel. He opened the door nearest the entrance, and Whitmore got out and reached a hand in to help Jan. The porter approached.

Whitmore handed his key to the porter. "Please show Miss Jameson to my quarters, Mr. Kanick. She'll be staying in my suite this evening, and I can be reached at my flat. Make sure some food is sent up to her when she's ready." Whitmore bowed slightly and took Jan's hand. "Rest, my new friend, for tomorrow you may have to report to work!"

Jan held onto his hand a moment longer than usually considered polite or proper. "I can't think how to thank you, Ralph," she said, her face a series of grimaces and frowns as she considered her good fortune.

"No need," Whitmore said. "As you said, we're all soldiers, now. I'll call for you at noon tomorrow, January."

The porter took the key and gestured with his arm for January to precede him. She had no luggage save her satchel, which contained precious little to freshen up with. Once inside the spacious quarters, Jan began to wonder about Mr. Ralph Whitmore. Who was he really? She made her way through the living room to one of two bathrooms, where she splashed water on her face and dried her hair with a towel. She brushed it fully dry, smoothed out her suit and poured herself a whiskey from Whitmore's well-stocked bar. After about twenty minutes, she realized she was starving. Whitmore had said the porter was to send up food, but Jan thought she'd rather be around people tonight and opted to dine alone in the hotel's cafe. As she prepared to leave the suite, she was surprised to find the porter waiting for her outside the door.

"Sir Ralph suggested I escort you to the dining restaurant," he said. "Once there, the maitre d' will see to a nice table for you."

Jan tilted her head slightly at the mention of her mentor, but she walked a step ahead of the porter, who, as promised, deposited her with a crusty maitre d' who seemed prepared for her. "Right this way, Miss Jameson. I am Claude Stanton, and I have the perfect table for you, discreet and off to the side but still where you can see life. Many people in London dine alone, so don't feel in the least bit awkward." With that, he led her to a lovely table, set for one person, in a small alcove that allowed her to view the entire cafe without actually seeming to be doing so.

Hmm. Not bad for a woman who just found out her mother isn't her mother and her neighbor is...her mother. I don't know why or how you found me, Sir Ralph, but I know three or four people who would never in a million years believe how I got here tonight. When the sommelier came around, Jan knew exactly what she wanted. “I'd like a nice champagne, this evening,” she said. “You choose for me.”

Strike against war, for without you no battles can be fought. Strike against manufacturing shrapnel and gas bombs and all other tools of murder. Strike against preparedness that means death and misery to millions of human beings. Be not dumb, obedient slaves in an army of destruction. Be heroes in an army of construction.

Helen Keller, "Strike Against War," speech at Carnegie Hall, January 5, 1916.

FOURTEEN

Tadley, July 27,1914

Rosemary leaned across the back of the front seat. “This will be fine, right here.”

“House number is down the street, ma'am,” the driver said.

“I know,” she answered, “but I want to walk. And you'll wait for me, is that correct?”

“Yes, I'll wait. I'll park over on that far corner under the tree,” he said, indicating an area half a block away with a canopy of shade trees that nearly formed a green bridge across the narrow street.

As Rosemary approached the address, she saw that it was actually two cottages on one small piece of property. A small yard and garden separated the bungalows. Somewhere she could hear a small dog yapping. She knocked on the door, and turned around to survey the area. She jumped when a voice came at her from the side

“Yes, may I help you?”

Rosemary searched for the source and saw a small

woman standing just inside an open crank window. The white lacy curtains billowed in the breeze, covering all but the elderly woman's face.

"Ah, yes, hello," said Rosemary. "Do you, by chance, know January Jameson?"

"I daresay I do, she's my daughter."

They stared at one another for a long moment, each taking the other's measure in terms of benefit and threat.

"Well," said Rosemary, "I'm pleased to meet you—Mrs. Jameson is it, then?"

The woman nodded.

"I'm...I'm, uh, my name is Rosemary Parker Pryce. Perhaps you've heard of me?"

"Nothing I'd care to repeat," said Mrs. Jameson, drawing herself up to her full short height.

"Right. Well...well, I need to talk to you. Could I come in and talk to you? Please, Mrs. Jameson?

Mrs. Jameson didn't answer but gave a long, appraising look at the woman who had broken her daughter's heart. Jan had so counted on that job. She actually loved going to work. Mrs. Jameson had not been able to work out why it ended, but she knew her daughter hadn't been the same since.

Without answering, she left the window and within seconds the front door opened. She motioned to Rosemary to come inside. Mrs. Jameson indicated that Rosemary should precede her into the parlor.

"Please sit down, Miss—is it Parker or Pryce or both?"

"Parker, Rosemary Parker, but please call me Rosie."

"All right, Rosemary, how may I help you?" Mrs. Jameson walked toward a chair but remained standing. She motioned to Parker to sit. Jameson was not a tall woman, but she used her stance to advantage as she peered, clear-eyed but wary.

"Mrs. Jameson, I truly need to find her."

"Why is that?"

"Because I've...I've done poorly by her, and I find..." Rosemary hesitated. She knew what she wanted to say before she arrived but, now here, she was stuck.

"You find?" repeated Mrs. Jameson.

"I find I miss her, Mrs. Jameson."

"Surely, you can find someone suitable to read your...your mail, Rosemary."

"There's no mail to be read anymore," she answered. "And even if there were, that's not why I'm looking for her. As you've noticed, I can see again. I miss her dreadfully, Mrs. Jameson. I grew fonder of her than I realized. As a friend, you understand." Rosemary lowered her eyes and her head drooped slightly. Her breathing was shallow. Audible.

"As appealing as it sounds, Rosemary," Mrs. Jameson said without a hint of irony in her tone, "I cannot help you."

Rosemary nodded but didn't look up. "I half expected as much," she whispered. "All right, well, I shouldn't have bothered you." She stood.

"Sit down, Rosemary. I cannot help you because I don't know where she is." Suddenly Mrs. Jameson felt her age as she sat down heavily. *I'm not going to lie, but I'm not going to tell her all I know either.*

"She sent me money in the post. It arrived this morning. No return address. No note. This is completely unlike her."

Rosemary turned toward the window. She saw that Mrs. Jameson must have seen her coming up the walk through the sheer panels.

"Mrs. Jameson, I have to tell you something, and I won't blame you if you throw me out immediately."

"Have *you* heard from her?" Hope asked, her interest in this woman increasing.

"No, and I'm not likely to. You see...hmm, how to put this."

"Try the direct approach. Jan says it's your style."

Rosie blinked and twisted her mouth a bit at the slight. "I told her you weren't her mother."

Hope sat as still as a block of ice, the sweat rolling down her scalp onto the back of her neck, the heat of astonishment melting the cold person within.

"I see. And under what circumstances did you happen to tell her this preposterous fiction?"

"I was...I was exceedingly angry with Jan," Rosie admitted. "She wrote a letter to me and left me to think it came from—from someone else. Someone who is, in fact, quite dead."

Hope laughed. She covered her face with both hands and laughed so hard the tears flowed down the front of her face as surely as the sweat rolled down the back of her head.

"It actually wasn't very funny at the time," Rosie said with a shrug. "But I suppose it does sound rather ludicrous now."

"And you couldn't tell the letter was not from your—from whomever you were expecting it to be from? How well do you know this person? Or knew...them."

"I knew her well. I knew her very well, and I suppose Jan didn't want to tell me she'd died, and so she wrote this rather amazing love letter from my Victoria and, yes, well, right, I didn't know it wasn't from Victoria!"

"That's my January," Hope said, smiling. "Always the perfect mimic."

"Anyway, I was so mad I said something along the lines of 'even your own mother won't claim you' and I—"

"Wherever did you get that notion?" Hope asked.

"From Margaret. Margaret Mills."

"I know her," Hope said. "Her sister Beatrice is

my...neighbor."

"Well, Margaret had told me many years ago about her sister getting in a family way without being married and how she let her neighbor, you, I guess, adopt the child and raise her as her own."

"Ah, right. Margaret believed that story. Well, we wanted her to believe it. Beatrice wanted her to believe it to protect me."

"Protect you?"

"Yes, I'm the one who got in a family way before getting married."

"Ah...no! Oh my God, what have I done?"

Rosemary listened as Hope told her that Beatrice had been her lover for about a year when Hope began seeing men, including Robert Jameson.

"I was frightened by the notion of becoming a social outcast. Then, of course, when I became pregnant, the reality of being unmarried and with child seemed suddenly worse than being called 'unnatural.'

"We married right away, and then I went to London for nearly a year to have the child. And Beatrice came with me. Robert stayed here."

"Did he—did he know?"

"Did he know what?" Hope asked. Her eyes gazed at Rosie with such intensity that Rosie looked away.

"Mr. Jameson was an honorable man," Hope continued, as though Rosie had asked about his moral stature. "He loved the idea of that child so much he said we must live as a family...even if not truly as husband and wife. Can I offer you a cup of tea, Rosie?"

Rosie hesitated. "I don't suppose you have anything stronger, do you?"

"As a matter of fact, I have some scotch whiskey, barely opened."

"Perfect," said Rosie, running a hand through her

hair. “Make mine a double, then.”

Hope continued with her story and Rosie took a small sip of her whiskey. “So Beatrice told her friends it was her child, and that Robert and I were adopting her. She felt responsible for my running off with Robert. She felt she hadn't adequately protected our relationship from the social stigmas that we were bound to experience–which, by the way, we never did experience because of how it worked out.”

Rosie took a larger gulp of her drink.

“Beatrice had bought side-by-sides, and when Robert and I moved into this one, Beatrice told people it was so she could watch her child grow up.”

“God!” Rosie cried. “So you really are her mother, and she thinks you're not. That's why she disappeared!”

“So I gather,” Hope said. Then, “But I wouldn't say she's disappeared. She's around. She's made mention of joining the Voluntary Aid Detachment, but we never took it that seriously.”

“Not as a nurse, surely?”

“All kinds of support staff join the VAD,” Hope said. “Jan talked about being a driver. I'm afraid the truth is she doesn't wish to be found just yet...but yes, I'm missing her too. As is Beatrice.”

“She's recovered then?” asked Rosie.

“Yes, fully. But I'm planning to move in with her.”

Rosie's eyes got big. “But why? You're right nextdoor and...” she drifted off and looked slowly around the small room.

“Because we are a couple, we are essentially married,” Hope said. “Better late than never, I suppose. And if January wants, she can live here.”

Rosie swallowed the last half finger of her scotch. “Where was the envelope posted from?” she asked

“I can't tell. The ink is blurry.”

"Sounds like Central London. Machines stamp the station name on the envelopes."

"Central London is a big place, Rosemary."

Hope got up and went to a small secretary desk. She thumbed through some envelopes and came up with a buff-colored one suitable for sending an invitation. It was small, note-sized, and Rosemary looked at the equally small, neat printing across the front. It was addressed to Hope Jameson.

"This is it," she said.

Rosemary turned the envelope around, opened the flap, looked inside and looked at the back again. There was a very minute number embossed on the point of the flap, along its edge. "Somebody must know who makes this," she said. "It looks custom. Possibly from a business. May I take it?"

"If you think it would do any good," Hope said, looking out the window. "I want my daughter to come home."

"So do I," said Rosemary. They looked at one another and knew they were talking about two different places.

***

When the sun broke through the thick bank of fog, London looked like any city about to have its loose grime and grit burnt onto it by a deceptively inviting sunshine. In the end, the heat would do little more than secure the permanence of the dirt and dust on an aging face that already bore the scars and sentiment of too much history gone terribly wrong. And wonderfully right. London was like that, though. Full of character, like a tall, proud old man who never airs out his suits, uses a bit too much pomade on his hair, has a prominent stain on his old school silk tie and who has that scent of the nearly dead that the still living can emit in a desperate, last-ditch sweat to beat the odds.

January smiled at her own condition as she walked down the street. A bit desperate, and yet, determined. She'd awakened at dawn after the most luxurious sleep in years and decided to take a walk before the city fully came alive. Even at this early hour, the commuters were scurrying to their stations, the buses were spewing sooty exhaust and at virtually every corner, soldiers, alone, in pairs or small groups, waited to cross the busy streets. They were headed somewhere, and most of them wouldn't come back, but one couldn't help but see the determination in their eyes. And the fear. Still, they moved along the boulevards with a smart step, shoulders back, eyes fixed on the way ahead. She smiled at one or two whose attention drifted toward her. Another time, another place, they would have stopped to chat her up. Another time, another place, she would have let them. But today she was on a mission. She had to make a plan.

Now, let's just say, as a for instance, that I stay in London for...for a while. Mother, or Hope, and Beatrice, or mother, will have the opportunity to see what they are to one another without having me around to provide them with a handy excuse to avoid whatever it is they needed me around to forget. What's everyone so damn afraid of? Look at Rosie! Bitch.

Jan giggled. It felt good. She continued her soliloquy, noting its limited success in providing her with clarity.

So, there's Rosie, afraid to death of Victoria and, as far as I can tell, the feeling is mutual. Then, of course, there's me. Oh really, do I honestly want to investigate that far?

Oh, just play with it.

Right. Well, I rather fancy Michael. But I will not be pursuing that.

Why?

I don't need a reason.

True, but if you had one, what would it be?

Fear.

Of? Losing?

Are you asking me or telling me?

Both? You're impossible!

I know. Let's say it is fear of losing.

Losing what?

I don't know because I don't experience it as fear of losing. That was just a guess. All right, an educated guess. But I experience it as, well, embarrassment. I think that's the right word.

Really?

Maybe. I'm reserved. I'm shy. I'm modest. Well, at first.

And isn't everyone—at first?

No, absolutely not! Some people are completely at ease with every circumstance. I'm not. Oh, I'm not getting anywhere with this plan.

You can't go forward until you stop running from the past. Well, actually, you can, but you oughtn't.

I'm fine with the past. The past has passed.

Hmm. Not quite. What about Rosie?

Rosie! I just found out my mum isn't my mum and—Rosie? Oh. Rosie. Right. The letter. Is it so different from what I think was done to me?

No, I suppose it's not. Not so different.

***

Jan continued walking. She wasn't sure where she was going, but the homes on either side of the street were stately, so she knew she was in a good neighborhood. After an hour, she thought she'd best turn around, so she crossed the street. As she began the trek back to Claridge's, she saw a small park set back off the street that she hadn't noticed when walking the other side of the street. It seemed to be a memorial park with some kind of war statue in the middle. And flowers. Many little beds of flowers, more benches than one usually sees, and it was quiet. She saw two other people across the park. One woman was feeding the birds, and another woman, about Jan's age, was reading. They glanced in her direction, but briefly.

She sat down on a bench that was half in the sun, half in the shade. As she sat there, the image of Rosie's mottled face full of indignation, even rage, flashed before her. As long as she could keep that image of Rosie's anger, she didn't feel so bad. Then she remembered the slump of Rosie's shoulders, the defeated downturn of her mouth, the sadness that shock couldn't hide.

Jan folded her hands on her lap and looked down at them. She was aware of the sweet scent of the flowers, the chirping of the birds and the warmth of the sun, but her heart was heavy. She wouldn't look at the prettiness around her. It didn't feel right that it should bring her happiness. The look on Rosie's face kept up its steady visitation in Jan's mind. In the first moment of comprehension, Rosie was at her most authentic beauty. The face was drawn and pale, and the eyes took on their previous cloudiness, but only for the moment it took for the fury of anger to blink itself to a dazzling, brightness. Then her eyes flashed with astonishing clarity.

She saw what I had done: I witnessed her grief...and as bad, I stole her grieving time. I am the thief of her love. It was intended for another. I kidnapped her lover, her dead lover, and gave her life again, became her, and became her words. I gulped down the responses greedily as though they were the rain for my parched throat, as though hearing them would make me loved, as though feeling them would make me whole. I am a fraud. I am the one who lives in fear. I was like a God, and I am the graven image I worshipped. I am so deeply sorry. Oh, Rosie, can you ever forgive me? No. Most likely not.

I understand. I understand what it's like to have one's grief taken away, ripped out of one's arms with someone else acting as though it hadn't happened, shouldn't have happened, anyway. As though the death of a baby isn't to be grieved for because of how it came to be. As though...ah, that would make sense, then. Since Hope Jameson isn't my mother, she wouldn't know what it's like to lose a child. She stole my grief because she's never lost a child. But I have no such excuse.

I stole Rosie's grief first to save her heart, and then to bask in the secret glory of knowing I had the power to write words that made someone feel loved. But I had none of my own heart in those words, not really.

Those words were for some mythical lover who was not mine, whom I've never had. Those words were the words written by a make-believe lover to and from her make-believe lover. I was both—I was Rosie to Victoria. I was Victoria to Rosie.

I could imagine what lovers would say to one another easily enough. Oh yes, it was easy. Easy to be someone else. But never myself. I've never said anything like that to anyone, and no one's ever said anything similar to me. I have completely stolen someone else's love affair.

And because of Victoria dying, I have caused irreparable damage to Rosie. Surely, this is one of the unforgivables.

January arrived back at the hotel by midmorning. She went to the suite, bathed and readied herself for lunch with Ralph. She tried to smooth out her cleaner clothing, but she still looked a bit worse for wear when she looked in the mirror. As she fussed with her hair, she looked at her reflection. Her cheeks were rosy from the walk, and her eyes were clear. She'd have to eventually make it up to Rosie, if she could. But on some level she felt better than at any time in recent memory, despite the realization that she wasn't any closer to figuring out what to do next. She did enjoy the irony of spending a night or two in a luxurious suite in a hotel where she would probably be folding towels and sheets within the week—if she were fortunate to land a position.

Her host greeted Jan at the door to the dining room.

"Ah, Miss Jameson, you're looking the picture of health this fine morning!"

"Thank you, I believe it's the London fog—I was out walking in it quite early."

"Was that altogether safe?" He motioned to the maitre d' who immediately showed them to a leather-covered banquette booth. "Thank you, Stanton."

"Oh, it was quite busy in the neighborhood," she replied. "A great number of soldiers, though. We must be getting closer and closer to declaring our intentions."

"I would hazard a guess that full mobilization is less than sixty days away. Which brings me to the next subject: your new position."

"My new position? What could that have to do with the War? Indeed, what is the new position?"

"Let's order, first, shall we?" Whitmore said.

Jan found she had a ravenous appetite. "Oh my! I guess my walk made me incredibly hungry!"

Whitmore chuckled. "Excellent! You'll be needing all your strength."

"Oh dear, am I to be doing heavy lifting?"

"No, but I have secured you a most coveted position in His Majesty's Voluntary Aid Detachment. They call them

VADs."

"Yes, I know of them, I was even—but I've no training..."

"Sure you do, and that's why you're to be a driver."

"A driver? Of what?" Jane felt her pulse quicken. She loved to drive. She hated folding sheets and towels.

"Eventually, the wounded, my dear. The chaps coming back from the front will have to be taken to hospital, to rehabilitation homes, to homes all over the country. There'll be plenty of places in Hampshire converted to facilities for the wounded. Large homes, estates, anyplace we can locate men where people can care for them."

"Yes, yes...I know of...such places." Jan shivered at the thought of ever having to take anyone to Parker House.

As if reading her mind, Whitmore added, "But of course, first, you'll be picking up wounded in Southampton and bringing them to London."

"Will anyone be riding with me? I mean any medical personnel?"

"Whenever possible," he answered, "which eventually means probably not. January, you are going to see the entire country change in the next two months. Virtually all able-bodied men will be going to war. Women will be taking their jobs, just for the duration of the war. We need women to work the farms, work in the munitions factories, drive ambulances, perform nursing and medical work, even...write letters."

"The military will have women who write letters?" she asked.

"Volunteers, yes, and quite a few of them will end up being very close to the front. These men will be badly wounded, Jan, many maimed for life, blind, without limbs. There is nothing redeeming about war, my dear, nothing."

Jan sipped her tea. She watched Whitmore's face as it

flushed with emotion. "What exactly have you to do with our country's war effort, if I may ask?"

He looked at her and his steady gaze penetrated her heart. It was filled with sorrow, with resolve, with concern. "Everything," he said. "I have everything to do with this country's war effort. I am a Special Envoy to His Majesty...well, having to do generally with Intelligence, but beyond that, I cannot say. But you are to have a special assignment, Jan. First, yes, you must take a very quick two-day first-aid course. It will be intense, and, I should tell you this now, it's far more than first aid. You could find yourself stanching blood, rewrapping wounds, no telling what horrors you may see. Are you of a temperament that can handle that? You seem to be. First thing I noticed about you."

Jan thought about it for a moment. "I believe I can handle it...Sir Ralph."

"Ah...well, I supposed you'd figure that part of my life out eventually. Yes, yes, I am Sir Ralph Whitmore. However, don't let that stand in the way of a few good laughs, old girl. Well, not old, of course!"

"Of course, Sir Ralph," Jan smiled. She really liked this man. He reminded her of the favorite uncle she never had. "But you said, 'first' I'm to take first-aid—what's second?"

"A special assignment. It's two-fold. For the near future, once you complete your basic training, you'll be assigned to the Special Envoy's Office—that's me. You'll drive me, some of my staff and various foreign dignitaries to meetings, evening social affairs, dinners, that kind of thing. Then, after two months, if you wish, you can join VAD as a regular driver. I've made all the arrangements to give you the most options. Once England declares war and the fighting starts, there will be captured enemy wounded. You are to bring wounded German senior officer prisoners of war from Southampton to hospital. These men should be under armed guard, but there might come a point during the war where we could become too stretched for that duty. You will be armed."

"I have no idea how to use a weapon!" she cried.

"Right, I shouldn't have thought you would. The second phase is you will spend one day learning how to shoot."

"At whom will I be shooting?" she asked, her eyes ablaze with disbelief.

"Any wounded German officer who thinks he wants to escape back to Germany."

"Well," Jan said, sitting back hard against the leather banquet. "When does my new life begin?"

"Aren't you even going to ask what your pay grade is?" he said, smiling.

"I'm getting paid? Oh! Very well, what is my pay grade?"

"For most VADS, it's a pittance, if anything. For you, plenty," he said. "Remember, it's a Special Assignment. Most of the girls get twenty pounds a year, but Special Assignment can receive as much as five times that. It's not enough, of course, but remember, the "V" stands for *Voluntary*."

"When do I begin?"

"Tomorrow morning at dawn. Just be near the concierge desk at 6 a.m."

"Will I see you again?" Jan asked, a shadow crossing her face.

"Not for a while," he admitted. "I'm pretty much constantly with His Majesty lately...but I'll keep tabs on you, young lady. I'm counting on you, Jan! I can always be reached through the Adjutant General's office," he said, handing her a card with a phone number and five other numbers printed on it. "Usually within an hour."

She looked at the card. There was no name, no identification of any kind. “What are these extra numbers?” she asked.

“If you ever have an emergency, just give the operator those numbers. You will be asked where you can be reached, and I will contact you.”

She shivered. “It all sounds very dangerous and intriguing,” she said. “Don't give that number to anyone, but if anyone gets it from you, don't reveal where they are calling. Don't let me down on that score, Jan.”

“I will never let you down! Never, Sir Ralph. And thank you.” She reached over and gave him a warm hug. He smelled like her father. A touch of rum, a touch of lime. A manly scent. A reassuring man, a decent man.

I shall not easily forget those long winter nights in the front line. Darkness fell about four in the afternoon and dawn was not until eight next morning. These sixteen hours of blackness were broken by gun flashes, the gleam of star shells and punctuated by the scream of a shell or the sudden heart-stopping rattle of a machine-gun. The long hours crept by with leaden feet and sometimes it seemed as if time itself was dead.

F. Noakes, The Distant Drum

FIFTEEN

Middlesex Hospital, July 27, 1914

Victoria was pacing up and down the halls, stopping every few rounds at the nurse's station.

"Are you quite sure Dr. Carter has not phoned in my discharge yet? It was to be before noon."

"No, Mrs. Smith, he has not. It's only 10:15, though, so it should be soon," the charge nurse said. "Oh, here's Dr. Sullivan. Perhaps he'll know."

"Know what, Miss Crutchfield? Oh, good morning, Mrs. Smith, how are we this morning?"

Victoria looked at him as if he were quite mad. "Doctor, if *we* were discussing *us*, I'd have to say that one of *us* is fine and the other not. I would be the one who is not fine!"

Michael Sullivan leaned up against the nurse's ledge. He crossed his arms and his legs at the same time. "Really, Mrs. Smith? You look positively glowing to me!"

"Well...if I do—thank you," she added almost

parenthetically, "but if I do, it's because I thought I was getting out of this institution today, and it cannot happen early enough."

Sullivan turned to Nurse Crutchfield. "Can you get Dr. Carter on the phone for me, please? Put the call through to my office if you reach him."

With a wry smile and a quick nod of the head, Sullivan turned and walked into his office. As he sat down at his desk, his phone rang. After a brief exchange, he hung up the phone, but then picked it up again. After a few moments, Mrs. Smith walked into his office. Without being invited, she sat in one of the two chairs in front of his desk.

"You wanted to see me?" she asked.

"I'm going to sign your discharge papers, Mrs. Smith...or whatever your name really is."

"Victoria Cabot-Jones," she said, extending her hand and giving him a conspiratorial grin. "How long have you known?"

"I believe I knew from your chart. NRN is an acronym we assign to persons of substantial social, political or financial standing. Not Real Name...for those among our citizenry who do not wish to have a public record of their hospitalization. It's fairly common in the psychiatric healing arts, Mrs. Cabot-Jones."

"Healing arts!" Victoria said, laughing. "Dr. Sullivan, I was essentially paralyzed, unable to walk without assistance or at best with two canes, I was unable to keep food down and I went into a full faint."

"And of course, you had that broken heart," Sullivan added nonchalantly.

Victoria looked away from him. "Yes, I did. Do."

"But you're walking rather well, I think."

"Yes."

"What do you suppose?"

Victoria sighed. “I'm not one to go on about things, Doctor.”

“No, I realize that. But you must be curious.”

“I'm grateful,” she said. “Grateful that whatever caused it is gone...”

“But?”

She looked at him, her eyes shiny with unshed tears.

“Mrs. Cabot-Jones—”

“Victoria, please call me Victoria.”

“Victoria, are you concerned that the paralysis will return, as mysteriously as it arrived?”

“Yes, I suppose I am. I have some familiarity with my own, what shall I call them, walls, I think. I put them up. Or demons—I befriend them.”

“Why is that? What will make you put up walls, Victoria?”

“When I care too much.”

“Ah, right. Caring too much, as you put it, must be frightening, then.”

“Yes, although I can't say it makes much sense when I look at it from this perspective.”

“This perspective?”

“Yes, from wherever one gets when one realizes that however frightening caring too much can be, not caring enough is surely worse.”

“Are you talking about your marriage, then?”

“My husband thinks I’m...he thinks I’m...lustless. And I think in many ways I am. I believe I am, yes. I thought...I thought Rosemary—that's who I'm in love with—well, I thought maybe it was something we would somehow have, and I would stay married, and it would all work out, but that's not what happened. I have begun to trust her, more than anyone. But I cannot have her and my husband in my life.”

“She's the one you care too much about, then?”

"Yes. Yes I do."

"And there's a lustfulness between you, I take it," Michael said.

Victoria hesitated. "Well, anyway, Doctor, thank you for talking with me, and mostly for getting me out of this place. A driver will be here to pick me up." She looked at her watch. "In less than a quarter of an hour." She rose and smiled at him. "It's Dr. Sullivan, isn't it?" she asked. "I know that name." She looked off into the distance, then shook her head as though indicating no memory of why she knew his name.

"Yes," he said, extending his hand. "Michael Sullivan."

"Well, Michael, you've been an awfully good sport about my...my tantrums. I apologize." She shook his hand and turned to leave.

"It wouldn't be Rosemary Parker Pryce would it, Victoria?"

Victoria stopped and slowly turned to him.

"Do you know her?"

"I am her physician."

"Of course! I remember now. I'm sorry. I wish I had known."

"Don't be, please...I just, I just put two and two together," he said. "You just now said her name..."

Victoria smiled. "But I said my own name at the beginning of this conversation. You knew then, didn't you?"

Michael lowered his gaze so she wouldn't see he knew even before she said her name. When he raised his eyes to her again, a smile spread across his face. "Yes, I knew then," he said. "And I should have said something, but...well, perhaps I was trying too hard to play cupid."

She smiled at him, briefly, and arched her eyebrows. "Hmm...not very professional, now, is it, Doctor?"

"Blasted unprofessional," he admitted, looking not at

all guilty.

"Well, Michael, your smile is disarming, your methods unorthodox, but your manner is quite charming and I forgive you. You won't be telling Rosemary what we discussed, will you?"

"No, I won't," he answered, his tone serious. "No, I won't do that, I assure you."

Victoria nodded. She had a look of wary confidence, as if she would handle it whether he did or didn't. "Goodday, Michael. I'll be seeing you around, sometime, no doubt."

"Victoria." He tilted his head slightly, in deference to her departure.

After she was gone he sat down heavily in his chair. *Can't say that wasn't awfully much like dodging a bullet. Oh, Rosie, you've got yourself a handful of woman there, my dear. You're going to need far more than your eyesight to handle this one.*

He closed his eyes as he sat back in his chair. Another smile spread across his face as he thought of Rosie's response when she found out he had just released her beloved from a world-renowned psychiatric facility. *Victoria Cabot-Jones. Probably one of the sanest women I've ever met.*

***

Jan nearly limped into Claridge's. Her uniform was covered in mud splatter, her hair was disheveled and her feet hurt so much she wanted to crawl.

The concierge looked up from his desk.

"Ah, Private Jameson! Another rough day in training, I imagine! Jolly good, and your king and country thank you!" he said, beaming as though word had come down from the King himself. "Shall I send your supper up, miss?"

"Yes, please Mr. Smythe."

"The usual, then, miss?"

"Please," Jan whimpered as she slowly walked to the elevator.

Once inside the suite, Jan laid out her bedclothes, stripped to the skin and left the soiled garments on the floor where they dropped. After the bathroom was warm and steamy, she stepped into the bathtub and though the water was hot, she sunk down below the water line. She sat up and soaked the aches from her body. She reviewed her day as she washed her hair. Weaponry was harder than first aid. One wrong move with those pistols and rifles and one could accidently shoot oneself. She turned on the faucet to rinse her hair. It felt good.

As she dried off with the thick Egyptian towels, one for her hair, one for her body, she felt a sense of exhausted triumph. A day ago, she was emptying bedpans, dressing wounds, giving injections and feeding wounded Belgian soldiers brought to England in the past week. Many were blind or minus an arm or a hand. She was shocked into silence when she saw the kinds of damage war wrecked on the human body.

She thought back to her second day in London when she took her walk...all those healthy, handsome young English men who walked proudly and confidently to war. If England joined the war, which seemed almost a certainty now, many of those same men would be brought home wounded and in a state of confusion, in a state of unbearable pain, in a state of partial manhood that would haunt them forever. Jan had heard of the wounded English female nurses, ambulance drivers, letter writers and even a few female doctors who had offered their services to the beleaguered Belgium military. Men and women who hadn't the good fortune to die fast on the battlefields consigned to a slow, uncertain recovery in rooms full of cries, sighs and tears.

The Belgians were grateful and inclusive to the British women whose own government thought women in war service a travesty beyond comprehension. The lessons learned in the Second Boer War, where the Empire's women served valiantly in medical and medical transport capacities, were all but forgotten until a few women of social standing prevailed upon the men in their lives to officially recognize, organize and reward the contribution of women during war. A solid knock on the door jolted her out of her reverie, and she put on her robe.

"Good evening, miss."

The waiter brought her tray to the table in the living area, with the discreet efficiency of one used to interrupting the privacy of private lives. He was gone as quietly as he arrived.

Jan looked at the food and wondered if she was too tired to eat it. She'd had nothing since breakfast but a hard scone and some lukewarm tea, brought to the shooting range by the instructor's wife. A dozen women and several men were in her weaponry class at a small farm near Henley on Thames. The wind was cold and the skies were blustery, but still they lined up at the range and proceeded to shoot at targets they could barely see. Jan took a spoonful of the creamy tomato soup. It was savory, hot and delicious.

She picked at the scrambled eggs but took a few bites of the thick cut bacon. Tomorrow would be a repeat of today. More guns, more bullets, more sounds of tin cans and bottles being blasted from their perches. Jan opened a small basket covered in a linen napkin and saw two dinner rolls, big, warm and fluffy. She eyed the leftover bacon and began to make a sandwich of the food. She wrapped her two rolls in the napkin and then again in a small hand towel from the bar. She placed it into her knapsack. If she had to spend the day killing bottles and cans, she thought she might get off a better shot with proper nourishment.

Jan left her tray beside her door where the night staff would remove it. She came back, poured herself a single shot of brandy and took it to bed. She had two sips of the liquor before falling asleep sitting up in her robe with the blankets wrapped warmly around her legs. Her dreams were red, like blood. Noisy, like bullets. Frightening, like war.

***

Two days later, Jan received her rifle, her pistol, her official VAD uniforms and two badges of high achievement for her first-aid and weaponry handling. As part of a Special VAD Unit, she also received the honorary red upside-down chevron of the Special Units. She sent the uniforms to the hotel laundress with instructions on where to sew the badging. She wasn't to report for first duty for three days, so she left a message with Sir Ralph's office that she would be free for dinner or sightseeing if he had time. At any rate, she'd like to see him before reporting for duty.

The first morning of her three-day weekend, Jan sat in the suite and wrote a letter to her mother. She included another ten-pound note.

Jan sealed the envelope and put on her walking shoes. The day was fair but chilly. Still, she decided on her raincoat, as that was the only civilian outer garment of any warmth that she had. She could buy some clothes, and maybe she would eventually. For the time being she expected to be in her VAD uniform most hours of most days. She had four uniforms consisting of trousers, a nicely cut short jacket onto which her badges would be sewn, a great coat, boots, and galoshes. She was issued a new knapsack and a small backpack, the latter to be kept in whatever vehicle she was assigned.

As she strode through the lobby, Mr. Smythe called to her.

"I have a letter just delivered a few minutes ago, miss. Would you like it now or shall we leave it in your room?"

"Oh thank, you Mr. Smythe," she said reaching for the letter. Before opening it, she handed him her own letter. "Remember, no return address on purpose."

"Of course, miss. I'll take care of it. When will you be reporting for duty?"

"Monday morning," she said. "I'm to be picked up here, and you probably won't see much of me except on the odd weekend. I'll be living in the barracks with the other VADs."

"Of course, miss. We'll keep your rooms ready just in case."

"Well, unless Sir Ralph needs them," she said.

"I doubt that, miss. Sir Ralph has another suite of rooms in the newer wing. He has those if he needs them, but I'll tell him you offered, just the same."

Jan blinked. Sir Ralph was some rare kind of special. "Well, in case he has other guests," she explained.

"Of course, miss." Smythe rarely smiled, but Jan could see the corners of his mouth turned up slightly as he turned away so she wouldn't see.

"Right, then, well, I'll be off for the day, Mr. Smythe."

"And returning in time for dinner with Sir Ralph?" he quizzed.

Jan looked at him blankly. He nodded at the note in her hand.

"His secretary called ahead this morning and made dinner reservations for the two of you at first seating."

"Ah, good." Jan stood there a moment longer than necessary. Finally she turned to depart.

"So, we'll see you at the maitre d' station at 6:30 then, miss." It was a statement.

Jan stopped and turned, a smile of relief lighting up her face. Smythe inclined his head one degree in acknowledgement and went back to the business on his desk. Jan walked swiftly out of the hotel. She felt like a peasant. But she was learning quickly. Outside the hotel, the porter walked up to her.

"Will you be needing Sir Ralph's car today, miss? I'm having it brought around, just in case."

"Yes, thank you Mr. Kanick, good of you to think ahead." *Oh my. I suppose I ought to look as though I have somewhere to go.*

At that moment, a woman walked out the door and stood under the canopy. She smiled at Jan.

"Gorgeous day for walk, isn't it?" she said as she looked up and down the street as though trying to decide which way to go.

"Actually," Jan said, "I'm off to take a little touring guide, but I don't know London well. I'm not sure where to go," she said offhandedly.

"Well, you can't go wrong with the Royal Botanical at Kew. Have you been?"

"I've not, actually. Is it far?"

"Not very, lovely drive all around it anyway, and then, so much to see, you'll have to choose something. I'm partial to the Chokushi-Mon gateway and the Japanese gardens, as well as the pink tulips, but you could go every day for a year and not see everything! Afraid it's a bit late in the year for the tulips, though!"

Jan saw the woman look hard at the Mercedes as it was driven into the alcove. "Well, have a lovely day," she finished and walked away.

Jan smiled but the woman had turned away. She thanked Kanick and slipped into the driver's seat. She breathed in the aroma of new leather.

Jan looked at the dash. Everything was familiar. Even the color of the dash was the same rich tobacco-colored leather surrounding a dark burl. The difference between Sir Ralph's car and Rosie's was a couple of years, with Rosie's being the older. In most respects the vehicles were nearly identical. Jan pulled out of the parking alcove and merged with the other vehicles.

The gas-cylinders had by this time been put into position on the front line. A special order came round imposing severe penalties on anyone who used any word but "accessory" in speaking of the gas. This was to keep it secret, but the French civilians knew all about the scheme long before this.

Robert Graves, Good-bye To All That

SIXTEEN

Tadley, July 28,1914

"I'm over it now, darling—it's been long enough," Beatrice said, waving away Hope's concerns.

"I know you are, my sweet, but Dr. Sullivan said avoid drafts just the same," Hope said, putting a thick shawl around Beatrice's shoulders.

"Darling, we're sitting in the sun, there is no wind, and I believe if I put another layer of clothing on, well, I'll just drop from the weight of it all!"

Hope smiled. "Oh, the drama!"

"What time is it?"

"Sweetheart, the mail will not be here for another twenty minutes earliest, and you've asked me the time every five minutes for a half hour."

"A watched pot and all that," Bea said.

"Exactly," Hope said, smiling.

They sat in companionable silence.

"It's still beyond me how that big fool could have told her I was her mother," Beatrice said, her fists curled in frustration.

"Which big fool, darling? Your sister or the big fool she works for?"

"Either. Both."

"It's not technically their fault, you know, Beatrice. They repeated the story we told them over three decades ago," Hope offered.

"I know. They're still fools, the both of them. Not once in those three decades did Margaret ever inquire as to the welfare of who she thought she knew was her niece. Am I right? If Jan was my daughter, then Margaret would have been her auntie!"

"Now, dear. Margaret couldn't very well have inquired about *that* without risking your wrath. You know it's true."

"Well, perhaps."

They sat in silence. Hope looked up just as Bea spoke. She seemed to expect the question.

"Did you write to His Honor when January disappeared?"

Hope looked at Bea, her gaze softening. "I called him actually. Yes, that same day she left. He was going to go to Paddington Station and expected to be there when she arrived."

"Good," Hope said. "I was hoping you would. I'm sure it's already been looked into. How could he ever hope to find her, though?"

"Well, I'm not certain he did. I gave him the arrival times from Reading. The first train hadn't arrived yet when we spoke. More than likely she caught it because it was delayed several hours with troop movement business."

They sat holding hands, each soaking up the warmth of unconditional love. "I told him she might look into the VADs, and he'd know about that, of course, and how to find out."

"Good thinking," Bea said. "Very good. Isn't it

amazing that someone you knew forty years ago has kept in touch all this time? And been a perfect gentleman. You do have good taste in...friends," she finished.

Hope looked at her and smiled. "He was a perfect gentleman when he danced me all over London, too," she said. "But our communication? Limited, really. A couple of letters early on, when Jan was born. You knew about that. But, I haven't called him in years. He's so busy, but he was always kind. I knew he would become someone important."

"Important is one thing," offered Bea. "Having the ear of the King as Sir Ralph does is something else entirely. He's a good man, a generous man."

"Ah, here's the post now—I just heard something dropping through Mrs. Cromwell's mail slot," Hope said.

"Hard to believe anyone writes to that old cow." Beatrice grinned and looked pleased with her own comment.

"Really, Bea!" Hope went into the house through the back door. She returned a few moments later with an envelope in her hand and a smile on her face.

"Looks like the same envelope," Beatrice said.

"I'm sure it is, and no return address again." Carefully, Hope used her finger to separate the flap from the envelope. "Ah, darling, we have a note!" Hope clutched the whole envelope to her breast. Beatrice reached over and placed her hand on Hope's thigh. She rubbed her leg gently.

"Oh, sweetheart, you do so miss her, I know you do! Let me read it, luv."

Hope handed the envelope to Beatrice. She pulled out the notepaper and a one-pound note fluttered to the ground. Hope leaned over and picked it up. "What an angel! Read it please, or I shall surely burst!"

"Right," said Beatrice, scanning the note. 'Dear

Mum—'"

"She's still calling me Mum!" Hope whispered.

"A child knows its mum," Beatrice said.

"Dear Mum,

I don't want you to worry. I'm in London working on a Special Assignment for the VAD. You may have heard of Sir Ralph Whitmore who hails from around us, but over near Highclere. He is some kind of high up person in the King's inner circle, and 'twas he who procured this position for me. I'm not allowed to say what it is, but I won't be going to war—that is, I will stay in and around London.

I heard things from Rosie that I don't understand. Perhaps someday, you will explain it to me. I hope you and Mrs. Graham are well, and I will stay in touch. January"

"Read it again, please, dear."

Beatrice read it again, but slower.

"Well, then, I don't suppose I should have actually expected her to sign it with love," Hope said, dabbing her nose with her handkerchief. "I've got to call that Parker-Pryce woman. I gave her the other envelope. Maybe this notepaper will be more helpful. Let me see that note, dear."

Hope held it up to the light. "Ah, what luck!"

"What? What is it? Don't tell me it's a watermark?"

"Yes! Looks to be the letter 'O' in a script-like lettering." Hope handed the letter back to Beatrice, who also held it up to the light.

"You know, I rather think that's a 'C' not an 'O.' Let's get Parker-Pryce on the phone. She can send her car for us."

"Us?" Hope asked.

"I'm not letting you anywhere near that den of iniquity without me," she said, getting up and throwing the shawl down on the chair.

Hope turned her head away to hide a smile. "No, of course not, darling, and I wouldn't dream of going without you. Besides, obviously Jan's now fully in the care of Sir Ralph. Technically, I shouldn't be meddling. But..."

"Hope?"

Beatrice stood straight, her hands folded in front of her. Her eyes were lowered and she spoke barely above a whisper. "Jan does love you, Hope, she loves you very much. As do I."

Hope moved closer and slipped her arm around Beatrice. "I know you do, darling, I've always known it."

***

Mrs. Tads walked nervously around the large dining table. She checked each place setting and moved a couple pieces of silver to some invisible standard of alignment that only she could see.

"One simply cannot expect hotel wait staff to be the same as one's own staff," she complained.

"Mrs. Tads," Mr. Tads said with a sigh. "No one expects that. We are in charge, tonight, dear, and mustn't think of ourselves as the wait staff."

"Well, I trust you will uncork the wine, Mr. Tads. We can't have some stranger pouring Mrs. Cabot-Jones' champagne!"

"Yes, of course, dear. I shall do the wine. Well, look," he said, taking his pocket watch out of his vest pocket, "only five more minutes before the guests begin to arrive."

"Exactly," Mrs. Tads said. "Thus my consternation."

Victoria floated into the room. "What is everyone

going on about?" she asked. "Mrs. Tads, there will never be anyone like you and Mr. T., so don't even compare yourselves. Dr. and Mrs. Carter know the limitations of hotel staff—even in a hotel as prestigious as this one."

"Yes, ma'am. Thank you, ma'am," Mrs. Tads murmured.

"Oh, for God's sakes, Dorothy! You know perfectly well you can call me Victoria when the guests aren't around."

"I know," Mrs. Tads said. "But I'm practicing. They are due any minute!"

At that very minute, the doorbell to the suite rang. Winston joined his wife in welcoming Ben and Camille Carter. Camille and Victoria were old friends, and they hugged like long lost ones. As the men walked over to the bar, the two women held onto each other.

"I've missed you so, Camille," Victoria whispered.

"Hells bells, me too, V!" Camille whispered back. "Let's get rid of these fuddies as soon as possible—I've got a lot to tell you."

"You?" Victoria laughed. "Well, you're not the only one."

"So I hear," laughed Camille, allowing her tongue to hang out and lolling her head to the side to mimic a mental patient.

"That's wickedly unkind," Victoria said, adding, "however deadly accurate!"

"It's me, V! The witch of inappropriate and outrageous. Besides, when one is a crazy as I am, it's like joking within the family."

"Oh, so you've heard I'm crazy?" Victoria asked, trying to hide a smirk. "Let's go drink to that."

Winston had walked Ben over to a sitting area alongside a large bank of windows overlooking a nearby park.

While the men shared a cocktail before dinner, Camille and Victoria wandered into a room that was set up as a small intimate parlor.

"Tell me everything and leave nothing out," Camille whispered.

"If I tell you everything, we'll miss dinner," Victoria said.

Camille lit a cigarette and handed it to Victoria.

"I shouldn't smoke, you know."

"Neither should I," answered Camille, "but I don't think a drink will be enough for this conversation. Is she still writing you?"

"Well, that's the oddest thing. In a word, no."

"No! I can't believe it! Why?" said Camille, taking a solid swallow of her cocktail.

"Well, of course, we've come to London from the house, but still, by now the mail ought to have been caught up to me, don't you think?"

"Why don't you telephone her?"

"Oh, good Lord, she just recently had a phone put in and refuses to use it. I did try to call her just before they released me from the hospital, and she actually answered."

"And? What did she say?"

"Nothing, I said 'Hello' and I heard a great banging around and muffled moaning and then she dropped the phone. I haven't tried again."

Victoria looked toward the other room. Camille followed her glance and saw that they had a perfect view of their husbands through the open door.

"I've not had a moment alone, Cam," she said. "And it's driving me mad. He doesn't leave for another two weeks, possibly longer."

"Do we know where yet?"

"Belgium, he thinks. It's all very hush-hush, you

know. I mean war's not even been declared."

"Yes, but have you seen the streets? Throngs of soldiers, just throngs of them. They are all signing up in anticipation. I don't think Ben will have to go. They need the psychiatrists here, you know, for when the men get home."

"Good God, Cam, what do you suppose Ben is telling Winston about...about me?"

"He shouldn't be telling him anything," she said indignantly. "That's a confidence between you and your doctor."

They took a sip of their drinks, looked at one another and burst out laughing.

"Right," said Victoria, "well it appears we *both* know where that leads!"

"What can he tell him?" Camille asked. "Ben doesn't even know! I mean you don't talk about *her* to him, do you, Vickie? Tell me you don't!"

"No, of course not, silly. He thinks I have some kind of war fear, which, by the way, I do. Also."

"Well, shit," Camille said, "I rather think we all have that!"

Victoria giggled. "Cam, you're so funny when you swear. You're not at all shy about it. What news do you have, by the way?"

"My husband is a psychiatrist," she said blithely. "One can't be shy around someone who lives in his head all day or I'd never have any fun at all, darling! And that's my only news, Vickie, I finally got my husband to make mad passionate love to me!"

"Good lord, do I want to know?"

"In your case, probably not," Camilla said with a throaty laugh. "Let's just say, I told him what American women really like."

Victoria raised her eyebrows. "Do tell! What do you

Americans really like?"

They both turned at the sound of approaching footsteps.

"We're hearing an awful lot of laughing in here," Winston said with a smile.

"And we think it sounds damn good," said Ben. "Any chance of getting any food around this place?"

They all moved to a dining table set up beautifully in the living room. The Tads stood a discreet distance away as two wait staff served the meal and cleared the table afterwards. Once again, after a respectful quarter hour, the two sexes separated, the men to the bar area, the women to a small sitting room.

"So, when is the next—what shall I—it seems far more important and permanent than 'assignation,'" Camille said as they sipped coffees.

"Well, it is, or would be, but, Cam, I'm still waiting for a letter. It's been nearly three weeks."

"Does she know you're here?"

"No, but I would have thought the mail would be sent on by now. I did say we were going to London for a couple weeks. I will write her tomorrow."

"And what's the plan?"

Victoria walked over to the table and poured them both another cup of coffee.

"I don't know. That is, I haven't decided."

"It's up to you, then?"

"Probably. Rosie is far too considerate to force my hand, as it were."

Camille giggled. "Oh Vickie, what *is* your problem! Just get on with it. You know you love her!"

"I wonder why it doesn't sound odd to hear you say it," Victoria mused.

"Well for starters, I'm not your husband. And second, well, there really is no second."

“Yes, well, Winston is being quite considerate. For someone who leaves for the front in less than month, he’s actually been quite chipper.”

“And?” Camille asked.

“And, nothing. I can’t, Cam, just can’t. He seems to have accepted it.”

“What about...what about before he leaves? Off to war?”

Victoria sighed but said nothing. She looked off to the opposite side of the small room.

“Well, anyway, darling, don’t fret about it. I'm sure he has no expectations.”

“I’m less certain of that than you, my friend...far less certain. Anyway! Tell me about those gorgeous girls of yours! Are they going to be femme fatales, like their mummy?”

Camille laughed a genuine throaty laugh. “You’re too sweet to be a lesbian,” she said.

“Oh, on the contrary, luv, I think I’m just too smart not to be!”

They both laughed at that and chatted about everything under the sun, old friends who had become such different people. The difference brought them together and, on some unarticulated level, kept them apart. Camille adored Victoria and would do anything for her. For her part, Victoria was happy to have a female friend who wasn't a love interest. Yet there was always an undercurrent of something neither could have named. They viewed the world differently. Victoria took nothing for granted; Camille assumed everything.

“Do you want me to drop in on Rosemary, Vicki? I will, you know.”

“Gracious, no!” Victoria said. “She'd faint dead away.” Victoria played with her sleeve.

“But?”

"Well...I suppose it wouldn't hurt to invite her to tea."

"I'll do it!" Camille agreed. "I will send her a note tomorrow. We've taken the flat near Marble Arch, so I'll see if she's planning to be in London any time soon."

"Oh no," suggested Victoria, "Don't leave it open. Give her a specific date, and remind her who you are."

"She doesn't know?"

"Darling, she's known of you since day one, but she forgets these things. She has too many things in that brain of hers. Lucky for me she remembers me!"

"Oh, I doubt she'd forget you," Camille said with a grin. "I'll send her a note tomorrow to meet me–where? At my flat, or someplace public?"

"Is your flat in order yet?" asked Victoria.

"Well, no, not entirely. Enough for tea, I suppose. How about the Savoy? Would she like that?"

"Yes, I think she would. She might say no if something's happened. She could have completely given up on me, you know."

"Impossible! Why on earth would she do that?"

"Well...you don't...well, she might have her reasons."

"Hmm. What might those reasons be–I mean if she actually had any."

"I don't know."

"Yes, you do."

"No, I don't"

"But if you did know?"

"Well, I don't know," said Victoria, a note of haughty discomfort in her voice. "But I suppose if I had to guess...I don't know."

"Well, the sex was great, you told me yourself."

"I did not say 'the sex was great,' Cam!"

"Well, something like that. I know! You said you've never felt so intimately possessed. I figured you meant sex."

“I wouldn’t know.”

Camille looked at her friend. Victoria's eyes were wide and damp.

“You wouldn’t know? Vicki?”

“What?”

“You wouldn't know because...?”

“Because I’ve never had sex with her.”

“What!” Cam screamed.

“Darling please keeps your voice down! I don't want them in here,” she said, motioning toward the men in the other room. “It’s true. We’ve never...we haven’t had...relations. That way.”

“But you said...”

“I know. We write...we make love in our letters, we—”

“Good God!” Camille said. “I need something stronger than this tea. Stay right here, I’m going to the bar.”

“They’ll follow you back,” Victoria protested.

“No, they won’t! Watch me.”

Camille returned with two large tumblers of scotch over ice.

“Christ, I’ll be blubbery in ten minutes,” said Victoria.

“You’ll want to be blubbery,” Camille said, settling deep into the couch. She took off her shoes and tucked one leg under her. “All right, so you write these letters—both of you?”

“Yes.”

“And...what about that week in London when all this supposedly happened.”

“I don’t know.”

“Vicki, you'll have to help me out a bit here, darling. Are you saying you didn’t kiss and touch and—”

“No, we did that. But...no, nothing more. Oh, Cam, we wanted to, that is, I wanted to.”

“And Rosie didn’t? I find that hard to believe.”

“No, she wanted to. All the time! I mean, yes, she

definitely wanted to."

Camille raised both her hands in supplication. "But it didn't happen because...you pick up here, Vicki."

"Because I was afraid."

"Of what, pray tell?"

Victoria gave a sad little shrug. "I'm not good at that kind of thing."

"What kind of thing? Vicki," she said softly, "I can't fill in these blanks on my own. Are you saying you're not good at...?" Camille turned to confirm where in the suite the men were. Seeing them where she last saw them, she continued, "Not good at making love?"

"Well, the actual act...it doesn't really move me. I don't think it does, anyway. I might...I would want to, I think, with Rosie, but I'm too afraid."

Camille leaned over and set her drink on the small table in front of them. She took Victoria's drink and did the same. Then she took both of Victoria's hands in her own.

"Darling, darling Vicki. You never told me. I understand now. Well, I don't understand, but I do. I understand that's how you feel."

"You do?"

"I do. What about Winston? Was it the same with him?"

"Well, no, I mean yes, but I just did it. It was rare enough once he gathered I lacked interest. He called it something, a condition. Cold. No... frigid."

"He actually said that?" asked Camille. When Victoria nodded, Camille flushed with irritation. "Well, isn't that up to you, Vickie? A man can't just call someone that even if he thinks so. I don't like that attitude–it reeks of entitlement. I simply do not like it." Camille took a large gulp of her drink. "Can't say they don't all have a bit of it, though," she added, more as an aside to herself.

Victoria smiled. Camille's perfect world was sometimes a bit less than perfect. But she looked at her friend for encouragement. When Camille smiled reassuringly, Victoria began again.

"I don't want to *just* be intimate, Camille, with Rosie or anyone. I want *to want* to do it, and I don't know if I ever will...want to, I mean. I cannot want something independent of the name I attach to it. Rosie is a lusty person, independent of me, or anyone really."

"The wench!" Camille teased.

Victoria nodded her agreement and smiled. "Yes, I'm very nearly proud of her for that! I'm afraid though that I am not a natural connoisseur of the pleasures of the flesh. It's different for me. I must feel deeply attached. And even then, who knows? But it does seem that my passions, if I can call them that, have Rosie's name all over them...so, well, maybe."

"Right, well, what does Rosie say? About all this, I mean? And yes, you can call what you feel passion."

"She says...she says she'll wait. But..."

"But will it ever change? For you, I mean," asked Camille softly.

"It...might. It...could, maybe. Maybe. You know, I don't think I know the answer to that myself. But maybe. I'm willing to find out. When I'm near her...when I'm near her, I want to possess her, to please her, to bring her inordinate amounts of pleasure."

"But you don't want that for yourself, Vicki? Is that what you mean?"

"No, I think I do. Want it for myself too, I mean. I've never really known how to give of my very private self quite that openly. Or maybe I just haven't allowed it. I think the anxiety about doing so does dampen whatever ardor I might have begun to feel. But, Rosie...she, well, you'll think I'm daft."

"I'll think you're a dead duck if you don't tell me!" exclaimed Camille. She leaned in close to Victoria, eager for something intriguing.

"Well, all right then. Rosie makes me laugh."

"What?" Camille's eyes got wide and her mouth became a grimace.

"See!" Victoria could not contain her giggling at the faces Camille was making. "But she makes me laugh when I'm most anxious, and even though we haven't...well, not yet, but I could imagine it. I like that she's not afraid to be a complete and utterly charming fool."

"Well, hell, she's got my attention," Camille said dryly. "Who wouldn't want a loud guffaw when on the very brink of orgasmic paradise?"

Victoria covered her mouth when she laughed. "Camille, you are a firebrand, a slut and an American!"

"Guilty!" Camille said. "But seriously, Vickie..."

"What?"

"What if you're wrong? If it doesn't change? Can you ask that of her?"

Victoria laughed lightly. "You say that as if it were up to me. No, I wouldn't ask that of her...but she'll ask it of herself. She'll say it matters, but not too awfully much. She'll say her love is stronger than her lust. That her heart is more reliable than her body. That her mind could not countenance being without one another. Either way, she'll accept whoever I turn out to be."

"So she'll refuse you your tragic ending?"

"That alone makes me want her!" Victoria said. She smiled and her eyes were glistening with happiness. Her shoulders relaxed and she looked smaller with the relief. "And yes, she'll refuse me my tragic ending, probably somewhat indelicately, but yes."

"Blimey. Hell of a woman," said Camille, fanning herself.

"It is never right to do wrong or to requite wrong with wrong, or when we suffer evil to defend ourselves by doing evil in return."
Socrates 469 - 399 BC

SEVENTEEN

London, July 29, 1914

The atmosphere in London was one of edgy excitement. Everyone seemed to know that which had not yet been declared: war was coming. Jan was pressed into service every day but not carrying wounded soldiers. Sir Ralph explained that the next two weeks were a crucial time in the history of the British Empire. There were hundreds of meetings, and it was Jan's job to drive the various diplomats, high-ranking government men and a few senior military officers to these meetings. On several occasions Sir Ralph asked her to provide transportation to these dignitaries in the evenings when they would meet at a private residence for dinner and, one supposed, more war planning. At least three times their wives accompanied some of the men. January listened closely for snatches of information about her country's intentions but references were vague, couched in terms of "the near future," and as often as not Jan gleaned little of import. Until July 21, 1914.

London seemed always to be trying to catch up with its drying out efforts following the wettest March in recent history. April, May and June were overcast, dull, damp and chilly. Some streets still had burlap bags of rocks and sand stacked up on either side of doorways from the March floods.

Finally, in mid July, the sun broke through for several days of uninterrupted summer. If the beating of the drums of war hadn't brought the citizens outside, the sunshine surely did. Lanes, sidewalks, courtyards and parks were filled with people ambling somewhat aimlessly to share their sunshine with strangers. People knew. People sensed. People nodded knowingly when the subject of Germany came up, and it always came up. Children stayed close, oblivious to the grave dangers ahead but intuitive to the fear in their parents' hearts. Mothers and fathers walked closer to one another, parents and children seemed to linger longer in cafes filled with other families. The noise level was subdued. People spoke in low voices and looked at perfect strangers for the mutual recognition in one another's eyes of what lay ahead. Lovers parted more reluctantly than ever, each clinging to the present which foretold no definite future. The country was alert, high-strung, and near to bursting with unexpressed resolve, anticipation and fear.

Jan drove to the front of Number 10 Downing Street, and was directed by armed guards to a parallel parking area directly across the street. She pulled in behind three other black Mercedes. None of the drivers left their vehicles and none of the vehicles were turned off. When the front door to Number 10 opened, Jan saw men and women milling about just inside the door. A moment later, two men exited and walked across the street to the first waiting car. Then three couples came out. They were escorted across the street by two military guards and got into the second and third vehicles. Finally Jan saw her passengers. She hopped out of the car and opened the rear passenger door on the sidewalk side. Sir Ralph walked with a handsome couple and they silently entered the vehicle.

"Claridge's, then, Jameson," Sir Ralph called out from the back seat.

Jan could tell by his tone that she was in full official work mode. "Sir," she said, saluting. She walked briskly around the car, got in and started the engine.

Jan looked in the rearview mirror as she pulled out of the space and she saw a luminous pair of eyes staring back at her. The woman sat between the two men, and though they were talking to one another across her, Jan thought she saw a glint of mischievousness in those eyes.

"Really, Sir Ralph, it's far more dire than anyone's saying, isn't it?" the woman asked.

Sir Ralph coughed lightly and nodded affirmatively.

"I knew it," she said. "I've always known it."

"How did you know, darling?" the husband said, a tone of amusement shadowing his curiosity.

"Any casual observer of recent history could have known," she said.

"She's quite right," Sir Ralph intoned. "However, most people have paid precious little attention."

"Too busy planning a holiday at the seashore," the woman offered.

"Damn worst place to be in a war, the seashore," Sir Ralph said. "Damn worst."

Winston shifted in his seat but said nothing.

No one said anything about Sir Ralph's reference to war. It was as if everyone already knew. War. A real war.

Jan pulled up in front of Claridge's and a hotel footman opened the rear door. The couple got out, but not before the woman gave Sir Ralph a hug and a kiss on the cheek.

"Stay well, my dear," he said to her. "You can do it!"

"I shall, Sir Ralph, I most certainly shall."

Jan drove out of the drive. "To Kensington, sir?"

"Oh, it's just us now, Jan, no need for formalities. But yes. How are you liking your new assignment?"

"I'm liking it very much, Sir Ralph," Jan said. "But when do I begin carting the wounded?"

"As soon as the Germans start shooting at them," he said. "Have you been to Hampshire?"

"Not lately, Sir Ralph."

"Might want to go soon," he said. "No telling when you'll get your next leave. Shall I put in for you for a three-day pass beginning Sunday?"

"That would be very nice, but entirely unnecessary," Jan said. She pulled up outside Sir Ralph's flat.

"Well, your mum might think it very necessary. So go on, take your time now, my friend, no telling when the opportunity will come again."

"All right, thank you, Sir Ralph."

"And take the car," he added. "I'll be leaving for Paris day after tomorrow."

"Paris?" asked Jan.

"Oh no you don't, young lady! It's all top secret, hush-hush and all that. But I need to calm them down. Easier said than done with the French. Even the men are emotional."

Jan got out of the car and walked around to open Sir Ralph's door. He beat her to it. "This is quite good," he said, waving her aside. She stood there, not sure what to say or do next. "All right, then," he said, his voice a bit gruffer than usual, "be off with you then to Hampshire tomorrow, and I'll see you on my return from Paris." He reached over and put a hand on her arm. "Go with your heart, Jan."

"My heart, sir?"

"Whatever's on your mind, go with your heart. I know something's going on in that heart of yours. And I'm not asking what it is. Don't need to know. Just go with your heart, Jan. You're a good young woman, and I'm proud of the job you're doing for England and...for me.”

Jan gulped. She didn't know what to say. She hadn’t done all that much for England yet, though she expected to do her part. It was almost as if Sir Ralph were giving her a little speech of some kind. “Right, sir. Good evening, then.”

“Take care, Jan. Take good care,” he said as he turned toward his building.

“You too, Sir Ralph. See you on...well, I’ll see you soon, I trust.”

He didn't say anything but he raised his hand in acknowledgement as he walked away from her.

***

When Rosemary walked into the public tearoom at the Savoy, she was wearing all black. Her hat, a small affair with a black velvet band, was also black, as were her gloves. Camille watched her as she walked the length of the dining room, escorted by the host.

When she reached the table, she extended her gloved hand. “Camille,” said Rosie. “So nice of you to invite me.”

“I went ahead and ordered a pot of orange pekoe,” Camille said, nervously. “But if you prefer another kind then—”

“No, no,” Rose answered, removing her gloves and waving away Camille's concern. “So, how have you been Camille? How was America?”

“Very well, thanks. America? The same, only better. Rosie, I've never seen my own country through someone else's eyes. Ben was positively smitten. Loves it there!”

“How nice,” Rosie said. “What exactly is it that he likes?”

“The energy, he says. He loves the way the entire

country has such forward momentum, such ebullience, such spunk."

"Yes, well, it's a young country, comparatively speaking," Rosie said. She picked up the menu.

Camille stole a glance at Rosemary as the other woman perused the menu. They had met before, of course, but Camille couldn't recall Rosie ever looking so dour. Usually she was upbeat, fun, even loud, but warm and welcoming. The woman before her was positively funereal.

They each ordered and exchanged small talk while sipping their tea.

"I wonder," said Camille, "should we order a glass of champagne?"

"Are we celebrating something?" Rosie asked.

"Well, let's celebrate life!" Camille said gaily as she motioned to the wine steward.

Once their champagne was poured, Camille proposed a toast.

"Shall we toast to our mutual dear friend?"

Rosie looked stricken but recovered quickly. "I wasn't quite ready to memorialize her demise, but all right."

They clinked glass and each took a substantial swallow. Rosie actually took two swallows.

"So, you're not prepared to join her, then?" asked Camille. "I had thought perhaps you might..."

Rosie looked at her lunch mate, the horror of the suggestion lingering in her eyes and on her face. She couldn't speak.

"Well, sorry, then," Camille added hastily, "I didn't mean that to be so, so cut and dried."

Rosie shrugged. "Well, I sometimes do feel I've not much to live for anymore. Perhaps we shouldn't talk about Victoria."

"Well, as you wish, though she certainly talked about

you non-stop!"

"She did?" Rosie was intrigued. "What kinds of things? I mean, if you don't mind me asking."

"Not at all, and given the current circumstances, I can't think it would hurt." Camille answered.

"No, I can't think it would," Rosie agreed.

"Well she always spoke highly of you, of course, as a person. Good moral fiber and all that. And she said you were very funny and that the two of you laughed a great deal."

"Well, we used to, yes," Rosie said, swishing her few remaining bubbles around in her flute.

"She said you were no good with modern marvels, like the telephone, and yet you took to the automobile immediately. I believe she was saying you're a bit of a contradiction. Oh, and she liked that! I didn't mean she didn't!" clarified Camille.

"The telephone? How odd that that would come up!" Rosie said.

"Well, she told me about that time she called you and you pulled the phone out of the wall."

Rosie set her champagne glass down and gripped both sides of the table. She leaned forward and glared at Camille. Camille pulled back.

"What? What? Really Rosie what is the matter with you?"

"That was her last phone call to me," Rosie nearly shouted. "That was just before she...that was only two weeks ago!"

"I know," Camille said, blithely buttering her small triangles of toast, "but I only heard this past weekend."

Rosie jumped up, threw her napkin down, reached over and nearly hoisted Camille right out of her banquette seat.

"Have you no mercy, woman!" Rosie shouted. By now

the entire restaurant clientele was openly looking their way. "I loved that woman in every way one can, and you're making a mockery of our intimacy."

"Your? What? Rosemary, stop shouting, please. Everyone is looking at us."

Rosie turned to face the other people in the establishment and then back to Camille. "I don't care! I don't care who knows! I love a dead woman and I always will!" The patrons gasped. Rosie leaned on the small table for support, her face flushed, the skin above her upper lip beaded with perspiration. She was shaking with anger.

It was Camille's turn to shout. "Well, damn it Rosie, I love her too, and she's certainly not dead. What a thing to say about someone you supposedly love!"

They stared at one another and the entire room including the service staff stared at them both. The room was deadly silent until suddenly an elderly lady in a corner booth rang a small bell that was placed on her table as a gesture of accommodation to her frailty. It was barely a tinkle, but it sounded like Sunday morning church bells.

"I'd like my glass of sherry now, please," she said in the softest, tiniest voice. Everyone turned to look at her, including Rosie and Camille.

The whole room released its collectively held breath, and Rosie sat down again. "Get the old lady her sherry," she said sotto voice.

Camille giggled.

"What the hell do you mean, she's not dead?" Rosie asked, her voice weak. "Winston sent back all my letters."

"He did what? Why?"

"He sent them all back with a note saying Victoria had passed. Died. Dead. That reader of mine knew for a week before telling me."

"Have I met her?" Camille asked, confused.

"No, no, just someone who read and wrote my letters

to Victoria when I was—when I was temporarily blind."

"You were blind? Oh dear. I had no idea. About any of this. You had someone write your letters to Victoria?"

"Yes, well, she's not working for me now, but, then, yes. I had no choice. I couldn't see."

They sat in silence until Camille motioned the waiter over.

"Two whiskies, neat," she said.

Camille reached over to touch Rosie's hand. "You realize, don't you, that Victoria knows none of this. She was in the hospital for two weeks, Winston's been called up for duty in Belgium and he stashed her in Claridge's just a few days ago. My husband, who is her doctor, and I just had dinner with Victoria and Winston three days ago. She's far from dead."

"Why hasn't she tried to contact me?" asked Rosie.

"First, I believe she did. She called you the minute she had a moment alone, from Claridge's. That's how she knew you pulled the phone out of the wall."

"That was Victoria?"

"The very same."

"The phone box fell on me, I either fainted or got knocked out, and when I came to, I could see. And the rest is too sordid to go into, but that reader of mine had been sending letters I couldn't see but then when I could, I realized they weren't from Victoria. Jan didn't want to tell me Victoria was dead."

"Jan?" Camille said.

"January Jameson, the young woman who was my reader. And writer."

Camille drank the rest of her drink and Rosie followed suit. They stood up and walked out of the tearoom.

"What's next?" Camille asked.

Rosie stopped walking and stood in the lobby of the hotel. She looked up at the ceiling and closed her eyes.

"Could you give Victoria a message for me?"

"Of course," Camille said, smiling uncertainly. "Anything."

"Tell her I said to go to hell."

Camille jerked back, stunned.

"Thank you for lunch," Rosie said as she turned and walked away.

***

Jan smoothed down the front of her uniform after exiting the car. She was given the Mercedes and ample petrol vouchers for her weekend leave. Sir Ralph saw to everything, it seemed. As she approached the front door, she reached for her key but thought better of it. Just as she raised her hand to knock on the door, it flew open and Hope Jameson reached out to pull her daughter inside.

"Hello Mum," Jan said.

Hope held her at arm's length for a moment. "Look at you! That uniform is most becoming, darling."

Jan nodded and set her carryall down in the living room.

Hope immediately picked it up. "I'll put this in your room," she said, "and the kettle's about to sing!"

Jan walked into the kitchen and was surprised to find Beatrice sitting at the table.

"Thank God you've come back," Bea said, a catch in her throat. "She's been worried sick about you. As have I," she added, reaching for Jan's hand. Jan bent down to kiss her hello.

"Glad to be back," Jan said stiffly.

Hope came up behind Jan and put her arm around her daughter's waist. "We'd narrowed it down to Claridge's," she said, as she pulled Jan closer. "But we couldn't figure out how you came to be there."

"Ah, good detective work. Sir Ralph, who I told you about, gave me his suite there."

Hope and Bea looked at her, eyes widening. Jan laughed.

"Oh, it's nothing untoward, I assure you, but—" Jan grinned. "Anyway, Sir Ralph, he's from over Highclere way, gave me a lift from Paddington when I first arrived in London in the worst downpour in centuries, and—"

"Oh my, you took a ride from a perfect stranger?" Bea said.

"Oh, he's not a stranger," said Hope. "I've known Sir Ralph for years. I haven't seen him in years, mind you, but we used to socialize a bit."

Jan looked at her mother. "You know Sir Ralph?" Her mother was full of surprises. "I had no idea. Isn't he just the most wonderful man? He's really taken care of me, Mum. He probably never made the connection…" January said, pausing long enough to decide how she wanted to finish that sentence. Bea saved the moment, although January couldn't have said from what exactly.

"I believe it's the most rain London has seen in years," Bea said, nodding to encourage Jan to continue her story.

"Yes, everyone is saying it is. So, anyway, we became friends—everyone shares rides in London, Mum, what with the cost of petrol and the war coming and all. I'd actually talked to him before—used to see him on the coach when I was going to Parker House every day, and we recognized one another. It turns out, I remind him of his deceased daughter—and he got me this position as a Driver in the VAD, but it's a Special Assignments position, so mostly I drive important dignitaries around London. I've been to Number Ten at least a dozen times," she added.

"Oh my! Did you go in? Did you meet our Prime Minister Asquith?" gushed Bea.

"Well, not yet," Jan said, trying to sound casual, "but with my Sir Ralph connections, it's fairly inevitable."

"You see, darling," Hope said to Bea, "I told you she would be doing something important!"

Jan laughed. "Well, I'm not sure driving important people back and forth from Claridge's and the Savoy to expensive dinners is important...but it certainly is...eye opening."

Bea got up to help Hope with the tea. "Sit down, sweet, I can do this," Hope whispered to her.

Jan looked at the two of them hovering around the tea service on the counter. "How have you been feeling, Bea?"

"Oh, much better, thank you. Your Dr. Sullivan is quite marvelous. And very handsome," she added lightly.

When they were all seated around the kitchen table, with tea poured and scones buttered and jammed, Hope spoke first.

"Jan," she began, "I want to get right to the heart of the matter that is on all our minds, I'm sure."

"Of course, Mum...well–"

"Yes, see, that's just it, Jan, I really am your mother."

"She really is," added Bea.

"I...I'm awfully glad of that," Jan said haltingly. She looked at Bea. "Of course, the other...the other way would have been fine, too...just a bit...confusing. To be honest, it's all a bit confusing. Why would Rosie tell me you weren't my mother?" Jan asked, turning to Hope.

Hope opened her mouth to respond, but Bea took up the baton and explained to Jan what happened those many years ago. She tried to give Jan a sense of what society was like over three decades earlier. "It was my idea, and I think a not very good one, in retrospect," she finished.

"Well, I agreed to it," Hope said. "I agreed because I was frightened. One couldn't really...it was...oh hell! I was a coward, Jan, a bloody coward, and your father covered for me and Bea covered for me."

"But, Mum? Who were you hiding from?"

"Everyone and…no one. It made no sense. Bea was my first…"

"Love," inserted Bea.

"Yes, Bea was my first love, and it was all so different from whatever everyone I knew was doing. I ran away."

"Literally," added Bea.

"I ran away to Devon and met your father. I went with several friends, and he was with a couple of his friends…and I wanted so desperately to be normal. Normal."

There was a long pause while Bea poured Hope more tea. Jan pushed her cup and saucer toward Bea and watched as the reddish brown liquid steamed into the cup. She poured in some milk and added sugar. They were each staring intently into their cups.

"She got pregnant."

"I did more or less figure that part out," Jan said with a half smile.

"But I wasn't in love," Hope said quickly. "I mean, not with your father."

"And he knew that?" Jan asked.

"He knew. He was hopeful, I think, that marrying might bring me about."

"But it never did," Bea stated. She looked at Hope for confirmation.

"No, it never did," Hope said.

Jan felt as though the two of them had had this same exchange many times, as if each time more forcefully confirmed what both of them needed to believe. *And who knows? Maybe it never happened between my parents again.* Jan decided she'd as soon not question it further. It no longer mattered.

“I feel as though there's a piece of this story that's missing,” Jan said. “Apparently, it was Margaret who first told Rosie. I have to wonder why Margaret needed to think I was Bea's daughter.”

Hope and Bea looked at one another, and then at Jan.

“Jan,” Hope began. She moved her chair a bit closer to her daughter, and as she reached for her hands, she crumpled into a shaking, trembling morass of tears and half-swallowed whimpers.

Jan stood up immediately and hovered close to her mother, bending to hold her, soothing her. It only lasted a moment.

“Mother,” Jan said when the woman stopped shaking. “I think perhaps you better tell me the truth. Tell me the whole story, Mother.”

“There’s so much more,” Hope said between sobs. “But not right now, Jan, please.”

No one said anything for a moment. Finally Hope spoke, her voice soft and tremulous.

"Bea and I lived together. It was a bit later that—that Mr. Jameson and I bought this house.”

“I owned both cottages,” explained Bea. One was to be my retirement investment. I wanted to have one to live in, one to let.”

Jan listened as both women tried to explain. The irony of Bea having provided for herself and giving it up for the love of Hope who would later criticize her for not having provided for herself was not lost on Jan.

As Hope recounted the story from her perspective, Jan was mesmerized at how utterly human her once distant mother now seemed.

"I can't begin to say how selfish and shallow I was," Hope said. She said she and Bea were having problems—nothing serious, or so it seemed. Bea thought it was just that Hope needed time to adjust. Hope knew her doubts were deeper than that. She loved Bea, there was no question about that. She simply could not see how their union would provide either of them with a happy life, or even a softly contented one.

"Mr. Jameson was the most decent among the lot of them, the young men in the area. He had a job, and he was a kind. We had...we got involved that week. He asked me to marry him a few weeks later. Or maybe I asked him, but he agreed. And that's basically what happened," Hope finished. She dabbed at her eyes with her cloth napkin, but the more she did so, the redder they became.

"Darling, why not go rinse your eyes in cold water," Bea suggested.

Wordlessly, Hope rose and left the room. As they sat there in silence, hearing the sound of running water somewhere off on the other side of the house, Jan wondered if they were thinking the same thing.

"It's always worse to find out something that shakes up everything you thought you knew," Bea said.

Jan looked at Bea. "How did you deal with the pain of it all?" she asked. "It must have been quite hurtful." She looked at Bea's hands rather than into her eyes.

"Yes, it was, at times, but I knew each bit of truth as it happened, or within a few days. Somehow that was easier and I had a good deal to say about how things would be handled. Too much power and not enough foresight. I'm deeply sorry that I have hurt you, too, January. I am."

Jan was looking at her own hands, head down, heart beating in her ears. She felt the skin on her hands, felt its softness, how taut it was, how clear of the telltale age spots of the women around her. She finally looked up. "I always cared about you very much, Bea. It was, I don't know, maybe something instinctual. I knew you were important to us, to mother. So you were important to me."

Bea reached over and took Jan's hands. "I know, I

know. You were always very kind to me, especially when your mother was trying so hard to pretend I was 'just the neighbor'."

"Why did she continue to keep that facade up?" asked Jan. "And what changed?"

"I think she was afraid that once you found out, she would lose you. Your mother...your mother is not all that good at expressing her deep emotions. But you are her world, Jan. You and me. And it's always been that way."

Bea let go of one of Jan's hands, but held onto the other one. "As for what changed? First, the chance came up for you to get a good job with Rosie, and Hope could not deny you that opportunity, despite its inherent risks of discovery, which, as we see, have been revealed. Then, I got sick. I think that frightened her more, or as much as, you discovering her past."

Jan got up and reached to refill the kettle to boil some more water for tea. "Or do we want a drink?" she asked.

"A drink sounds good to me," Hope said, walking into the kitchen, looking better than when she left.

"I'll have what she's having," Bea said, smiling.

"You two go on into the parlor, I'll bring the drinks in," Jan offered.

She brought out a small silver tray from an upper cupboard, and a small serving goblet. She opened a tin of mixed nuts and poured them into the goblet. She mixed some whiskey, some lemon juice and a bit of sugar in a tall tumbler that she covered with her hand. She poured the three strong whiskey sours over some ice and placed everything on the tray. There was a tablespoon of the cocktail mix left in the tumbler and Jan drank it straight from the glass.

***

"Ha!" said Victoria. "I *knew* it!"

"You knew what?" Camille asked. She twisted her silk scarf nervously.

"She wants me to come get her."

"I didn't get that impression," Camille said, lowering her eyelids.

"No, I'm sure you didn't," Victoria agreed. "Rosie would be believable because she half believes it herself. Think about it, Cam."

"I'm rather valiantly trying not to," her friend answered.

"Oh, it must have been positively trying for you. I'm so sorry. I should have gone to Parker House myself. But we didn't know she thought I was dead, for Christ's sake! I'm going to kill that Winston if the Germans don't."

"He was only trying to protect what is his," Camille said.

"I was never really his," Victoria said. She paused. "Well, I was at the beginning, a little, but not after I met Rosemary. But I know what you are saying. Frankly, I didn't think he had it in him. I can't imagine he actually thought it would work, though."

"Maybe he didn't," Camille said. "Maybe he just wanted you to know he wanted his wife back."

"Yes, there's that of course. But to say someone is dead? That's a bit beyond the pale, isn't it?"

"You'll have to talk to him about it, you know. I mean before he leaves for the front."

"Yes. I'll speak to him this evening."

"And Rosie?" Camille asked. "What will you do about her?"

"I will go to her. It's the only way. I owe her that. I owe myself that."

Camille stood up, preparing to leave.

"You don't think I'm doing the right thing by Winston,

do you, Cam?" Victoria asked.

Camille thought about the question a while. Finally, she looked directly at Victoria. "You know, I thought I was all for you and Rosie. It was exciting to hear about. I was rooting for both of you. But now that I've seen what Winston has done to keep you—oh, I don't know Vicki, it's just all so sobering."

Victoria walked to Camille and hugged her. "I know, dear, and don't think this very subject hasn't haunted me from here to utter distraction every day for several years. Winston's done absolutely nothing wrong. Nothing."

They stood holding one another. "You're crying, Vicki!" Camille said, holding her friend at arm's length to look at her.

"I know," Victoria said. "Pathetic isn't it?"

"Not at all."

"Cam, I have to follow my heart. I've never done that. I've followed my fears, I've followed my insecurities and I've followed every rule I was ever taught. But I cannot do that any longer. It's made me ill. It's made me nervous. And it's made me inconsolable."

"I know," Camille said, tearing up. "I know. Yes, my friend, you surely must."

***

Rosemary hopped out of the Mercedes without waiting for Betters to open her door. She stomped up the front steps and pulled on the locked door.

"God damn it, Margaret, open this door! I live here, you know!" Rosie hefted the heavy doorknocker and banged it several times. She gave up and began pacing back and forth on the landing. Immediately the door opened.

"If you live here, you ought to at least have a key,"

Margaret said, a dour but worried look on her face.

"And how much did *you* know, Margaret?"

"Rosie, what the devil are you bellowing about?" Margaret leaned out the door after Rosie swooped in and waved Betters on.

"She's not Goddamn dead, Margaret, that's what!"

"Who's not dead?"

"Victoria! Victoria is not dead, God damn it!"

"Well, stop sounding like you're sorry to hear it," Margaret groused. "Now tell me the whole story." Margaret turned to go into the kitchen and Rosie followed her, flailing her arms as she tried to undo her black silk scarf from around her neck.

"And me dressed in mourning like a Goddamn fool! I'm so mad at Victoria I could spit!"

"Actually, you are spitting," Margaret said, pointing to a chair at the kitchen table.

"Can't we go into my library? I never come in here," Rosie sniffed.

"Normally, we would," Margaret answered, "but I'm baking soda bread today, so either sit here and talk to me or go to your library and sit alone."

With a sharp intake of breath, Rosie landed hard on the chair. "I don't recall you having such a mouth, Margaret."

"Well, then you weren't paying attention, and besides, I learned it from you. Now what happened and how do you know Victoria is alive?"

Rosie told her story in colorful detail with all the appropriate dramatic flair. Margaret laughed at the part where all restaurant patrons froze with forks midair as Rosie and Camille yelled at one another.

"Where did you leave it? I'm surprised you didn't march right over to Claridge's!"

"I told her to tell Victoria to go to hell," Rosie said,

smiling coyly.

"Right. Well, that'll bring her running in no time," Margaret said. "I suppose I should disappear in this case."

"Oh, Christ, stop it, Margaret. You'll do no such thing."

"She doesn't like me."

"Well, we have you to thank for that, don't we?"

"I'm sure I don't know what you're talking about."

"Oh, Margaret, it's me you're talking to. I've never held it against you, but whatever Winston's suspicions, it took you to confirm it for him."

"I didn't know you were going to fall in love with her!"

"It was not your business to say anything to him. You know that. I also understand you felt quite indebted to him for giving you such responsibilities around here."

"That was your father did that, now, wasn't it?"

"Yes, and Winston continued to uphold Daddy's trust in you."

"Well, anyway, that all got ruined, now, didn't it."

It wasn't a question. Rosemary looked at Margaret as if seeing her for the first time.

"It meant...I didn't know it all meant so much to you, Margaret. I'm sorry. I didn't know."

"Of course it meant the world to me, Rosie! Why wouldn't it? I'd had no real education, no connections, nothing."

"You were good with numbers, Margaret."

"Your father said I was a born manager."

"Well, you are. And if this all gets sorted out between Victoria and me, I'm going to want you to be the official estate manager."

"Well..." Margaret's face was flushed with embarrassment. "It can't really be afforded, now can it, Rosie? No need, no need."

"Actually, Margaret, it can be afforded."

"How?" Margaret said, raising an eyebrow of interest.

"I've decided to sell Papa's china bowls."

"You mean the green ones? You can't possibly be willing to part with them. They are museum pieces! They've been in your family for—"

"For a couple of decades, Margaret, not centuries. Daddy bought them, or let's say, came by them, before I was born. They are museum pieces, and that's exactly where some of them will go. The rest will be sent to Sotheby's. That ought to carry us through another decade or so until you can get those fallow pastures fruitful again. You can do that, right, Margaret? With the proper help, the right equipment, the right crops?"

Margaret stared at her wide-eyed. Finally, she blinked. "Yes," she said, in a whisper. "I can do that. I can do the management of it, hire a farm manager who can hire a crop manager, who ca—"

Rosie laughed a full, throaty, happy laugh. "Let me sell the family jewels, first, Margaret! Come here." Rosie stood up and held her arms out to Margaret, who hesitated, frozen in shock.

"All right then, I'll come to you, my Major Domo!" Rosie took a couple steps forward and gave Margaret a warm, tight hug. Margaret's mouth quivered and her body began to shake. "There, there, now, my Major Domo, don't go all soft on me. I know how loyal you are. I do. And it's time I repaid you in kind. You will never be without a roof over your head or food in your belly or a warm fire and a good strong cuppa so long as Parker House remains mine."

Margaret sniffled. Her face was all blotchy red and her eyes rimmed with tears. But she smiled large and full, her missing teeth no longer stopping her. Rosie saw that smile and hugged her again.

"Right," Margaret said, pulling away, "well, we best

get on with it."

"Thank God, these chairs are killing my bottom. Take me to my library, Margaret."

Margaret put her hands on her hips, looked at Rosie, and they both laughed.

"Sorry, Margaret. I completely forgot I could see."

"No you didn't. I've spoiled you. Rotten."

***

Winston came into the suite dripping wet. He handed Tads his umbrella and raincoat, stamped his feet on the rug and rubbed his hands together.

"Damn bloody chilly rain for the end of July," he said, holding onto to one of Tads' arms while he pulled off the rubber shoes. "Ah, better. Where's Anne, Tads?"

Mr. Tads did not answer but fiddled with hanging up the wet rain gear in a small closet just inside the door.

"Tads?"

"Oh, sorry, sir. I'm not quite sure. I believe Mrs. Tads might know, though."

"Tads, I believe I mentioned when we arrived that you were to—"

"What? Keep an eye on me?" It was Victoria, standing in the center of the room, dressed in a mauve suit.

"Oh, there you are, darling!" Winston said. His slight frown revealed his surprise to see her.

"Would you fix me a drink, dear?" she said.

"Capital idea, my dear."

While Winston fixed the drinks, Mrs. Tads hovered nearby in the library, dusting and re-dusting the same row of books. She glanced at Victoria, who acknowledged her with a slight inclination of the head. Mr. Tads hovered near the entryway, wiping up errant drips of rainwater from Winston's boots and clothing.

"To us," Winston said, smiling as he raised his tumbler.

Victoria took a sip of the drink and placed her glass on the table. "No Winston, not to us."

He looked at her, his smile fading, his eyes narrowing.

"I know what you did. I can understand you wanting Rosemary out of our lives, but sending back all my letters and telling her I was dead was a bit much, wasn't it?"

"Not if you actually do understand that I wanted her out of our lives." He took a large gulp of his drink. They looked at one another in silence. Finally he set his drink on the table. "I see," he said. "She is not going out of our lives; I am."

"It's for the best, Winston," Victoria said.

"Whose best, Anne? Yours or mine?"

"Ours," she answered evenly. "I don't like this, Winston, sending you off to the front with this...this news, but I can't send you off with a false hope, either."

"No, I suppose not," he said, bending down to pick up his drink. "You're sure of this, then?"

"Winston. Winston you know that you have done nothing wrong in our lives together. Nothing at all. If you don't know it, I want you to know it."

"Yes, well, I'll go to war with that reassurance at least."

"Winston?"

"What, Anne?"

"Please call me Victoria."

"Why?"

"Because that is my name, the name I've always gone by. I don't use Anne, and I know why you chose to. It's unnecessary now."

"Now. Now because you've made up your mind, is that it?"

Victoria smiled and acknowledged his thrust to her

parry.

"All right, Winston. It's not that I've made up my mind just recently. No, I had to make myself and you and...her, sick and frightened and just...sick."

"Are you telling me this paralysis is all about Rosemary Parker Pryce?"

"The same way her blindness, though temporary, was all about me. And you."

"Me? However on earth could you two getting sick be about me, pray tell?" He laughed cynically and poured himself another drink.

She watched him mix his drink. She could explain, she could justify, she could even convince him. But that's not what he needed right now. Right now he needed to believe he had some semblance of his dignity left.

"Well, anyway," she said, "I thought maybe we'd go out to dinner this evening."

"A final fling, Victoria?" he said. But his voice had softened; his demeanor was not so rigid.

"Well, I don't think we should call it a fling, exactly, but—"

"I'm not serious, Vicki. I'm just trying to add a note of levity to an otherwise difficult moment."

She smiled at him as she rose from the davenport. "Well, then, Winston, let's have a lovely dinner. You're leaving...when?"

"Day after tomorrow. But you don't have to—"

"Winston!" A note of warning gilded her tone.

He nodded, and offered her his arm. Mr. Tads was near the front door to the suite, Victoria's coat across his arm. Mrs. Tads was in the closet, pulling out Winston's raincoat.

"This almost looks orchestrated," Winston said under his breath.

"It almost is," Victoria said, laughing.

After the door closed, Mrs. Tads looked at her husband. “And what will happen to us, then, Mr. Tads?”

“Don't worry, Mrs. Tads. Mrs. Cabot-Jones has already advised me that we're to return to her home in Hants.”

“And why haven't I been told of this very happy result?” she asked.

“I had to make sure this evening wouldn't reverse itself.”

“Reverse itself? What do you mean? That she'd stay with him?”

Mr. Tads shrugged as if to indicate the possibility.

“Oh, Mr. Tads,” she said, shaking her head.

He shrugged again. “Anything's possible.”

She smiled at him. “Not that,” she assured him.

EIGHTEEN

London, Claridge's, July 30, 1914

The phone rang in the staccato pattern of bullets firing. Jan had not used the phone while staying in Sir Ralph's suite, and this was the first time she'd heard it ring. She ran out to the living area and picked up the receiver.

"Oh, good morning! No, well, yes, but I was awake. Well, of course I was; it's almost noon!"

She stood listening, and then picked up a pen. She took a couple of notes.

"Here?" she said. "She's staying here? No, no, nothing. Yes, certainly. Has Sir Ralph returned from France yet? I see. No, of course not. I shouldn't have asked."

Jan replaced the receiver. She walked around the suite deep in thought. *This can't be true. If I were awake, I'd have a drink.*

She paced for another few minutes, holding a coffee cup. She looked out the window, then with a start headed for the bathroom and a quick bath. She'd have forty minutes before she had to be downstairs, with the car at the front door. Within ten minutes she was fully dressed, hair brushed, though still a bit damp, and her messenger bag on the table at the ready.

Although it looked innocent enough, the bag held a pistol, extra ammunition, an ID card and her Special Services letter signed by Sir Ralph that allowed her easy access and egress to all the military bases, hospitals and converted hospital homes, as well as priority for petrol. Petrol!

Did I refill? I was going to, but did I? She determined that she must have done, as it was protocol to always have the vehicle at full-tank ready before having it parked for the night. She headed for the front door of the suite, but stopped. *I'm not coming back here. I don't know how I know this.* She backtracked into the bedroom and quickly threw all her belongings into a dark green duffle bag. She opened the closet door, took down a small satchel and packed her personal items in that.

Jan stood outside the front of the hotel, ready to open the rear passenger door. She looked at the time. Her passenger was not yet late. Another three minutes. With a minute to spare, Jan saw the elevator doors open and a baggage handler rolling a cart with luggage and hanging bags. Behind him, in a mauve suit, black hat and crisp white blouse, Victoria Cabot Jones walked her way. *This cannot be happening. I'm taking Rosie's dead lover to Hampshire. To Rosie. Except she's not at all dead.*

"Good morning, Private," Victoria said. "Lovely day for a drive to Hants, don't you agree?" She stepped into the rear compartment of the Mercedes. Jan only nodded, shut the car door swiftly and helped the porter put the luggage into the trunk.

Jan adjusted her tie, smoothed down the front of her uniform and checked to see that her shoes were glistening with shine. She slid into the driver's seat, adjusted the rearview mirror just a touch and slowly pulled out of the hotel roundabout. Within a few minutes they were on the main road to Hampshire. Jan heard the click of a cigarette lighter.

"You don't mind, do you?" Victoria said. "I'll crack a window."

"Not at all, ma'am," Jan answered.

"Would you like one? It's a good hour to where we're going, I think."

"No, thank you, ma'am. Yes, it's an hour and a quarter unless we hit rain. Then it could take a bit longer."

"Do I detect a slight Hampshire accent, then?" asked Victoria.

"You do, ma'am." Jan put both hands on the steering wheel. *Do I tell her? Do I not? Won't she find out eventually? 'Oh hello, ma'am, I've read all your love letters.' Has a ring to it. Or, 'Oh by the way, that last knock-your-knickers-off letter you got from Rosie? I wrote it. Not bad, don't you agree, ma'am? By the way, your husband says you're dead. The cad!'*

"Which village?" Victoria asked.

"I beg your pardon? Oh, uh, Tadley," Jan answered, the sweat dripping down her hairline into her collar.

"Ah, yes, I've been through it a few times. Charming place. Wonderful little pub on some street or another where they serve the best fish and chips I've had in ages."

"Yes, ma'am," Jan said. "That would be *The George and Dragon.*"

"Yes, yes, I believe it was."

They drove in silence the rest of the way. Although the weather was mild, Jan felt the thin sheen of perspiration sticking to her back. *Nerves. My God, she is a beautiful woman. No wonder Rosie was in such a state.* Jan glanced in the rearview mirror just as Victoria removed her sunglasses. Their eyes met, and Jan switched her line of vision to the road ahead. *She has a look. There's curiosity in her eyes. They dance. Her eyes dance.*

As they turned down a long lane that led to the even

longer drive into Parker House, Victoria spoke. “I think you've been here before, Private. You've never even glanced at a map.”

“Yes, ma'am,” Jan said. “I've been here before. Living around here, of course, one gets to know all the estates.”

They were almost in the semicircle that took the vehicle to the front door. “Well, here we are!” Jan brought the car to a sudden stop and Victoria was thrown forward, then back. “Oh, sorry, ma'am.”

“I suppose you might want to use the facilities, Private? They...uh...they don't know I'm coming, but I'm sure you'd be welcome to do so. It's a long drive back.”

“Oh, no thank you, ma'am. I'm just fine!” *I've never had to pee so much in all my life. Lord, just get me out of here.* Jan hopped out of the car, walked briskly to the opposite side and whipped open the door for Victoria, who was gathering her things off the seat. “Did you want me to wait, then, ma'am?”

“Oh, no thank you, Private,” Victoria said, distracted by movement in one of the upstairs windows. “Have a good trip back, then!”

“Thank you, ma'am.” Jan smiled and tipped her head but double-stepped to the driver's seat. Just as Victoria was raising the heavy doorknocker, Jan made it all the way to the end of the long drive when she remembered the luggage. *Oh, Christ! Bloody hell!* She backed the car up and turned around. She left the luggage on the front doorsteps and took off again. *Well, no point interrupting anything. Might as well find a bathroom, have a bite to eat and then go on over to Mum's house. That'll be enough confrontation for one day, I've no doubt.*

***

Jan pulled over to a small pub on Pamber Copse

Road, parked the Mercedes at the back of the building and entered the dark interior from the rear. A couple of men sat at the bar, and the waitress told her to sit anywhere. She chose a small table near the bar. After ordering a roast beef sandwich, Jan asked for a glass of wine. She sat in the warm, smoky darkness and thought about the evening ahead. She supposed she should have let them know she was coming. But it was just for the night. Drive back to London the next day.

The front door of the pub opened and in the shaft of light, Jan saw Dr. Michael Sullivan walk in. His eyes obviously hadn't adjusted to the darkness as he went straight to the bar. She decided she would say hello to him and rose from her table.

"What could bring you to this out-of-the-way road stop, Dr. Sullivan?" she said as she approached him.

He turned and smiled broadly. "I might ask the same of you! But you asked first. So as not to be discovered by anyone I know, but now that I have been, I'm not at all unhappy about it."

Jan looked around as if to see who he was talking about. She smiled and invited him to her table.

They chatted amiably and Jan found herself laughing at Michael's self-deprecating humor. They had that in common. They had a love of books in common too, and Jan wondered that she hadn't actually considered the value of having things in common with someone.

"You know," Michael said, "We've several hours of daylight left. Would you fancy a walk around? Get some fresh air?"

"I would, actually. Should we leave our cars here?"

"Well, I'm not in a car!" he said. "I was just on my way to Parker House to see Rosemary for dinner this evening. I left Reading by train a bit early and decided to stop here for a bit."

“Here? In Tadley, you mean?” Jan asked, surprised. He nodded.

They walked out into the sunshine and Michael stopped and stared at her. “Good Lord, you're in uniform! Are you a VAD then? Crikey!”

Jan laughed. She looked at her shirt and tie, pressed trousers, and began giggling. “I suppose I do look rather official,” she gasped. “Well, I'm Special Assignment VAD.”

“What, pray tell, is that?” Michael asked, laughing. “Do you drive the lords and generals around?”

“I do, kind of!” she answered brightly. They walked along the lane and arrived at the main square. “Let's go this direction,” she said, pointing west. “That will take us to Towns End Road, and it's a pretty stroll. Then we'll circle back.”

Michael looked at his pocket watch. “I have two hours before I'm due to arrive. The walk sounds perfect. Say, why don't you join me at Rosie's for dinner–I'm quite sure she wouldn't mind another guest at all! I'll even call ahead if you'd rather.”

Jan hesitated. “I believe Rosie already has a guest she didn't expect,” she said.

“Don't say? And who might that be?”

“Well, my special assignment today was to bring Victoria Cabot-Jones to Parker House.”

Michael stopped dead in his tracks. “Really? I am stunned!”

“As was I when I discovered she was to be my passenger this morning. She was a Special Assignment. Evidently, her husband is high up in the military and he's left for Belgium just today.”

“Convenient,” Michael mumbled.

“I beg your pardon?” Jan asked.

“Oh, no, nothing.”

“No, what did you say? Did you say it was

convenient?"

Michael looked at her sheepishly. "I did say that."

"Then you know Victoria? You know about Rosie and—"

"Yes, I know Rosie, and I've met Victoria, but not through Rosie."

"Oh, that's intriguing, Doctor!" Jan said.

"Michael. You agreed to call me Michael."

"Yes, Michael, I did. I will."

"Thank you. Well, I can't really go into it, but I met her professionally. I mean, in my capacity as a professional. Hell!"

Jan smiled. "I wasn't born yesterday, Michael. You're a psychiatrist, and you met Victoria as a patient. I think that's what you're trying awfully hard not to say."

He shrugged. "Well, then, I have you to thank for making that goal so much easier." They laughed together and walked a block or so in silence, stopping every once in a while to look at someone's pretty yard.

"And what do you think of the union of Victoria and Rosie, Michael? Do you think they will...well, become as one," Jan asked.

"Oh, I think so," he said. "I think it's their destiny. Rosie's determined to have her, and Victoria is fated to fall eventually."

"Hmm. So you think Victoria is the holdout?" she asked.

"Not at all," he said, smiling at her. "I think it's Rosie."

"But you said—?"

"I know it seems all opposite doesn't it? Rosie's more frightened than Victoria, I'd venture. Victoria is attracted to the vulnerability that lies at the base of that fear. She'll be the one to bring it all about, sooner or later. Although they're both skittish, I'll grant you that."

"Hmm, I think I'm going to have to put my money on

Rosie being the one to bring it all about. Nothing seems to stop that woman when she sets about to make it happen."

"You're on!" he exclaimed and stuck out his hand. They shook hands over the wager, and the contact seemed to put them both at ease.

Jan laughed. "And how do you come to know so much about lesbians, Doctor, and I use the word purposefully."

"Which, lesbians or Doctor?" He took her arm and put it through his own. "I don't know," he said. "I deal with people's feelings. Women seem better suited on a lot of levels for expressing their feelings. All women," he added.

"Well, I was raised by lesbians, after a fashion," Jan offered.

"Well, there's one I wouldn't have guessed!" he said, stopping to look at her. "And you're...is it..."

"Am I all right with it? Yes, I am, actually. Of course, I just recently found out because it's not one I would have guessed either! Not in a million bloody years!" she said, laughing.

Jan didn't know how long they walked, but it must have been for over an hour. She couldn't recall the last time she enjoyed talking to someone, a man, so much. Michael was delightful, unassuming and intelligent. At first Jan didn't know how to respond when he'd say something amusing or ironic—she wasn't sure if he was serious or not. Little by little she thawed, and halfway through their walk she was laughing, loudly and freely. She was relaxed, even spontaneous, at one point grabbing his arm when she stumbled on an errant rock while pointing to a bird in the trees.

"A bird in the hand," he began, as he held her up, both of them laughing like fools. When she stood upright, they were face to face, leaning on one another. "You know, Jan, if I knew you better, I'd try to kiss you right now."

She looked up at him. The smile on her face slowly

faded but the warmth in her eyes increased. She felt as though they'd always known each other. "Let's pretend you do know me well," she said.

***

Margaret met Michael at the door.

"Oh dear, please come in. I'm afraid dinner has been cancelled, but you're welcome to dine with me in the cozy kitchen, Doctor."

"Nothing serious, I hope—is Rosie feeling unwell?"

"Well, I thought not, but she sent a note downstairs with the housekeeper saying she was not to be disturbed. Had a bit of a flushed face, Hannah said."

"Hannah?"

"The new cleaning girl."

They stood together in the entrance hallway, both uncharacteristically awkward.

"So...you don't think I should check on her or anything like that?" Michael asked. "Because, if not, I believe I'll go 'round to January's house and check in on Beatrice. She's been a bit under the weather."

"Yes, yes of course," Margaret said. She fidgeted with her hands. "I can have Betters drive you over. I assume you got dropped off. I heard a car but didn't see one when I let you in."

"Actually," he said, blushing, "that was VAD January Jameson giving me a lift. Ran into her in town."

"My, she's a regular taxi service today!" Margaret exclaimed.

"I beg your pardon?" Michael pretended not to know what Margaret was talking about.

"Oh, nothing, nothing. Just that Hannah was out in the cutting garden, off to the side out front, and said Jan came by earlier. Whoever she dropped off must not have stayed long. I suppose Rosie answered the door. I was out in the back garden fighting with the roses. It's not altogether unlike fighting with Pryce, now I think on it."

"Well, then," Michael said, smiling, "sounds like a perfect match all 'round!" Michael reached over to Margaret and put a hand on her arm. "I'm going to rain-check that dinner. Will you tell Rosie, next you see her?

"Of course," she answered, her eyelids lowered in self-consciousness. "Doctor, you know what's worrying me? What if when the war starts and the wounded soldiers get here, they're going to need more than we can give them."

"Surely you can't mean medically, Margaret! They'll have the finest that I and others can give them."

"No, not that," she said. "I worry about the blind ones." Margaret wrung her hands and shook her head.

"Margaret. If we go to war, yes, there will be some horrific wounds. But blindness is the one condition you have a great deal of experience with. Remember when Rosie couldn't see?"

"I never quite understood that," Margaret mused. Then, "I don't think these boys are going to be getting their sight back."

Michael opened his mouth to answer, but shut it again at the solemn truth of her statement. He nodded, squeezed her shoulder and turned to let himself out.

"Come into the kitchen with me and have a quick cup of tea, Doctor. It'll take Betters a few minutes to get himself sorted out."

Michael gave her a broad grin. "Damn, I was hoping you'd offer a hot cup!" he admitted.

"Oh, go on with yourself," she said, blushing, "I know you came for the soda bread all along."

"Best in the country," he said as they headed for the kitchen.

"I thought Bea's health had improved," Margaret said,

placing the tea cozy over the pot.

"Oh, yes, yes, it has," Michael said. "This is just a follow-up call."

"You like her, don't you, Doctor?"

"Who? Bea? Yes, she seems a jolly one. I like her quite a bit."

"I don't mean my sister, Doctor."

Michael looked up, his mouth full of a generous bite of soda bread. He nodded as if he understood. She poured him a cup of tea and he took a sip, the steam warming his face.

"Oh! You mean January. Yes. Yes I do, actually. Don't know her well, of course."

"But you'll remedy that, I trust," Margaret said.

Michael nodded and made some kind of guttural sound. "I will, yes," he said. "Hope so, anyway." He grinned at Margaret.

"Well then, it's looking like everyone has themselves sorted out."

"What about you, Margaret? Are you sorted out?"

Margaret looked off toward the back door. "Rosie's making me the manager of the estate, such as it is," she said.

"Oh, that's wonderful, Margaret. You seem suited to it."

"Well, I'm certainly not suited to love," she said.

He looked at her, surprise spreading across his handsome features.

"Now, why do you say that?"

"Some people are just like that, Doctor. You must know, seeing as how you handle brains."

Michael laughed. "Well, that's a description I wouldn't have come up with on my own," he said.

Margaret blushed. "You know what I mean. I tried it, once, and I lost."

They sat in silence and sipped their tea. Michael felt his neck getting hot, just as they heard a tap on the door.

"Oh, that'll be Betters."

"Perfect," Michael said. "Any longer and I'd eat the whole loaf."

"Next time you see me, I'll probably have my own little office somewhere on the property," Margaret said.

"I can't tell if that makes you happy or not," Michael said.

"A bit of both, I suppose. A person gives up one dream, but another comes along and you realize it's what you wanted all along. It's what I'm suited to, managing. Big waste of time spent with feeling about the other."

Michael turned and took Margaret by the shoulders. "Margaret, feelings are never a waste of time. They are the expression of one's soul as well as one's heart."

"No use crying over spilt milk," she said. Her lower eyelids were red. Her nose was turning scarlet.

"You're the estate manager, now, Margaret. Get someone over to mop up that milk!"

Margaret laughed. "Thank you, Doctor, I think I will."

"I'm to be Michael to you now, Margaret. It would please me to be your friend."

Margaret eyes grew wide. "Thank you, Michael, you're a good man." With that she turned and walked to the back door to greet Betters.

"Take care of Michael on the road," she said. "You know driving at night is not your strong point, Betters."

Betters' eyebrows shot up in mock indignation. But he mumbled, "I will...ma'am. I certainly will."

"Seems like everyone's heard the news about your promotion," Michael whispered as he passed her.

She pulled herself up to her full height, gave him a crooked smile and nodded. *Margaret Mills, Estate Manager. Had a nice ring to it, didn't it now?*

NINETEEN

Kingsclere, July 31, 1914

Margaret came stomping in through the back door, and Hannah the new cleaning girl was at her heels. She motioned to a chair.

"Sit down, Hannah, I'll fix you some nice Sunday tea."

"Oh, no thank you, ma'am—"

Margaret gave her a look. "No thank you, Margaret," she corrected herself. "Thank you, but you wore me out on that walk—think I'll take a small break and rest a while. Rain check?"

"Yes, of course," Margaret said absently. "Rain's bound to happen sooner than later around here."

Hannah passed through the kitchen and gave January a nod.

"Nice young girl," Margaret offered. "She'll do anything I ask."

"Seems to be, yes," Jan answered.

"Can't say I thought I'd be seeing you here any time soon," Margaret said. She set out two cups.

"Well, I've thought things over. And my mum is my mum, by the way."

"Yes, I've heard. Sorry for my part in all that business," she said, her back to Jan. When Jan didn't respond, she turned around. “So, are we all back to being settled, then?”

“I think so, yes, if you and Rosie are...”

“Oh, hell, January. All she’s done is mope about you being gone.”

“I haven’t been gone a full month,” Jan said.

“Really? I could’ve sworn it was a year!”

Jan pushed her chair back, stood up and walked up to Margaret. She put her arms around the woman and smiled. “Felt like a year, didn’t it?”

“Well, this tea won’t serve itself,” Margaret said, blushing.

They sat at the table together and had their tea, each reading a section of the day’s newspaper.

“It’s going to be soon, Margaret. The war.”

“I know. I feel it. Are you pretty certain, then?”

“Yes, I’m afraid so. I don’t know everything, but let’s just say I know enough. I see movement is underway to get the house ready.”

“If we’re called upon, yes, we’ll do it. I actually want to do it, have some life around here, even if it’s broken. Oh, by the way, Dr. Sullivan will be around Monday. I think Rosie invited him to lunch.”

Jan continued reading her newspaper, looking up only to take a sip of tea.

“Actually, Rosie mentioned inviting you to join them.”

“Me?” Jan was startled. “Why me?”

“Why not? All that uncomfortable business is behind us, Jan. And you know Pryce is so much more bark than bite. She’s missed you greatly.”

“Oh, I don't know, Margaret—I'm meant to take a couple officers from Aldershot to Reading to catch the train to London. I don't think I'll be back until...” Jan mentally calculated the time and distance of her task. “Shortly after noon,” she finished weakly.

"Perfect," Margaret said, wiping her hands on a dishtowel. "I'll tell Rosie the luncheon will be served about 12:30. Perfect, she'll be so happy."

"Speaking of Rosie," Jan said, changing the subject somewhat, "where is she? How long did Victoria stay? Did they get it all sorted out?" She took a bite of the soda bread. It just seemed to get better every time Margaret baked it.

Margaret stopped in her tracks. "Victoria? Here? When?"

Jan looked up startled, her mouth full. Finally, "I dropped her off here yesterday afternoon! I thought you knew!"

"No! She sent a note down with Hannah that she was going to bed early and was not to be disturbed. In fact, Dr., uh, Michael came by last evening for dinner, and I had to apologize for cancelling last minute."

Jan said nothing about Michael's visit to her mother's house. He didn't come by until after the dinner hour, so Jan assumed it had been an early dinner at Rosie's. She and Michael had no moment alone, with Hope and Bea hovering over him, so she never got a chance to ask how the dinner had gone.

"Didn't you speak to her when you went into the library?" Margaret asked. "Or didn't you go in?"

"No, I mean, yes, I did. She wasn't there. I came out here for a cup of tea thinking you'd know where she was."

Margaret started toward the hallway and Jan followed behind her. They looked in the parlor.

"It doesn't even look as though she was in here this morning," Margaret said. She put her finger to her lips.

"What?" Jan asked.

"Nothing, just trying to remember, the order of things this morning. I got up, came downstairs and went to the kitchen. Had tea, then joined Hannah and Doreen, making the rounds we call it, walking through the supply closets, that sort of thing. Then, we practiced changing bandages on one another, and then Hannah and I came back to the kitchen, just now when you saw me.

"And you hadn't seen Rosie this whole time?"

"No." Margaret frowned. "What happened is that Hannah asked me to show her the gardens. Reminded her of her mum's in Cornwall."

Margaret and Jan looked at each other, and then turned and ran up the stairs to the second floor.

Rosie's room door was closed, so they both knocked urgently. Nothing. Jan reached for the doorknob, and as soon as she turned it Margaret barreled into the room.

"She's gone!"

"Look!" Jan said. "She left every drawer open. There's a suitcase she decided not to take."

They turned in a complete circle and looked around the room. Everything was in disarray, the departure hasty.

"Looks like a couple of wolves slept in that bed!" Margaret said. She walked over to a nearby secretary desk while Jan inched closer to the bed. She stopped suddenly at what she saw.

"Margaret?"

"What?" Margaret was leaning over the desk looking at something.

"Margaret, does Rosie usually wear pajamas *and* a nightgown to bed?"

Margaret looked up, alarmed. "What the devil are you talking about, Jan?"

"Come here."

Margaret walked toward Jan who pointed at the bed. "Oh!" Margaret said. "Well, those are definitely Rosie's pajamas."

They looked at one another, eyebrows raised, eyes wide.

"And the white silk nightgown?"

Margaret didn't answer at first. She reached over and fingered the neck of the nightgown. "Hmm," she said. "There's only one person I know who would have a Fortuny nightgown..."

"Who?" She looked at Margaret, and in her eyes, she saw the answer. "Victoria."

Margaret nodded, turned around and walked back to the desk.

Jan was stunned. She heard Margaret rustling some papers, and she jumped at the sudden sound of Margaret laughing. "Oh my good God!" Margaret screamed, waving several sheets of paper above her head. "They've run off together! They finally did it!"

"Did...it...did...what?" Jan said slowly. Her face was white as a sheet. She couldn't have said for sure what had struck her, but she felt left out somehow. Not left out by Rosie and Victoria—left out of life. Left out of loving someone so much that moving heaven and earth to be together seemed an inconsequential task compared to the reward. Left out of the singular feelings of being in love. Left out of knowing even what it meant to be in love.

"You have to read this, it's—"

"No!" Jan whipped around and headed for the door. "I don't want to read it. I'm sick of reading their letters. I'm sick of caring for them. I'm sick of..."

"Love, Jan? Are you sick of love? Because that's exactly what we have here, Jan. We've got the biggest, strongest, death-defying, war-trumping, society-frowning love I've ever seen...except maybe one other time."

Jan looked at Margaret, her eyes narrowing. "Are you going to tell me you've had a bigger love, Margaret?"

"No, not bigger...not quite big enough, in fact...but the biggest of my life." She lowered her eyes, and Jan felt a pang of compassion. She couldn't imagine who would find

Margaret attractive. Her mouth was too small, her nose was too big, and her height was certainly not the classic feminine picture of beauty.

“You know, Margaret, about the only thing you could say now to cause me more anxiety is that the big love of your life was my mother.”

Margaret turned slowly, her shoulders back, her face contorted in something between grace and grief. Jan's mouth opened. Her body froze. Her eyes glazed over.

“Don't be bloody fekking ridiculous, Jan!” With that, Margaret swept out of the room, throwing the letter up in the air. As it floated down toward the floor, Jan knew. *Perhaps I ought to read these letters. Obviously, I don't know the first damn thing about love.*

TWENTY

Kingsclere, July 31, 1914

Jan walked over to the writing table. She held the pages in her hand and looked around at the room, its disarray almost comical. *Should I read this? Am I trespassing again? How can I not read it? It was left here to be read. There's no possibility Rosie didn't realize this letter would be read. I'm reading it.* She looked at the first page, at Victoria's beautiful cursive handwriting...Jan sat down.

Darling, oh darling!

I received your note, and there is only one possible response. I've had the same response within my heart since first we met. It's the same response that's been kept alive these many years later. I've always written about the same response. Written about, thought about, felt about. But not acted on. That will change. Immediately. Yes, of course I shall come to you, my Bliss.

Sir Ralph Whitmore (he lives out our way in a small castle with magnificent grounds and no one to share them with—lovely older man, you'll like him immediately and I can't fathom how you haven't met him before, but maybe you have! I'm so excited I'm tumbling all over myself here!) —but Sir Ralph arranged a driver for me, though I can hardly see how he's pulled that off as I phoned in my request this morning upon receipt of your letter only to discover he'd gone to Belgium. Something about the war effort, no doubt. Somehow, though, a call came in within the hour: my driver will bring me to you tomorrow. I imagine it will be around Noon. My body, my spirit, my soul, my mind, my entire being is in a heightened sense of awareness. It started to frighten me...again, as before...but each time I put your heart back into the equation, and the fear left. It tests me, certainly, and I doubt I'll sleep much tonight, but it matters not.

Darling...? You must surely know beyond any doubt that I love you. I am in love with you. I give my heart to you and you must never give it back to me. Never, sweetheart. I have been so silly, so fearful, so difficult, and yet...and yet, you continue to love me. You say you adore me though I can't imagine I deserve it—indeed, I've gone in and out of wondering if I've merely affected your brain with fevered imaginings or is it truly love you feel for me? But no more, darling. No more will I wonder about that. I don't know what will happen with us, but if it fails, it won't be because I haven't given my entire self to you. If it succeeds, perhaps it will be because of that decision. Or maybe it will come down to luck or Divine Intervention (yes, darling, I know you laugh at my dithering about God sometimes, but seriously, I do firmly believe He has had a strong hand in my decision!) But whatever the force or power, divine or otherwise, behind us, behind you and me, behind you and me as one, I am encouraged—no! I am positively alive with optimism that ours is a rare and special gift beyond describing.

Yes, I want you to love me, in all the ways two people do, and I will love you back, darling. I will kiss you, hold you, and touch you in every possible expression of love, and in your response, I will know your love for me. And darling, I will await with open heart your loving of me...all of me. And you will know my love for you.

And more! Much more because we will live our lives together at Parker House, and I will help you to bring it back to its former glory and beyond. We will make your estate—dare I call it ours? I'm giggling, for I know you will insist that it is ours, but only after I refuse when you suggest and offer making it all mine—No, my heart, it will be ours. Full stop.

We will make our estate a showplace of lives well lived because we will open our grounds to others, darling. I would love to perhaps have a small orphanage—there will be so many children left parentless by this awful war, and we will find them and bring them to Parker House and love them until someone else can.

And yes, as we've mentioned before, we must make this land rich and fruitful again. Darling: I know that Josephine is Margaret Mills, so don't deny it. You are so very silly, too, sometimes! She did us an enormous favor, whatever her motivation, which I do believe was something honorable, if a bit obtuse. (By the way, Tads let the cat out of the bag on that one—how he came to know, I didn't inquire. And speaking of the Tads, I'm sure we will find plenty for them to do at Parker House.) Nevertheless, as for Margaret, I quite think that she would make an outstanding Estate Manager. Would you consider giving that some thought?

Finally, I was wondering something. Would you be receptive to having a driving school on the grounds? I really believe that vehicles are the key, or a key, to the independence of young women. When the men return, you know as well as I do that the jobs women are doing now will be returned to the men. It's the way of the world, at least for now. But if women have access to mobility, they have access to opportunity.

So darling, I know you have some things you'd like to accomplish too—you mentioned starting a lending library with all your father's volumes, and I believe you have given some thought to using some of the land for another school, given the grossly reduced circumstances of the country school since most of the male teachers are leaving for war. And what of that young lady, January Jameson? She quite amused me with that over-wrought, over-written love letter (Darling: You surely didn't think I thought that was from you! Good God, sweetheart, you blush when I come within a meter of you!) Anyway, I'm quite sure there will be plenty of places around Parker House for her abundant and, may I say it, over-ripe imagination.

All of these things, darling, all of these things are what I want to do while sharing my life with you.

So thank you, darling, thank you for your refusal to give me my tragic ending. I can't exactly characterize your refusal as delicate for fear of losing all my credibility, but I say 'thank you' nevertheless. Oh sweetheart! Don't frown: you know I tease you, and all right, somewhat mercilessly, for your strong-willed ways, your forthright demeanor, your abrupt and succinct honesty, your intrinsic fairness to all. It's what makes you you! *If it sometimes lands you on your knees in supplication to the humility gods, well, sweetheart, I fall to my knees with you in prayers of gratitude for the unique and wonderful person you are. I could not love you without loving the passion of you.*

I am yours. I am fully yours. I will bring myself to you tomorrow. I will be yours always, forever and ever, amen. V

Jan held the letter in her hands and closed her eyes. *What on earth had Rosie said to her?* Jan looked at the table and saw Rosie's stacks of old mail, her pens, her writing pad and her stationery. But nothing else. She turned to look out the leaded glass windows and saw that this area of Rosie's suite gave her an unobstructed view of the prettiest part of the Parker House estate. The softly rolling hills, the estate gardens, the circular drive—*ah!* Jan stood up and moved toward the window. She saw that Rosie could look down and see anyone arriving. She had a clear view of the front door from her second-story room. Jan shook her head and turned to leave.

As she did, she glanced down and saw sheaves of ink-stained stationery crumpled up into balls. *Of course! Rosie would have had a rough draft.* As she smoothed the pages out, she saw a few crossed-out words, but mostly ink drops and ink smears, a testament to Rosie's haste and careless abandon as she rushed through the words to get it all out. Jan began to read...

Dearest Victoria,

If you go to hell, I will follow you there. But you won't. You will come here to Parker House. You will be my mate. You will share my life. You will continue to be my heart, my blessed gift, my Treasure. I do not write the beautiful love letters like those I have received from you. It is not really my way, is it, darling? You've known that all along haven't you darling? Knowing how shy I am, you've let me take my time, and I've taken far too long.

But I am no longer afraid to make love to you, to be with you in all ways, for all days. I was afraid, yes, but it was the fear that I could not please you, and not for anything wanting in you. I was afraid that I was a clumsy oaf. That I was awkward and given to outbursts of unrestrained passion of expression that, more than anything, scare people away. That I would not know how to love you, as you needed to be loved. That you would leave me in my ineptitude, walk away silently without telling my why, knowing I'd know why. That I would pursue your beautiful soul only to stumble in the face of it, landing unceremoniously on my bottom, or worse, on your leg. That I would turn too rapidly as we walked in the garden and knock you to your knees amidst brambles and thorns...that my indelicately raised voice would frighten away your hummingbirds and possibly your heart.

And something else, my sweetest one. There is no right way to love someone, to make love with someone, to give love to someone, to feel love for someone. There is no basic skill save the desire to unite. No amazing technique, save the desire to elicit pleasure or contentment or happiness—there is nothing new to learn or tricks to acquire. The elegance is in the simplicity, darling, and we shall stumble and bumble and tumble ourselves into one another's arms laughing, crying, knowing and loving. Speaking strictly for myself, were I to die in your arms, having done nothing more than land there, I would die happy.

So if you are scared, (oh, I suppose you must be—how could you not be!) let me tell you: You have loved me exquisitely each day...your visits, your words and later, your letters. You found me charming. You found me attractive. You found me needing someone like you. And then you died on me! Well, my life was over. I was dead, too. I was in Hell and wanted you to join me, even there. And now? Now I have a singularly miraculous opportunity to have my life back again. Come home to me darling. Come the minute you get this letter tomorrow. You have my heart, and I should die twice were you ever to return it to me. Come home to me darling, for I am yours, forever and ever, amen. R.

TWENTY ONE

Tadley, July 31, 1914

Hope and Bea were waiting up for Jan when she returned home. Opening the door, Jan was startled to see the two of them sitting on the couch sipping brandy.

"Ah there you are, Jan," Hope said. "We were rather hoping we'd last until you returned"

"Hello, Mum, Bea," Jan said, taking off her jacket.

"Can I get you a brandy, January?" Bea asked.

"Oh, thank you, Bea, yes, I think I'll join you."

Bea went to the kitchen and Jan sat down heavily on the winged back chair across from the couch.

"Were you waiting up for me, then, Mum?" Jan asked.

"We were, darling, but as Bea took the call, I'll let her tell you."

Jan sighed and sank back further into the chair. She wondered what could be more surprising than seeing the bed Rosie and Victoria just left.

"You'll never believe who called you, Jan!" Bea said handing her a brandy. "That lovely Sir Ralph. He said it wasn't urgent and asks that you drive over to Highclere tomorrow to pick him up and bring him back to London."

"Oh my, I didn't realize he was even in Hampshire,"

Jan said. “What time does he want me to arrive?”

“He wants you to come for breakfast, dear,” Hope said.

Jan raised her eyebrows and grinned. “Really? Does he now?”

“He sounds very pleasant dear,” Bea said. “And he sounds genuinely fond of you.”

“And I'm fond of him,” Jan agreed. She took a sip of her drink. “He's a very unusual man. Like a wise old uncle or even grandfather.”

***

When she arrived in Highclere, Sir Ralph was standing on the front steps to the mansion with two personal valets on either side of him. Next to them, the houseman stood ready to great her. He walked toward the driver's side door and was clearly planning to open it for her when she hoped out.

And that set the tone for the entire morning. Sir Ralph laughed.

“Welcome to Highclere Manor, Private Jameson!”

“Happy to be here, Sir Ralph!” Jan said with a big grin. They shook hands and the two valets slid their glance sideways toward each other. The houseman stood next to the car with his mouth half open.

“Come in, come in,” Sir Ralph said.

The doors were open and Jan entered a huge foyer with Carrera marble statues, crystal chandeliers and ceiling to floor paintings of important looking ancestors, men and women in full military or formal dress posing with small dogs or, in one case, two small children in sailor suits.

“Pay them no mind, January,” Sir Ralph said seeing her looking up at the oil paintings. “If they didn't have some money and political connections, they wouldn't have had anything, most of them. I'm from a long line of lucky bastards who curried the favor of queens and kings and private pirates who could make them a lovely living robbing for the same queens and kings. Institutionalized piracy, all of it."

"Well, there must have been some decent among them," Jan offered. "After all, they produced you!"

"Ah, well, thank you my dear, but I'm just a horse trader who happens to deal in the whimsies, foibles and vanities of powerful countries led by egotists, marauders and playboys. My job is to fashion them all a new deal after they've mucked it up and try not to kill off too many innocent people while doing so. I'm afraid I'm failing lately," he said.

"Why do you say that? The war?"

"Exactly. The war. I fear it could be a massacre of historic proportions of more innocent lives than the world has ever seen. Well! Enough depressing talk. We're to have a nice breakfast and then I'll show you around. My ancestors had good taste, at least, if not good judgment."

Jan walked alongside Sir Ralph and into a sunny room. A table was set for two, and fresh flowers were everywhere.

"I love white roses," Jan said. "Are these from your own gardens?"

Sir Ralph looked at the display of roses and nodded.

A houseman served breakfast. It was delicious, and afterward they had a fresh cup of coffee. Sir Ralph pushed back a bit from the table and looked off in the distance through the glassed in breakfast room. "Jan, I want to talk to you about something."

"What is it, Sir Ralph? Your tone of voice worries me."

"Sometime in the next year, maybe sooner, I'm going to be doing a great deal more traveling. More than now, even. This war business, you know."

"Is there something I can do for you while you're gone?" Jan asked.

"Yes, Jan, I want you to let me rescind your VAD commission."

Jan was raising her cup to her lips and stopped in mid-air. "Why? Why, pray tell, Sir Ralph! I love my work!"

"Jan...Jan hear me out. You love your work now because it's not very hard work."

"I've nothing at all against hard work," she said. She lowered her eyelids and ran her finger long the edge of her napkin.

"No, you don't. You work very hard, and I think you always have. But that's not the kind of hard I mean. I mean young men without limbs, I mean blind young men, I mean young men driven nearly insane by the fear and the noise—and the death they don't feel worthy having escaped. War is a monster, Jan. It is a monster that will eat away at your spirit, your soul, your heart. At everything you thought you knew, at everything you were sure about."

Jan watched him rise from the table. He walked to the end of it, stood for a moment then turned around.

"I'm frightening you. I'm sorry. It's just that..."

"What, Sir Ralph?"

"I see you as a teacher, Jan."

"Sir Ralph, I'm not nearly qualified! I love children, but—"

"Not just children," he interrupted. "People of all ages. The elderly, babies, youth, the middle aged. You have something that war would take away, and though there'll be no avoiding some of it, I just think if you didn't have to see the worst of it..."

"Sir Ralph! I'm English. We handle these things. I can handle these things." Jan rose from her chair and turned to the windows, which served as a picture frame for an exquisite garden.

Sir Ralph walked over to the window and stood next to Jan.

“It's so lovely here, Sir Ralph. Do you enjoy it?”

“Not as one ought,” he admitted, rubbing the bridge of his nose. “It's an awfully big place to be alone. An awfully big place to waste on one family, on one man, really. I stayed on after my wife died because she loved it so. Well, she loved the gardens.”

“When did she pass, if I may ask?”

“Oh dear, must be nearly twenty years now. I miss her dreadfully, but the House of Saxe-Coburg-Gotha keeps me busy.”

“Is it true, the rumors about the King changing the Royal Family's name?”

“There's talk,” Sir Ralph said. “King George V is very sensitive to how despised anything Germanic is. He's even mentioned changing it to the name of one of the castles. Windsor. We'll see what happens.”

“I'm sorry about your wife, Sir Ralph. You must miss her every day.”

“I do, I do. Well, we can't all live forever.”

Something in his voice made Jan turn to face him. “You look the picture of health, Sir Ralph. I doubt you'll be leaving us anytime soon.”

“Well...”

“What? Good God, you're not ill, are you?”

“I mean simply...the war, you know. We think that when—*if* we declare war—there will be attacks on London and the coastline. A lot of our own civilians could perish. It's all such an unknown, Jan."

Jan waited for him to elaborate but he didn't.

“I suppose I ought to let you drive me on into London,” he said suddenly. With that, he turned toward the door. One of his valets handed him his raincoat and his bulging briefcase. “I haven't really shown you the property, or even the whole house, Jan, but there'll be time enough for that.”

“I should love to spend more time exploring,” Jan said, “and my mother's friend Beatrice would simply faint at the sight of those gardens!”

“That's what we'll do when I return,” he said. “I'll have you and your family down for the day. Are you sweet on anyone, Jan?”

Jan hesitated. “Not exactly...well. Maybe. It’s very recent. I didn’t think he knew I existed,” she said.

Sir Ralph laughed as he put himself into the back seat of the Mercedes. “I doubt that, January, I doubt that very much. Be a fool if he hadn’t noticed!”

Jan smiled at the way Sir Ralph's comment obviously entertained him. It felt good to hear the old boy laugh. She scooted into the driver's seat and turned the engine over.

“And what would you suggest I do to determine one way or the other,” she asked, their eyes meeting in the rearview mirror.

“Just be you,” he said. “Who is he? Do I know him?”

“Oh, I rather doubt you do, Sir Ralph. He's a...he's a doctor friend. Acquaintance, really. In fact, he's Rosemary Parker-Pryce's doctor.”

“I see. Is she ill?”

“Not that I know of—well she was blind. That is, she was somewhat blind. Evidently she wasn’t *really* blind but she'd worried herself into a state of some kind where she couldn’t see clearly.”

“Hysteria they call it. It’s this war. All the anxiety.”

“Hmm. Even Rosie's friend has some kind of problem where she can't walk. And yet, she can, kind of. It's complicated.”

“Rosie's friend?”

“Yes, Victoria Cabot-Jones.”

“Ah, yes. I didn't realize they knew one another.”

Jan looked in the rearview mirror. He was looking out the window.

“Makes perfect sense, though, now I think on it,” he said.

Jan nodded. She wondered if he knew how much perfect sense it made. Jan turned on the wipers as the fat drops of rain came down fast and loud. She loved the way the vehicle handled in inclement weather. But she had precious cargo, so she slowed the vehicle and turned on the headlamps.

“You all right driving in this muck, Jan?” Sir Ralph called out from the back seat. “I shouldn't have brought you out here on such a dreary day, should have caught the train.”

“Not at all! I love driving this car, and I've had a lovely morning with you.” As she peered into the thick encroaching fog clouds up ahead, she did wonder what Sir Ralph had brought her out here to tell her but hadn't done. Something was on his mind. He seemed preoccupied, maybe melancholy. The talk of war, she supposed. It was getting to everyone.

TWENTY TWO

London, August 5, 1914

The Guardian

Great Britain declared war on Germany at 11 o'clock last night.

The Cabinet yesterday delivered an ultimatum to Germany. Announcing the fact to the House of Commons, the Prime Minister said: "We have repeated the request made last week to the German Government that they should give us the same assurance in regard to Belgian neutrality that was given to us and Belgium by France last week. We have asked that it should be given before midnight."

Last evening a reply was received from Germany. This being unsatisfactory the King held at once a Council which had been called for midnight. The declaration of war was then signed.

The Foreign Office issued the following official statement:-

Owing to the summary rejection by the German Government of the request made by his Majesty's Government for assurances that the neutrality of Belgium will be respected, his Majesty's Ambassador to

Berlin has received his passports, and his Majesty's Government declared to the German Government that a state of war exists between Great Britain and Germany as from 11 p.m. on August 4, 1914.

A statement made in London last night said the British Note to Germany was sent direct to Sir E. Goschen, the Ambassador in Berlin.

German troops have invaded Belgium. The Premier informed the Brussels Chamber yesterday, after King Albert had addressed the Deputies in a speech calling on the nation to defend its integrity. Mr. Asquith knew of the invasion when he made his statement in the Commons.

As she ultimately agreed to Sir Ralph's request that she resign her VAD appointment, Jan did the next best thing to helping out with the war effort. She fell in love. January and Michael were married three months after England joined her allies and declared war on Germany.

EPILOGUE

On April 6, 1917, the United States declared war on Germany, after holding to a neutrality position as long as it could. Toward the end of September 1917, the Germans launched a significant number of raids on the southeast coast of England and over London on the 24th, the 25th, the 29th and the 30th.

September 12, 1917

"What is it darling?"

"It's a telegram. For you."

Jan looked up from her list of library books. She was cataloguing Rosie's entire library in anticipation of opening a new lending library in the old horse barn. The barn had been cleaned, painted and divided in two, with a library on one side, and The Parker Pryce Primary School on the other. Neither was set to open for several months, but the excitement was in the air.

Michael brought her the telegram and stood off to the side, a worried look on his face. Jan looked at him.

"They always bring bad news, telegrams," he explained, shrugging.

Jan stood up and walked over to him. “Unless the stork has decided to come three months early and telegrammed to say so, which would be bad news indeed as I'm not at all ready, well, otherwise, I'm too happy to be sad.”

Jan raised herself on her toes and as he put his arms around her, she felt a soft crush of love between them as her rather large belly got in the way.

Jan laughed. “I better open that,” she said, “because that child just kicked me.”

She opened the envelope, scanned the contents and grabbed Michael's arm. “Oh dear,” she cried. He took the envelope from her.

“Ah, Jan darling, I'm so sorry. I know you were quite fond of him.”

“But I think he was a better friend than I was. I didn't even know he was ill.”

Michael sat forward, his elbows resting on his knees. He looked at his wife. “If he was, that’s not what killed him, Jan. According to this, he was killed in Belgium. Passchendaele.”

“What?" Jan cried. "He was a diplomat, he was on the King's mission, he was—how?"

“I don’t know, darling.”

“He was a lovely man,” she answered through her tears. “I reminded him of his daughter. I never knew her name.” She paused to think. “I don't believe I ever asked. I should have done.” She took the envelope back.

“Who sent the telegram?”

Jan looked at it again. “Oh! The Prime Minister's Office!”

“I wonder how they knew to send it here?”

Michael and Jan had moved into Hope's cottage after they were married, a marriage that took place within a few months of their meeting in the tavern. Although Michael was made an officer immediately upon his enlistment, he was assigned to treating the patient overload throughout Hampshire. He went from hospital to manor house to small clinics every day. His patients were suffering from a combination of physical wounds and mental breakdowns. Shortly before they were married, Jan wrote to Sir Ralph and allowed him to decommission her from the Special Assignment corps of the VAD and the VAD itself. She had served her minimum three-month commitment, and was ready to help Parker House and the other area homes, large and small, that were taking in soldiers. They all had to be taken by ambulance to the various destinations, and Jan took care of that as an employee, once again, of Parker House.

Hope and Beatrice continued to live next door in Bea's bungalow. It was proving to be a most felicitous arrangement, even more so, the young couple thought, once the baby arrived.

"That is a mystery," Jan said.

A second knock on the door made them both turn. Michael leaned over to peer out the window.

"Say! Another delivery! Who delivers mail on Sunday?"

"The Government? But the man must be a special messenger. Michael?"

Michael nodded, drew the belt on his robe tighter and opened the door.

Michael signed for the envelope. "It's for you, darling."

***

"They've had another delivery, Bea," Hope said as she peered out the slatted shutters.

Hope and Bea exchanged a long look.

"It's all right, darling. She'll be fine."

Hope looked toward the closed door. "Maybe I should have—said something first..."

"He kept his promise to you all these years, Hope. Now you must keep your promise to him. This is how he wanted it."

"Yes, he did. Yes, I suppose you are right. I only hope she understands that we both wanted it this way."

"He'll tell her," Bea said. "He's been an honorable man all along. I don't suppose that will change now."

***

Highclere, Hampshire, July 31, 1917

Dear January,

I know a few things about you, dear girl, and I hope you will allow me to make a couple of observations. As you now know, I have met both you and Rosemary, off and on throughout her earlier years, and you, more recently when first we used to meet on the coaches and trains and later, when the Gods of Fate, and your mother, brought us together one rainy night in London.

You and Rosie are remarkably similar—oh, not in your personalities, not in your temperament, certainly, and not even in your experiences. I shouldn't wonder that you'll end up splendid friends in the end and the little setbacks will seem like nothing more serious than a few raindrops on a sunny copse. (May you always be surrounded by close friends and loving family.)

However, in your caring, Jan, in your absolute inability to do anything half-hearted, lies your future, your strength, your victories. In addition, here I must add a single notion of caution. Do not let interim setbacks, failures or losses cause you to swear off caring. Sometimes in life, one is fortunate merely to throw some mud against the wall and see what sticks. An inelegant metaphor, perhaps, but life can be dirty, deadly, muddied up by misunderstanding, by neglect, by fear and yes, even by caring.

Still, what's left of life after all that, what gives one a second chance, and another and another, is caring of the right kind. Our war has been "caring distorted" preceded by "caring not at all." Our less than splendid isolation has led almost guiltily, irresistibly to an overabundance of alliances that strained our resources, if not our credibility.

Yet, when the moment called for courage, England was there. When the moment called for decisive humanity, England took the side of saving humanity. When the moment called for involvement, England sent her youngest, her strongest, her purest, her bravest.

England, for all her glory, for all her magnificence, for all her history, is not unlike each of us. We might do many things wrong, but what history remembers is what we have done right. There is precious little that does not affect us, and much that does. We must find the balance that enables us to care. As Mr. John Donne said: "If a clod be washed away by the sea, Europe is the less. As well as if a promontory were. As well as if a manor of thine own. Or of thine friend's were."

If there is a world left after this war, cherish life, Jan. There is so much more I could say, but I will leave it at that. I think you can recall our brief times together, and in remembering, I hope you find they mean as much to you as they eternally mean to me.

I have left you my manor house and all its grounds, as well as an annual stipend to keep its beauty and, hopefully, its usefulness, intact. ("As well as if a manor of thine own...".)

You may do with it as you will, but it is my fondest hope that you will want to share a large part of it with all of Great Britain, or all of her that wishes to partake. Make gardens, make schools, make music, make people care. And as you have found someone who makes your world come alive with laughter, love and loyalty—caring then—make love. Make babies, and love who they become. Make memories, and cherish them. Make happiness, and share it.

You've been a good friend, January Jameson Sullivan. You will find a small rose garden on the estate filled with white roses, which I know you love. I was blessed that someone like you came into the end of my life for I surely could not face the end without knowing you. I met someone very much like you a long time ago, at the point where I was becoming a man. And I have the fondest memories of that joyful time in my life. Your mother has always had a very special place in my secret heart, Jan, but until you, I had not met such a person since. I hope you will want to keep the garden.

I am very ill, Jan, and will not see you again. I thought I'd tell you that and another thing or two that morning I asked you to Highclere for breakfast, but I couldn't bring myself to do it. I felt I shouldn't disrupt your life, and that, at best, it should be a deathbed kind of revelation. And now, ironically, it is. I told your mother that I wished to be the one to tell you what you are about to learn, and, though she worried, she felt that since I once kept her secret, long, long ago, that she would keep mine until I could reveal it. Then, as it turned out, I lasted far longer than I had a right to, but this past six months...well, I've known I'm dying for a while now, but I wish to go the way our young men are going: in battle, in passion, in caring.

Thank you for being my friend.

With love, your father,
Ralph David Whitmore
Highclere

The End

*An Excerpt from the author's next book, The Girl With Two Hearts**

THE GIRL WITH TWO HEARTS

By T. T. Thomas

Chapter 1

"Private Dormier, I want you to take this message to the first officer you see on the front line, and since you'll probably die doing it, I guess this is goodbye, then."

"Yes, Ma'am."

"'Yes, Ma'am' what, Private?"

"Yes, Ma'am. Thank you Ma'am. Goodbye Ma'am."

"That's better, Private. Now go!"

Captain Rosemary Privet kept her smile to herself as the citizen-soldier gunned her motorcycle. They were brave, these Red Cross drivers, and this one was pretty. Terrible to waste lives like this. The Boers wanted their freedom and Britain wanted its empire. The Germans, pretending to be neutral, managed to side with the Boers and be provocative at the same time. The Germans were itching to have a war with Britain, but Kaiser Wilhelm II hadn't settled his sights on his grandmother's homeland just yet—not until His Majesty's naval fleet was as impressive and deadly as Her Majesty's. No, for now the Germans were content to favor the Boers with weapons and information on England's troop movements and Parliament's plans. With South Africa as the theatre, no telling who knew what.

Captain Privet headed back to her tent. She slowed as two soldiers passed her carrying a litter with a deceased soldier on it. The morgue was filling up. Soon the ambulance drivers would have to stack the bodies inside their lorries and make a run for it behind the lines. Some might not make it: a wayward cannon ball, a lucky sniper. Any number of things could keep the living from carting the dead to a proper burial. It had happened. A couple of snappy drivers, a truck full of corpses and without warning, the drivers were dead and the dead were as good as twice dead. But the drivers! Young, all of them: dedicated, full of courage, full of fear. Doing it anyway. Driving the dead. Dying for the dead.

Privet hopped up the three steps to the officer's tent. Inside, Jones was sleeping, or trying to, Montgomery was reading and St. James was polishing her toenails. All four of them were officers, with Privet the senior. Juliet Montgomery and Clare St. James were physicians assigned to the Nurses Brigade, and Abigail Jones was in charge of operations.

"Did you send another soldier off with your usual fond farewell?" asked St James.

"Of course."

"Why do you do that? You know it makes the riders more nervous than they already are."

Jones stirred in her bed and covered her head. "Why do you talk so loudly, St. Bitch?" she mumbled.

St James raised her index finger in the direction of the mound of blankets.

"Because," answered Privet, looking at the formless heap of army blankets covering Jones, "we really don't know if they're going to make it."

"We've lost exactly one rider to the front in a year," said St. James.

Juliet Montgomery put her book down and looked at Privet. Privet saw the movement out of the corner of her eye. "Don't worry, Montgomery," she said, "St. James is just trying to toughen me up."

Montgomery opened her mouth to speak then closed it. She swallowed hard. "Still," she said softly, "it must hurt awfully much, even after all this time."

St. James continued working on her toes, her head down.

Privet gave Montgomery a quick smile. *'Thank you'* she mouthed silently. As Privet turned toward her bunk, she was thrown to the floor by a huge explosion coming from the direction of the front a quarter mile away. The percussion waves rocked the wooden foundation of their tent. In her daze, she saw Jones jump out of bed fully clothed and grab her helmet. St James and Montgomery did the same. Privet froze. It was a second's hesitation, a moment of indecision, a flash of fear darkened by awareness: *Good God! Dormier?* As the others ran out of the tent and down the four wooden stairs, the smell of smoke and gunpowder filled the air. Privet made the sign of the cross as she exited the tent. *Yes, Ma'am. Thank you, Ma'am. Goodbye Ma'am.* Another pretty one probably gone. Another letter home to stunned parents. Privet didn't even know her full name.

***

Dormier adjusted her goggles, leaned low on her seat and gunned the motorcycle up a small hill. Once there, she could see the layout of the entire valley. The Boer flanks were in a straight line to her right and around an elbow of small earthen mounds further to the right. She had to roll silently down the steep incline, staying close to the edge of the road in the hopes that the sickly grove of beat-up poplars would help hide her. Once at the bottom of the incline she'd have to traverse a narrow gully that would take her up behind the large hill on her left and to the allies' front line command post. From the gully, she'd have to gun the bike up another incline. That would be the dangerous part. She would be clearly visible from the enemy outposts behind the small mounds to her right.

She'd made this trip a week earlier, but that was before the Boers extended their flank behind the grassy molars, creating a danger zone between the allies' front line and the hospital encampment a half-mile to the side of them. Privet had told everyone they were moving the main camp a mile to the west to be directly behind their troops, but it hadn't happened yet. *Privet. Holy hell, Ma'am! So, this is goodbye? I don't think so. I don't damn think so.*

Dormier looked around before beginning her silent descent. To her left the allies were safely behind two major hills, and behind them another, even higher hill. As Dormier watched the smoke from the enemies' cannon volleys, she saw that all of the shots hit right below the hill in front of the line. None of the cannons seemed to be in striking distance of the trenches. Was the slow Boer encroachment to the right, behind the smaller mounds, a prelude to setting up cannons that would crest the allies' two hills and cause a frightful amount of damage? Had anyone actually looked at this newer enemy layout from the perspective she had at that moment?

As she mentally prepared herself for the descent, the sun glanced off something in the sky and shot a stream of intense light right onto the ground in front of her. Laying her bike down, she crawled into the bushes to the side of the road, and that's when she saw it. A German dirigible was approaching the allies' front line from behind. A spying ship! They hadn't seen it. They couldn't see it. Suddenly the volleys from the Boer side increased in frequency. Their accuracy was still ineffective but the noise and smoke alone was frightening. The Boers had seen an airship friendly to their cause creeping silently up behind their enemy.

Dormier knew it was a deflection: They don't want anyone to turn around and look up. She reached inside her leather jacket and felt in her interior pocket for her leather case. Drawing it out, she opened the case slowly. First, she picked out the small metal arm and attached its clipping mechanism to her watch, then took out the mirrors and attached them to the arm. Would she have the time?

She raised her left arm and positioned one mirror to capture the German airship. Then she attached another mirror to the first at a forty-five degree angle, and a third mirror directly facing the second. The most she could hope for was that she could send the hologram so close to the allies' front line that they would have to turn around and look up. Her timing had to be perfect. Her hands shook with the adrenalin rush of knowing she was the only person on earth who might be able to save her countrymen. The downside was that the mirrors would give away her position. Once the allies had seen the hologram, she'd have to get down off her hill quickly: she was in range of the snipers if not the cannon volleys.

As she aimed the first mirror at the dirigible, she set her watch for a ten-second exposure. Then she moved the holographic image that resulted from the first mirror to reflect off the second mirror. She pushed a small screw on her watch and projected the holograph as close to the front line as she could. *Look up, damn it, look up!*

Maybe it was someone lying on his back. Maybe it was someone daydreaming about home. Whoever saw the holograph started firing up into the air. In a heartbeat the allies' cannons were turned around and pointing up into the sky. By now they should be seeing two zeppelins, one of which was real. Dormier knew their cannon shots wouldn't reach the altitude of the real or the holographic zeppelins and the small arms fire would only leave small holes in the real rig's skin—nothing serious enough to deflate the huge sky menace. No, only one weapon could do that.

She reached into her lens case and drew out a small crystal prism. Placing it in front of the mirror pointing in the direction of the actual dirigible, she turned the crystal toward the sun and held it aloft with her right hand until she saw a smoking horizontal line tear across the skin of the zeppelin. Within seconds, the big ship was shooting flames and billowing black smoke. Dormier knew it would blow at any moment.

With the split-second timing of experience, she closed down the holograph, placed the mirrors and crystal back into their case and crawled over to her bike. She jumped on it and stepped on the gas pedal. As she throttled forward, a massive explosion shook the air in all directions. At almost the same time, a searing pain ripped through her right shoulder. She held onto the bike with her left hand, and made it halfway down the hill before the loss of blood, the pain and the adrenalin-coated fear threw her into a state of shock. The bike went down, landing on her left leg, and the last thing she remembered was the echo of the Allied troops shouting a huge hurrah.

***

Every driver started her engine. Nurses and medics were scrambling for seats in the back of the ambulances, medical bags on their laps, helmets on their heads and a breathy fear in their whispered voices.

"Five coaches in each contingent!" Second Lieutenant Agnes Jones yelled loudly to the nurses milling around. "Make me six groups of five and plan to leave in five-minute increments."

Thirty ambulances rolled into a rough configuration of six groups. Jones was in charge of the drive to the front, with Montgomery organizing the two tent hospitals, each capable of holding about thirty beds.

Privet stepped out of her officer's tent, and waved away the dust kicked up by the running feet and moving tires. "Hold on Lieutenant," she shouted. "Let's send a couple cyclists up to see what we're in for."

"I'd say we're in for hell," yelled Jones, unable to hide her look of disbelief at the delay.

"True enough," agreed Privet. "Let's just see whose hell it is." She motioned to a couple motorcyclists, were sitting astride their bikes ready to go. "Soldiers? Head on up that hill where the messenger went, and see what you can see. Ought to take ten minutes up and back." She looked at her watch and waved them forward.

Everyone watched the two cyclists until they were out of sight. Jones gave the order to turn off the ambulance engines. "Turn 'em off ladies, save the petrol."

Privet walked over toward the nearest hospital tent, where Montgomery was.

"Notice anything funny, Monty?"

"Only that it just became awfully quiet."

"Exactly. Where's the firepower we've been hearing all morning?"

"What do you think? Is the enemy creeping up on us as we speak?"

"Hope to hell not," said Privet. She reached in her jacket and pulled out a pack of cigarettes. She pumped the pack and held it out to Montgomery.

"Thanks, think I will."

Privet lit both their cigarettes and noticed how Juliet Montgomery's hand shook as she cupped the flame. Privet lit her own and looked around the camp. There was an eerie stillness. Montgomery took several deep drags of her cigarette, then threw it to the ground and snuffed it out with her boot. "Things'll kill you, Privet."

"Something's bound to," she said quietly, enjoying another puff. She blew the smoke out slowly and let it hover languidly in the air between them. "Say, Monty, want to join up for a lovely candle-lit dinner in the canteen tonight?"

Montgomery looked at her. Privet noticed a wry smile creeping across her face. "You're just trying to get my mind off the blood and guts I'm mentally preparing myself to be tending to this evening," said Montgomery.

"Is that a 'No'? Damn."

"Was it really an invitation, Privet?"

"'Rosie, or, if you're feeling formal, 'Rosemary,'" said Privet.

"I like both."

"Yes, actually, it was an invitation," Privet said, snuffing out her cigarette at the sounds of the returning motorcycle. "Shit, where's the second rider?"

She walked briskly to the front of the ambulance line where the rider was gesturing towards the direction from where she had come. St. James was listening, and looked back to find Privet just as she approached.

"Dormier's down," said St. James. "We need to send an ambulance up. Sounds like she got shot returning here."

"Doesn't seem like she's been gone long enough to have delivered the message to Lt. Pierce," said Privet.

"Doesn't, does it?" said St. James.

Privet looked up the hill. "Alright, then, let's get Dormier back here. Better take the rider so she can drive Dormier's bike back."

Before the ambulance was out of sight, Privet saw two male soldiers running down the long hill toward the camp. She knew they were allied troops because the ambulance didn't slow down as it came upon them.

She walked toward the front of the ambulance brigade to greet the envoy.

"Captain!" the two soldiers saluted as they slowed. They were out of breath and red-faced.

"What's going on up there, soldiers?" asked Privet.

"Somebody just shot the hell out of a German dirigible," said one.

"Yeah, thing went up in flames. And Captain, wasn't any of us that shot it. Hell we didn't even see it creeping up behind us."

"Them," the other man said. "There were two of 'em, Captain."

"Two?" she said. "They both got shot down?"

"Well, that's the strange thing. One caught on fire and crashed and the other just disappeared."

"Into thin air," the first soldier said. He was almost whispering. "Like it wasn't even there!"

"What did the Boer lines do?" she asked.

"They started running," one soldier said. "They broke up their front lines and backed way up. At least a half mile."

"Hunh," mumbled Privet. "That doesn't make a lot of sense. They'd be backed up to the river. Unless they plan to cross it and lose their front lines all the way."

"Captain," said one of the soldiers, "Lt. Pierce told us to tell you it's safe to move your encampment back behind our lines now."

"Good," said Privet. "We don't much like being flanked by both friend and foe with nothing in front of us but open territory. You men rest a bit, get some grub and water, and tell Lt. Pierce we'll be moving out tonight under cover of darkness. Tell him we'll set up about a quarter mile behind his last trenches."

"Yes Ma'am, thank you Ma'am."

Privet looked off into the distance where the blast had occurred. The blue sky revealed nothing. She walked back to the infirmary and lifted the tent flap. She saw Montgomery scrubbing up, two nurses alongside her doing the same. "Date's off, Monty," she called out. "Right after you finish fixing up Dormier, we're packing up to move behind the lines. Looks like the Boers saw their ally's flying cigar blow up and took off running."

Montgomery turned slightly and grinned. "I knew you were all talk, Rosemary."

Privet smiled. "Not quite. I'm rain-checking that dinner."

With that she dropped the tent flap and walked away. She knew Monty had a very serious relationship with a young man back home. She knew the good doctor was teasing her, playing along. Trouble was, Privet wished Montgomery wasn't teasing. She wished Montgomery were as available as she was accepting. *Watch it, Privet. The woman likes you, as a friend. She knows what you like, and she likes you anyway. Don't mess it up.*

Chapter 2

Dornier had a fever-driven delirium that Montgomery had seen too many times. The bullet, now removed, had gone deep. But no major arteries had been damaged, no bone fragments had splintered into tissue, killing muscle, and the infection, kept spotlessly clean by the nurses, would clear up soon. Monty looked at the bullet in the pan. "Looks like a sharpshooter got her. Wonder how far away he was?"

"Close enough to hit his target," mumbled one of the nurses.

"But not close enough to kill her," said Monty. "Or maybe he wasn't trying to kill her."

"That would be a first," said the nurse.

"I know. It's curious. This bullet should have killed her or at least caused a lot more damage. It stuck right under her rotator cup. She's sure gonna be sore for a few weeks."

Dormier weaved in and out of consciousness. "Sorry, Auntie," she said.

Monty looked at the nurse.

"Sorry, Auntie," Dormier repeated.

"Nurse, when we're done here, will you ask Privet to look up her record? We'll want to advise her parents."

"Get your bloody royal ass over here!" Dormier cried out.

"You a Royal now, are ya?" the nurse said to Montgomery.

Monty smiled. "Not even distantly related," she said. "Give her another shot of morphine in ten minutes."

After the second shot, Dormier went into a deeper sleep. Within the nether land of memory, imagination and metaphor, the dreams came to life, dreams now distorted by the opiate...*her aunt Queen Victoria had called for her. Again. Apparently, she was in trouble. Again. She looked at her father who smiled benignly.*

"Toria, whatever are we going to do about you, darling?"

Victoria Dormier hung her head. It had only been for a lark. What's the harm in that? She liked the docks, she loved the big ships and she adored the lowly dockworkers and hangers-on she met there. They didn't know—or care—who she was. They didn't call her Lady, or Princess, and they didn't ask why she was there. Everyone already knew because everyone was there for the same reason. "Go'a smoke on ye, now, lad?" they would say. She always did, and she always shared.

She'd sit around the indigents' steel barrel fires for hours, warming her hands, filling her imagination and learning everything she could about everything. Those poor folks knew far more than anyone gave them credit for, she decided. They were smart in a way Dormier's brothers, sisters and cousins would never be.

"Sorry, Daddy," she whispered. "I didn't mean to worry you."

"You didn't worry me, child, but your auntie is all in a roar because you were arrested for stealing."

"I did not steal anything, Daddy," she said. She never lied to her father, and he knew it. "The money in my pocket is money you gave me weeks ago. Remember?"

He did and he nodded. "And the cigarettes, young lady?"

"Ah, well, bartering. Traded them for...things."

"What kinds of things, Toria?"

"Information, mainly. Auntie is in a fidge because she thinks I'm cavorting with the wrong kind of people. It's true, Daddy, that's what she said to me last time."

"You don't think it's the way you were arrested wearing a lad's breeches, coat and hat, with your hair all pinned up, your face dirty and your feet swathed in old shoes held together with strips of rags?"

Dormier shifted from one foot to the other. "Perhaps, Daddy. But that's how they dress down there, and I wanted to fit in."

"For what purpose, child?"

"Maybe I could help...?"

"Now, Toria, we've talked about this before. You're not to speak of your royal rare gift in anything other than matters of life and death. You promised your mother, you know."

Before she could hold them back, tears gushed out of Dormier's bright blue eyes. "I miss Mummy, Daddy! I miss her so much."

Lord Randolph Charles William Andrew George Dormier pulled his daughter close and held her slight and sobbing body until she calmed. He expelled a groan and his face contorted into a grimace of pain as he held her close.

"What is it Daddy?"

"Nothing, sweetheart, just the old shoulder wound." Nevertheless, he dropped his arms to his side and sat down heavily. He closed his eyes for a moment. He wasn't gong to be able to keep this from his child for much longer.

"You're ill aren't you Daddy? Seriously ill."

He looked at his daughter and nodded to the ottoman in front of his chair. "Sit down, Toria, Daddy wants to talk to you."

Dormier sat on the ottoman but never took her bloodshot blue eyes from her father's face.

"It's a bit more serious than I would have wanted," he began. "In fact, the doctor says..." He waved his good arm as if to dismiss whatever the doctor had said. "Nothing is for certain in this life, daughter, and especially not life itself."

"I could help you Daddy!" she cried.

"I'm afraid it doesn't work that way, darling. Your—your gift—can only heal you. Oh, it can help others, but when it comes to the body your gift can relieve others' pain, and it can heal, somewhat, but, no, it's too late for me, daughter. And I would ask that you be strong for me."

Dormier's eye widened. He sounded as though he were dying. That's it! He was dying. First her mother and now her father? It couldn't be. She couldn't bear it. "Could I not try, Father?" she said, trying to sound like an adult.

"Toria, it will be soon. I've meant to tell you, but there was never a good time. It's gone into my bones, now, and it's starting to be very painful."

"Oh, Daddy! If I hadn't run away for three weeks, I might have been able to do something!" She looked at him, the paleness of her face framing the lightness of her eyes, the darkness of her long lashes.

"Daughter, listen to me. First, you must go see my sister. Erm...Her Royal Highness Queen Victoria. Your Auntie, darling, has been very worried about you."

"I will, Daddy. I will go on the morrow."

"No, sweetheart, after you've freshened up, you must go immediately. I've sent 'round a message and she's expecting you for dinner."

"I can't do one of those palace dinners, today, Daddy, not with what you just—"

"No, it will be just you and your auntie."

Dormier looked at him suspiciously. He patted her hand, then sat back in his favorite chair and closed his eyes.

"And what's second, Daddy?"

He took another moment before answering. He reached over to his side table and pulled something from the book he had been reading. It was two pieces of paper, folded in half, worn. "For when you can't actually hold the crystal your mother gave you," he said, handing the papers to her. "Read it, memorize it, and then destroy it."

Dormier took the note and read it quickly.

"Your mother gave it to me, sweetheart. I don't have the gift like the two of you, but I helped her to delve deeper into that gift, to make it more, ah, shall we say, convenient."

Dormier glanced at the two-page set of instructions. "It seems easy," she said.

"It's not, darling, it's very hard. One must be tremendously focused. You will need to practice a great deal. Promise you will do that. And tell no one, of course."

"Auntie knows," she said.

"Auntie knows something," he answered with a wan smile, "but she's far too practical to believe such a gift actually exists, so we never told her. Curious, since it actually came from her own aunt."

"And yet you don't have the gift, Daddy. Are you quite sure?"

"Positive, Toria. It passes mainly to women through women. We've had one instance of a male having the gift,

but that was decades ago. But your mother's grandmother, your great-grandmother, was my half-sister Victoria's, eh, the Queen's, aunt. Auntie Adelaide, er, Queen Adelaide, had no children of her own, but she taught the gift to another of her nieces, my beloved Elizabeth, your mother."

"And why didn't she teach it to Auntie?" asked Dormier.

"My sister, the Queen," he said, "didn't believe in things like the gift. She called it hocus-pocus. I think it frightened her."

"What is it properly called, Daddy," asked Dormier.

"We don't know. Never did, really. Your mother's sense of irony set in when she heard that Victoria thought it daft, so she began calling it hocus- pocus. So, that's what we both called it. Besides, calling it that has the added benefit of disguise. It's a bit like that story in Greek mythology where the name of the daughter of Demeter and Poseidon couldn't be revealed except to those initiated into her mysteries. So, she was called Desponia. Basically Desponia means mistress of the house, which doesn't reveal a whole lot does it?"

"And," added Dormier, "Desponia wasn't her real name anyway! All right Daddy, hocus-pocus it is!"

***

Dormier's hair and body were scrubbed clean and tingling and sparkling with the sweet scent of gardenia. She looked at what her maid has set out for her to wear and made a face. It was a dress. Oh, how she hated dresses.

"Hello? Dormier? Wake up soldier!" Montgomery turned at the sound of Privet's voice. She saw Dormier pull herself out of the dream and open her swollen eyes.

"You crying for God's sake, Dormier?" asked Privet.

"No, Captain Privet. No, Ma'am."

"Well, good, because we're going to be moving camp tonight and I'll need your help."

"Help Ma'am?" Her body felt as though a few rounds from a Mauser rifle had hit her, but slight movement in the cot confirmed to her that the worst of it was her right shoulder.

"Yeah, I want you to help pack up," said Privet. "I'm kidding Dormier."

"Oh, good. Thank you Ma'am for just kidding."

"Dormier, I'm having you moved to a bigger field hospital near Port Elizabeth—"

"Oh! No, please! Please Ma'am, let me stay. I'm almost completely recovered."

Monty continued to watch this exchange and smiled. Privet was a natural-born leader with a sense of humor—rare to have both qualities in the same person.

"Right, I see that. Seriously, Dormier, I'll do the joking around here. We're moving tonight around midnight. I just need you to fill me in on a couple details."

"Details, Ma'am?"

"Details, Dormier. Like next of kin. Where I can send a letter to let your family know you've been hit but you're going to live. For now," she added, grinning.

"Ah, right. Well, just send my father a note then," said Dormier, "but don't say anything to frighten him, of course. Please Ma'am."

"Naturally," said Privet. "Of course frightening him might prove slightly difficult since he's dead. You did know your father was dead, right Dormier?"

"Dead," she repeated. "Right. Dead Daddy. Yes Ma'am, I do know."

"And so then am I quite right in reminding you that he's actually *been dead* for a couple years now?"

"Yes. Yes, Ma'am. March 21, 1897."

"So, Dormier, good, now that we've got that cleared up. Next of kin?" Privet took her small notebook out and wetted the tip of her pencil with her tongue. She held the pencil at attention, reading to write. Her head was down. There was nothing but silence. She waited. Finally, she looked up.

"Next of kin, Dormier?"

"Ah, yes, well, I suppose that would be the Queen, Ma'am."

"The Queen?"

"Yes, Ma'am, Queen Victoria. My auntie."

Montgomery watched as Privet turned on her camp cot and called out to her.

"I thought you said she was no longer delirious, Monty?"

Montgomery stood up and walked slowly across from her makeshift desk to Dormier's makeshift ward. "The Royals bit?" she asked.

Privet nodded. Even Dormier nodded.

Montgomery shrugged and waved one arm as if to call forth some higher power. "She was talking the same way when she was delirious," she said. "Who's listed as her next of kin?"

Privet looked at her book. "Some fellow named A.V. Guelph."

"That my auntie," Dormier said. Her full name is Alexandrina Victoria. Guelph is her family name. All House of Saxe-Coburg and Gotha, of course."

"Oh, of course," said Privet. "Monty, would you step outside with me a moment?" As Privet stood to leave the infirmary she asked another question. "Is this address correct for your auntie?" She held the notebook up to Dormier's face. "Is that right, WinCas?"

"Yes, Ma'am. That's short for Windsor Castle."

"Auntie's house. Right?"

"'Fraid so, Ma'am. Let me ask you, Ma'am, if I were to be all recuperated, I mean completely well, mobile and irrepressibly coherent by midnight, would you be willing to forego the letter to next of kin? I'd so hate to worry the old girl."

Privet looked at Dormier closely, but she nodded. "Not a problem, Dormier. Let's see how you're doing around midnight."

Privet turned to exit the tent and rolled her eyes at Montgomery and the nurse standing at a dressing station just inside the flap. Before following Privet outside, Monty turned toward her patient just in time to see that Dormier rolled her eyes too.

Other Novels by T.T. Thomas

<u>Two Weeks at Gay Banana Hot Springs</u>

<u>The Blondness of Honey</u>

<u>Vivien and Rose</u>

www.ingramcontent.com/pod-product-compliance
Lightning Source LLC
LaVergne TN
LVHW010605100826
845148LV00014B/2855

* 9 7 8 0 9 8 3 9 1 8 0 8 0 *